"You have a life, Ozzy. What are you doing in mine?"

"I'm here because it's where I want to be," he said finally. He lifted a hand to her face, stroked her cheek. "You're amazing, Jo. You're stunning, and fun, and challenging."

He could see the doubt swimming in her eyes.

"We're just so impractical a match. I mean, I'm older than you. And not by a little."

"What does that even matter?"

"It just does."

"Not to me. And I don't care what other people might think."

"Of course you do," she countered and hit a nerve. "The changes you've made in your life, the man you've become, it's partially because you want people to see beneath the shell. I'm just another shell to hide behind." She pushed away from him. "I'm further along in life than you are. I know who I am. I know what I want and where I'm going. And where I'm going is away from here."

Dear Reader,

It's hard to believe this is my tenth Butterfly Harbor romance. I think, in a lot of ways, this is the story I've been waiting to tell.

Ozzy Lakeman was in the very first book of the series, and since then, he's popped up in just about every story, moving along with his life as it seemed like everyone else in town found their HEA. He's been a sentry, standing guard until his time came, and now it has. He's a changed man from who he was then, both physically and mentally, inspired by unexpected events and people. Whoever was going to steal his heart would have to be very special.

The idea of Jo Bertoletti came in a bit of an explosion. She was just there. *Bam!* And she didn't arrive alone. Writing a pregnant heroine, a heroine whose independence is as much a part of her as the air she breathes, was a change of pace for me and I loved the challenge.

But like I said, Ozzy is special, and from the second he sets his eyes on Jo, he knows this is a woman who will have an impact on his life, baby and all.

I hope you enjoy Ozzy's story and getting to visit with old friends.

Anna

Heartwarming

Building a Surprise Family

—

Anna J. Stewart

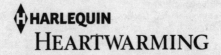

HARLEQUIN
HEARTWARMING

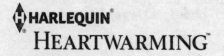

ISBN-13: 978-1-335-42634-5

Recycling programs for this product may not exist in your area.

Building a Surprise Family

Copyright © 2021 by Anna J. Stewart

This edition published by arrangement with Harlequin Books S.A.

For questions and comments about the quality of this book, please contact us at CustomerService@Harlequin.com.

Harlequin Enterprises ULC
22 Adelaide St. West, 40th Floor
Toronto, Ontario M5H 4E3, Canada
www.Harlequin.com

Printed in U.S.A.

Bestselling author **Anna J. Stewart** can barely remember a time she didn't want to write romances. A bookaholic for as long as she can remember, stories of action and adventure have always topped her list, especially if said books also include a spunky, independent heroine and a well-earned happily-ever-after. With Wonder Woman and Princess Leia as her earliest influences, she now writes for Harlequin's Heartwarming and Romantic Suspense lines and, when she's not cooking or baking, attempts to wrangle her two cats, Rosie and Sherlock, into some semblance of proper behavior (yeah, that's not happening).

Books by Anna J. Stewart

Harlequin Heartwarming

Return of the Blackwell Brothers

The Rancher's Homecoming

Butterfly Harbor Stories

A Dad for Charlie
Always the Hero
Holiday Kisses
Safe in His Arms
The Firefighter's Thanksgiving Wish
A Match Made Perfect
Bride on the Run

Visit the Author Profile page at Harlequin.com for more titles.

For Stacy Crum.

Friend, fan and cheerleader.

Readers like you are why I love this job.

CHAPTER ONE

"AND SWIPE RIGHT." Ozzy Lakeman waited for a ping of excitement, a ping of…*something* as the app responded and added another name to his list of potential romantic matches. Even as he set his phone down to finish his breakfast, that something never materialized. Instead, amidst the aroma of frying bacon and brewing coffee of the Butterfly Diner, the anticipation he hoped for was replaced with an odd feeling of, well, dread.

It was official. His dating pool had dried up.

"Who's today's lucky lady?" Brooke Evans set the coffeepot on the black speckled Formica counter and leaned her chin on her hand, the gold band of her wedding ring glinting against the florescent lights. "Oh, come on. Let me see." She mock-frowned and sighed at Ozzy paying meticulous attention to the last of his egg-white veggie omelet and fresh fruit. "You have to know you're considered a hot commodity in town, Oz. Sheriff's deputy turned firefighter, eligible bachelor. Homeowner." Her grin had him chuckling. "Trust me, that last one is a definite plus. And you're a nice guy to boot. That's a pretty rare combination these days, my friend."

"Be careful, Brooke. Taken or not, you might end up on my wish list." Fat chance. If there was one thing Butterfly Harbor, California, boasted about, it was their happily-ever-afters. And Brooke was newly married and very, very happy.

Six months ago, six *long* months ago, after spending years bearing witness to most of his friends getting married and starting families, Ozzy had, after attending yet another town wedding solo, decided to take the full-on plunge into the dating scene. He'd been paddling ever since.

From internet dating sites that required sign-up fees and hours spent filling out his profile, to cell phone apps with fifty character description limits, he'd gone all in. The results had eroded his bank account and left him wondering if he should accept the final challenge of letting his now-married friends start setting him up.

Nope. He wasn't that desperate. At least, not yet.

"You only love me for my coffee," Brooke teased. "You've worked hard to improve yourself, Oz. I'm just saying you should maybe enjoy the dating game a little more. It should be fun. Not a chore or obligation."

Ozzy swallowed the sour thought. "Improving himself" was town code for his having lost seventy pounds over the past two years, which allowed him to move into a career—and life—that not so long ago he'd have thought impossible. The only thing missing was having someone to share that life with. His friends all had someone to go home to at night and were adding children to their happily-ever-after equation. Was it so wrong for Ozzy to want the same thing? "Who says I'm not enjoying it?"

"That expression on your face, for one." Brook circled a finger in front of his nose. "Potential romance should bring out a smile. Hope. Excitement."

"My excitement is internal." Not to mention buried under twenty-seven years of insecurities and reality. Even at his heaviest, he'd dated occasionally, but he'd never experienced much of a spark. There had been crushes, of course, aptly named as that's what had inevitably happened. Nothing crushed a heart faster than being put in the friend zone.

That said, the friend zone was a very safe place to reside. Easy. Comfortable, actually.

Friends meant romance wasn't involved and the chance of getting romantically hurt was zero. But now? He glanced again at Brooke's engagement and wedding rings and sighed. He was really tired of playing it safe. "I like to save it up," he added with a forced smile.

Brooke glanced around the smattering of sunrise customers. The main breakfast crowd would start trickling in around seven-thirty, but for now, the orange upholstered booths and stools were occupied by early risers, postexercisers and, in Ozzy's case, a firefighter just off a twenty-four-hour shift. "You know," Brooke continued, "I heard a rumor there's more than one single lady in town hoping for an invite from you to Monty's wedding next month."

"You don't say?" Appetite extinguished, he dug through his wallet for cash. It was like the universe was reading his mind. He really hoped Brooke wasn't about to offer to play matchmaker.

"I do say. I bet you heard the same rumor, didn't you, Urs?" Brooke stood up straight and called back to Ursula, the diner's long-time cook, who slapped her metal spatula on the bell with her trademark scowl. "Something about a bet or a pool or something?"

"Might've heard something like that." Ursula's suspicious eyes were barely visible behind the counter as she slid a bacon breakfast special onto the pass-through window. "Order up. Table four."

"On it." Brooke offered Ozzy an encouraging smile. "I mean it, Ozzy. Try to enjoy yourself a bit more with this. The right woman's out there. Probably where you least expect to find her."

Brooke moved off, her blond ponytail swinging behind her. Ozzy swallowed his standard response. Despite a rather drastic change in appearance, he was still the same Oswald Lakeman he'd always been: the same Ozzy who had been born in Butterfly Harbor and had grown up here. He knew everyone and everyone knew him. On the one hand, there was no hiding anything given he'd lived in one place his entire life. On the other? It was more than unnerving to suddenly not be quite so…invisible.

His cell phone buzzed. After tossing money onto the counter, he picked it up, saw that his latest swipe had counter-added him to her "check me out" page. Ozzy's shoulders sagged.

The howdy bell over the door chimed as a new early breakfast devotee strode in.

"Hey, Oz." Fletcher Bradley, co-deputy at the sheriff's office, offered a warm, if not tired, smile. "You just off shift or heading on?"

"Off, actually." Ozzy's last shift had been relatively uneventful. Other than rescuing Mrs. Hastings's new cat, Blinky, who had taken refuge in the tree in the front yard because of her neighbor's half-blind retriever, his shift at the Butterfly Harbor Fire Department had proceeded without much fanfare or drama.

"Yeah, me, too." Fletcher smothered a yawn. "I've been getting in some overtime before Paige has the baby. Hoping to grab a jolt of caffeine before I head home to take Charlie to school."

Ozzy frowned, thinking of Fletcher's active and independent ten-year-old stepdaughter. "It's not raining, is it?" He glanced out the window just as the sun began glinting off the ocean that lay beyond the stone retaining wall across the street. "I thought Charlie always rode her bike to school."

Fletcher grimaced and wiped a hand down the side of his face. "Usually. She had a bit of a wipeout the other day."

"She okay?"

"Skinned her chin pretty badly. Thank goodness she was wearing her helmet. But the bike's totaled. Poor kid's heartbroken. It was the first thing Paige bought her when they moved to Butterfly Harbor."

Ozzy remembered. Charlie had been an instant bit of spark for their little Pacific coast town. No one could be cranky or have a bad day with the little spitfire around, but for Ozzy personally? Ozzy's heart tilted. Ozzy would always have a special place in his heart for Charlie. If it hadn't been for her impulsive actions a few years ago, he might not have changed his life—and his health—for the better. "Bikes can't be that expensive to replace, can they?"

"Charlie does not want just any bike," Fletcher declared in a formal tone as if a new law had been passed. "She wants *her* bike. Never mind she pretty much outgrew it last year and that I've spent the last two days scouring online marketplaces to find one identical to it. Looks like for now, or until I find one she approves of, I'll be driving her to school."

Ozzy finished his coffee, slapped a hand on his friend's shoulder. "You're a good dad, Fletch. I can't wait to see how you're going to juggle two kiddos."

"Well, our good Sheriff Saxon will be my role model in that area. If he can manage his three…" Fletcher trailed off as he looked outside. "Hey, that's something you don't see every day."

Ozzy followed his friend's gaze toward Monarch Lane where a substantial blue pickup was towing what looked like a house down the street.

"What the…" He moved past Fletcher and pushed open the front door. Sure enough, a plank-sided structure with a slightly slanted roofline rolled its way through town behind a large pickup truck.

Ozzy blinked. It wouldn't take more than a few minutes for its arrival to be the main topic of conversation not only in the diner, but all around town.

"It's like one of those home improvement channels is coming to visit," Ozzy said as other morning diners peered out the plate glass windows as the truck and cargo made their way slowly out of sight. "I've never seen one of those in real life. Any idea who that might be?" Fletcher shook his head. "Brooke?" Ozzy asked as Brooke joined them at the door.

"Afraid not. I've been off the last few days. Ursula?" Brooke called. "Have you heard anything?"

"Might've." Ursula rose up on her tiptoes. "I bet it's the new construction supervisor here to do damage control with the butterfly sanctuary site. Word is the town council overrode the mayor's choice and hired someone Leah Ellis recommended. Joe something."

"Really?" Brooke's eyes were still wide when she looked back at Ozzy and Fletcher. "I bet that was an ego blow for Gil."

"More like a wake-up call." Ozzy couldn't muster much sympathy for their mayor. But Brooke was right about one thing. If the town council had gone with the suggestion made by Gil's only rival in the upcoming election, there was probably trouble brewing in more ways than one.

"I guess I should head up to the construction site and see if they need help." Fletcher glanced at his watch. "I don't have to be home for a bit yet."

"I'll go." Ozzy grabbed the coat he'd hung up on one of the hooks by the door. "Get some coffee, relax. Anything comes up or I need help, I'll call you."

"You sure?" Relief shone in Fletcher's tired eyes. "That'd be great. I'll owe you, man."

"Don't worry about it. I'll add it to your tab." All Ozzy was going to do was sleep, anyway. Fletcher had people waiting at home for him.

Ozzy bid a quick farewell to Brooke and the diner's patrons and headed out to his new SUV, which, after more than ten years driving around a clunker, he was still getting used to.

The construction site, located on a plot of

land just north of the nearby organic farm and eucalyptus grove, had been closed in late March due to an unfortunate accident that sent four of the crew, including the foreman, to the hospital with minor to severe injuries. The ensuing investigation had kept the project shutdown for over a month and revealed the initial materials purchased for the project had been substandard. With lawsuits pending and accusations flying, speculation was running as rampant as water through newly installed pipes. Whether there was enough money in the town's treasury to absorb the cost of delays was a big topic of debate, a debate Mayor Gil Hamilton seemed determined to avoid having. The person ultimately responsible? Chances were the voters would make that decision come November.

Personally, Ozzy didn't think they could afford not to complete the project. So much of Butterfly Harbor's future depended on this new tourist destination, from various businesses to real estate prices. Their small coastal town had finally emerged from its long economic slump and was thriving again. New shops and services were popping up, and a lot of those places had planned their grand openings for the weeks surrounding the sanctuary and education center's completion. Whatever debt the town needed to take on to get the project finished should be accepted so they could move forward, as far as Ozzy was concerned.

He took the long way around to the site and pulled into the gravel parking area on the other side of what looked like crime-scene tape stretched between and around thick-trunked trees. He heard the rumble of the serious truck heading up the hill as he climbed out of his car. Headlights flashed into view and he held up a hand to signal the driver.

He couldn't stop grinning. That home on wheels was something to behold—practical with an elegant, streamlined luxury-cabin design. He could imagine how it would look nestled among the eucalyptus trees that outlined most of the area. A supervisor who brought his own house with him was someone who meant business.

The truck's engine suddenly went silent. Ozzy walked over to greet the driver. "That is a thing of beauty," he said as the door opened and the driver dropped to the ground in front of him.

Every thought he had disappeared straight out of his head.

Tall, curvy and with sun-streaked blond hair knotted into a messy pile on top of her head, Butterfly Harbor's latest arrival faced Ozzy with a wide, welcoming smile on her round face. Beneath the barely-there sunlight of the May morning, her skin seemed to glisten in the chilly air. She had light brown eyes, almost amber with flecks of gold that sparkled when she smiled. She wore snug jeans that accentuated everything a man like him enjoyed, sneakers that looked as if they'd been worn into the ground and a snug short-sleeved turquoise T-shirt that displayed a surprisingly round stomach.

The new foreman was a woman?

A *pregnant* forewoman?

"Didn't realize there'd be a welcoming committee." The woman closed the truck door and stepped up to him. "I know I wasn't expected until next week, but I wanted to get a jump on settling in. I'm Jo Bertoletti. You are not Mayor Hamilton." She gestured to Ozzy's T-shirt with the BHFD logo on the front peeking out of his jacket.

"Ah, no, ma'am." Ozzy shook her offered

hand. Her skin felt rough and calloused, proving she was someone who was used to getting her hands dirty. Beneath that observation, a dull buzz shifted through his system. "I'm Ozzy Lakeman. I was in the diner when you drove down Monarch Lane. Just thought I'd come up and be the first to see what was happening here." His own smile widened as something oddly definitive dinged. "I guess that makes me the welcoming committee."

"I appreciate that, Ozzy Lakeman of the BHFD." She beamed at him before her expression shifted into a knowing one. "Judging by the look on your face, I'm betting you weren't expecting someone...like me."

"I...uh." There had to be a way to answer that without sounding like a complete sexist or jerk. "Like you?"

Jo snickered. "Don't worry, Ozzy. Not the first time I've seen that reaction when I arrive on a site. And it's not because of the little bun I'm baking in here. *Bun in the oven*. That's such a weird phrase. Although come to think about it, I have spent my fair share of time waiting for my sourdough starter to develop."

Ozzy could only nod. His ears were buzz-

ing and his heart did an odd little skip and
jolted in a manner he'd never felt anytime
he'd swiped right.

"You still in there, Ozzy?" She waved a
hand in front of his face. "If you're trying
to cling to political correctness, don't bother
with me. I've been living and working on
construction sites since before I could walk
and long before I got this little one. I've heard
it all and a lot worse that would make that
cute face of yours blush six shades of red."

"Okay." At some point he was going to not
sound like an idiot, right?

Jo stepped around him and moved toward
the yellow tape. "They sent me pictures of the
site. Man, when the frame collapsed, it did
some damage, didn't it?" She pointed toward
the expansive grove of trees where scarred
trunks and barren ground were the only remnants of the originally assembled structure.
"We've got, what, nearly two months of construction to try to make up in a few weeks to
get back on schedule?"

"The mayor is still counting on us opening
in late October, early November. In time for
monarch season and the butterfly festival."

More like in time for the election, but Ozzy held his tongue on that point.

Jo sighed. "It's not the best situation I've dealt with, but it's not the worst, either. With the right crew, we'll get it done." Hands planted on her hips, she walked the perimeter. "You expecting more problems with the site?"

"No, ma'am."

"I'm no one's ma'am. The name's Jo or boss. Since you aren't crew, make it Jo."

"Nice to meet you, Jo." Something flickered in her eyes, something he couldn't quite identify, but he hadn't imagined it. "I was coming off shift when I saw you, or rather, your truck, rumbling through town."

"From the diner, right." She nodded. "Okay, firefighter from the diner, I'm glad you're here. You want to help a pregnant lady hook up a house?" When she faced him, her smile told him she was teasing him. "I'm kidding." She ripped down the yellow tape and crushed it into a tiny ball. "I've been hooking up this trailer for the last three years. I see the sewer line's right over there, near the construction office. And I can plug it into that generator next to it for backup power."

"So…you don't need help?"

"Never have, never will." She patted his arm and then headed back to her truck. "Stand back, Ozzy. This mama-to-be is making her nest."

THERE WAS LITTLE Jo liked more than a challenge and there was nothing more challenging than coming to a city or town to fix a problem that others were responsible for. Shocking one of the hometown boys into relative silence definitely ranked up there on her list of favorite things. Though, no, not a boy, she corrected herself.

A very handsome hometown *man*. She'd hoped to roll into town undetected, be set up and ready to go by the time anyone turned up on-site, as if she'd somehow appeared by magic. It seemed, however, that this town— or at least Ozzy Lakeman—had other ideas.

He also had her feeling a bit off-kilter with that charming, shell-shocked smile of his. Typical. She'd met enough firefighters to know that, like a lot of men in construction, they often came loaded with testosterone and more than their fair share of hero syndrome. She shook her head. Nope. Not even going to let herself contemplate any man's testosterone level. Clearly, she should have taken her doctor's warnings about her own amped-up hormones seriously.

Between her expanding business, this job and her baby on the way, the last thing she needed was to add anyone, especially a man, to her life. She'd learned her lesson. From here on out, she was on her own.

That said, firefighter or not, Jo imagined Ozzy Lakeman threw a lot of women off-kilter. How could he not with that thick, curly brown hair and eyes the color of a forest, dark and deep? As she moved around the truck, she couldn't help but take inventory of Ozzy's muscular build. It spoke of attention to fitness. That broad chest was perfect to display his firefighter logo and— Good heavens, what was wrong with her?

She wasn't in Butterfly Harbor to ogle men or, even worse, have a fling with one of them.

Like anyone would want to fling her anywhere, anyway. Still, that didn't stop her from glancing at the firefighter's hand to verify he wasn't attached. At least not legally. *It doesn't matter!* He was clearly younger than she was, and at thirty-five, Jo was beyond the time of helping men in their twenties find themselves. Besides, she'd be doing plenty of reassuring and guiding once her baby was born. But she had another four-plus months before she had to start fretting about that.

She ducked her head, hiding her smile as she removed the trailer from her truck, unhooked the cords and cables and got her home connected to the appropriate lines. As if by rote she then stretched out the industrial power cable to the trailer office on the off chance her solar storage decided to get temperamental.

Jo patted the back of the house. One of the main considerations she'd paid attention to when she'd built the structure was its ease of mobility. Taking her home with her from job to job, while it created some issues, had solved far more. One flip of the main power switch had the automated trailer pylons lowering and the porch steps popping out. She reached into the truck bed. Remembering the amount of effort it had taken her the last time to haul out her toolbox, she hesitated.

"Let me help," Ozzy quickly offered.

Jo's first instinct was to say no, but there was no denying the happy, almost jubilant expression on Ozzy's fine face. "You just couldn't wait for me to ask, could you?"

"No, ma—No," he corrected when she narrowed her eyes. His smile seemed genuine enough. Friendly, accepting, warm. He picked up her toolbox and turned to the trailer. "I've never seen one of these houses up close before."

"It's my pride and joy. Built it myself. Have some upgrades to make, of course, but I've got all the necessities, including a washer and dryer." Her stomach growled—maybe not only her own. "I hate laundromats," she added with a laugh.

"You'd love ours," Ozzy said. "We have old-fashioned arcade games in the waiting area, along with a reading room. It's also next door to Chrysalis Bakery. Best doughnuts in…well, best ones I've ever eaten," he added with a quick grin as she pulled out the key to her front door.

"If you'd leave my toolbox right down there." She pointed to the floor once she was inside. He leaned around the doorframe and waited for her to wave him forward to deposit the box. Out of habit, she retrieved a framed photograph from a kitchen drawer and set it on the counter, so that it was the first thing she'd see whenever she came home.

"Is that you?"

"Sure is." Pride had her straightening. "With my grandfather and my father. Joseph Bertoletti Senior and Junior. I was four here, I think? It wasn't my first day on a construction site, but it was the first day I actually remember. The crew bought me that 'Boss's girl' hard hat I'm wearing." Her lips twitched at the memory even as her heart clenched. That hat was one of the few items she'd kept from childhood, and there was a fifty-fifty chance she'd soon have a reason to pull it out of storage.

"Now you're just the boss," Ozzy teased. "So that makes you Jo—"

"The third. It's also a great fit, my dad thought, since it's likewise the name of my grandpa's favorite baseball player."

"DiMaggio?"

"Got it in one. You a Yankees fan?" Impressed, Jo turned and braced her hands on the table behind her.

"Not even close." Ozzy chuckled.

So he wasn't perfect after all. "The name was an ode to my grandmother, as well.

She loved Marilyn Monroe so much." She shrugged. "It was a twofer."

"Will this one be Jo number four?" Ozzy glanced down at her stomach.

"As much as I love the family tradition, I think I'll be giving my baby his or her own identity."

"You won't be naming the kid after the father, then?"

"No." That was enough cold water to douse the sparkling conversation. "Thanks again for your help, Ozzy. And the welcome. If you'll excuse me, I need to grab some sleep before the day really gets going."

"Sure, yeah, of course." He reached into his pocket for his wallet and pulled out a card. "I'm sure you'll be meeting plenty of people soon, but in case you need anything. Like someone to move things for you before your crew's back on the job." Ozzy gestured to the small but well-organized space. "I'm usually out and about. And if you can't find me, call the station house. I'll get the message."

"Good to know. Thank you, Mr. Fire-fighter."

His cheeks went red. "It was nice to meet

you, Jo." He backed down the steps. "I'm sure I'll see you around."

"I look forward to it." She stood in the open door, welcoming that fresh sea air. It was nice, she thought, having someone to talk to after more than three days on the road. Someone new and hospitable and, well… *Let's face it.* Firefighter Ozzy Lakeman was pretty darn nice to look at, too. She couldn't wait to see what the rest of the town had to offer. Not that she'd be sticking around long enough to gain much of an appreciation. After this, she'd be off to her new life—job, house, baby and all.

With her arms crossed over her chest, she waited until he drove away before she returned to the kitchen to find something to eat.

CHAPTER TWO

"KNOCK, KNOCK!" a familiar female voice called out.

Jo stopped midslurp of her peanut butter protein shake as the front door opened and Leah Ellis stepped into her house. "Hey!" She set her glass down and waved Leah inside, then gave her a quick hug. It never failed to amaze her how her longtime friend could wear designer suits and make them look both practical and elegant at the same time. The sky blue pants and blazer were tailor-made, while the casual white shirt and familiar solitary gold chain and charm around Leah's neck displayed professionalism, success and sentimentality. "I only got here this morning. How'd you know I was here?"

"Are you kidding?" Leah laughed and tucked her stylish bobbed dark hair behind her ear. "You drove your house past the diner. Everyone knows you're here." Leah reached out and rested her hand against Jo's baby bump.

What was it, Jo wondered, with people wanting to touch her stomach?

"How's the little one doing?" Leah asked.

"Swimmingly," Jo laughed as the baby kicked. She still got this odd zing of exhilaration whenever she felt her child move. "Not letting me sleep, that's for sure. I was hoping for a few more hours since I drove all night, but nope. Not having it." At some point she and her child were going to have to come to an understanding about the definition of what's comfortable. "Please, say you want coffee just so I can smell it." She missed coffee, but caffeine had been one of the things she'd had to eliminate from her diet.

"Coffee would be great. Thanks." Leah settled on one of the two bar stools at the narrow breakfast bar. "I see you took my advice." She pointed behind her to the transom windows Jo had opened to let in the morning breeze. "That ocean air's great, isn't it?"

"You did not lie." Jo took an extra beat to draw in a long breath and embrace the moment. She was a city girl, born and raised, and most of her professional life had been spent amidst the steel and concrete of the country's most populous spaces. What was it about fresh ocean air that made the reality of life fade away for a few blissful seconds? "I've been looking forward to it for the last three days. Hang on." Jo held up a finger, went to the small bread box she kept by the full-size stove and pulled out a brown paper bag. "They're probably a little stale, but…"

"Rudolf's bagels?" Leah practically threw herself onto the counter in dramatic gratitude. "You brought me bagels from Seattle?"

"Well, I brought you one." Jo grinned. "Don't ask how many I actually bought on my way out of town." Or how many she'd eaten since. She cut the one blueberry and the one everything bagel in half and popped them into the toaster, then retrieved the last of the cream cheese out of the fridge.

"How many mornings did we roll out of bed in our pj's to go buy a bag of fresh baked ones?" Leah sighed.

"So many that I'm still carrying the calories around on my hips." The aroma of brewing coffee and toasting bagels filled the air with nostalgia and sweet memories. "You were a hard flatmate to replace," Jo said.

"Impossible, actually." Which was why she'd eventually given up trying. They'd met in spin class shortly after Jo had graduated college and Leah was finishing law school in Seattle. Instant friends, they'd decided to pool resources and become roommates until Leah graduated and moved back east to work for a prestigious private law firm. They hadn't seen each other in, what? Eight years? They'd kept in touch, of course, via email and video chats, but looking at her friend now, it really was as if no time had passed.

"Ha, my mother always said I made a lasting impression." Leah's smile disappeared as soon as it happened. "So." She sipped the coffee Jo slid in front of her. "You going to tell me about it?"

"It?" Jo wasn't the greatest at playing innocent. Instead, she busied herself fixing the bagels.

"What happened with Greg, Jo?"

"Short story?" Jo took her frustration out on the cream cheese. At least Leah was the only person familiar with her history. "He doesn't want to be a father. Like *really* doesn't want to." She scraped the remaining cheese off with her finger. "On the bright side, at least we didn't get married."

"You came pretty close."

Six weeks and two days close. Jo turned her head, still confused that she felt more disappointment than anger at being dumped. But that was quickly replaced by irritation. She didn't plan to give Greg any more thought than she absolutely had to.

"I see you aren't wearing his ring anymore."

"Nope." The observation was enough to kick her out of self-pity mode. "I sold it." When Jo plunked the paper plate holding Leah's bagel in front of her, her everything-is-fine smile was solidly back in place. "Used the cash to upgrade my solar power system for this place." It probably hadn't been the nicest thing to do, but Greg's behavior certainly warranted it. "One guess which gives me infinitely more pleasure."

"Jo." Leah did that infuriating headtilt that often happened when Jo told a tale of heartbreak. "I'm sorry."

"Don't be." Jo shook off the remaining melancholy. "Apparently I needed a reminder that people I'm romantically involved with always let me down. This—" she pointed to her belly

"—wasn't supposed to happen. Doctors always told me I couldn't have kids. Who knew being infertile was one of the things Greg liked best about me." It hadn't struck her as ironic until after she realized that her biggest heartache—her inability to have children—was, at least to Greg's thinking, an asset. "It's okay, Leah, really." What she wouldn't give to erase that sympathy from her friend's face. "I've got the one person I've always been able to count on and that's me. That's all my baby will need. We're going to be fine."

"But you know you aren't alone, right? I mean you have me for crying out loud and you're here in Butterfly Harbor now." She smiled in a manner that had Jo suspecting there was more to that statement. "No one's ever alone very long in Butterfly Harbor." Leah hesitated. "What about your mom? Have you told her?"

"Had to. Mainly because I knew at some point I'd run into someone she knew and I didn't want to be on the receiving end of that phone call." Jo tried to ignore the pang of disappointment whenever she talked about her mother. "She wished me well and offered the obligatory 'if I needed anything' platitudes." It was, Jo realized, the most her mother was capable of. Any contact with Jo only reminded her mother of the loss she'd never gotten over. Not wanting to be dragged into the depressing topic that was her familial experience, Jo pushed the regret aside and focused on the present. "I'm supposed to let her know if it's a boy or a girl so she can get an appropriate gift."

"You don't know yet?" Leah's eyes went wide. "Aren't you around that time?"

"My last appointment got canceled and before I could reschedule, this job came along. I couldn't say no. Don't worry, I'll catch up." She waved off Leah's concern.

"When you're ready, we've got a great OB here in town. Cheyenne Miakoda. She hired a nurse practitioner and expanded her practice last year, set up her office just off the main street. From what I hear, she's amazing."

"Noted." And she did make note of it, on the pad on the counter. "So." Jo finally chomped down on her bagel and moaned at the goodness in her mouth. "Are these bagels as good as you remember?"

Leah ate some, furrowed her brow and, after a moment, nodded. "Not bad."

"Not bad?" Had Jo arrived in a parallel universe? "What's the deal?"

"Sure, it's good. Don't get me wrong, but there's a bakery in town that, I'm sorry, puts these to shame."

"Let me guess. Chrysalis Bakery?"

Leah's brows shot up and disappeared under her hair. "You heard about it already? From who?"

"Ha, I read about it online first," Jo admitted and finished the first half of her bagel, then washed it down with more protein shake. "But Ozzy Lakeman mentioned it this morning. He's a hottie. You and he ever—"

Leah choked on her coffee and reached for a napkin.

"Uh-oh." Jo frowned as her friend cleaned up. "That's an unfortunate reaction." Many tight knots formed in her already crowded belly, confusing her. "What's wrong with the blushing firefighter?"

"Nothing, actually." Leah wiped her eyes. "I'm just surprised is all. I assumed I was your first visitor, but I guess I should have known. He does seem to be everywhere these days."

"He saw me drive into town and thought

he'd play welcoming committee." The more she watched her friend, the more curious Jo became. "Okay, seriously, Leah. What? He seemed really sweet. Not to mention seriously hot." She smirked at her unintentional firefighter joke. "Hormones," she added at Leah's expression. "It's hard not to notice these things. Let me guess. He's secretly a serial killer. Oh, no. Don't tell me he still lives with his mother."

"No." Leah cringed. "I think he moved out of his parents' house before I moved here."

That sounded convincing. "Then what?"

"I'm just comparing him to Greg, I guess. I mean Greg is so…" Leah flicked out her fingers as if something exploded. "And Ozzy's so…" She shrugged and dropped her arms. "Ozzy's a sweetheart. One of the nicest guys I've ever met. You ever need help with anything, you need advice or a great conversation or someone to watch your kids, he's who you call." There was something else, something more Leah obviously had trouble putting into words.

"Well, he is a firefighter. They are reliable and trustworthy."

"He's also a former computer tech and sheriff's deputy."

"Really?" So Ozzy Lakeman had even more layers than she'd realized. He also sounded as if he was still trying to find himself. Yet another man who had issues with commitment. Yeah. Nothing to see there— she should move on. "Interesting."

"You tend to have a type, Jo." Leah hesitated. "Trust me, Ozzy's not a Greg."

"Another point in his favor, then." Despite her piqued interest, Jo downplayed her notion of Ozzy. "You've actually confirmed my first impression. But don't worry. I'm here to do a job and move on. And I'm definitely not looking to get personal with anyone." Personal created ties and Jo was done tying herself to anyone other than her baby.

"Oh? Where are you headed to next?"

"Montana. If all goes well here." Jo didn't want to jinx it. "There's a female-owned-and-operated construction company that's reached out. They're looking for a new partner to buy into the business, and apparently my name came up in discussion. We're talking. If it works out, I'll be heading directly there after the New Year."

Leah set her coffee down. "Montana?"

"I know." Jo knew exactly what Leah was thinking. Wide-open spaces weren't exactly her forte, and Montana had plenty of them. "It would be a big change." A huge change, Jo reminded herself. But the idea of a home base for a while appealed. She'd need some downtime once the baby got here and before she hit the road again. "And don't worry. I know how important this election is, Madame Mayor."

"Stop it." Leah winced. "I'm nowhere near elected yet. That's months away."

"But the town council took your suggestion to hire me. That must mean something."

"It means Gil ran out of excuses and alternate plans." Leah rested her jaw on her hand and looked almost forlornly at her bagel. "I never intended to do something like run for office, but I just couldn't sit back when no one was moving in to stop him. And don't think my recent move here has won me very many devotees. My opponent's lived here all his life and still has fans on every corner. What support I do have comes mainly from people who are tired of having a Hamilton running this town. I could have been a circus clown and they'd have put up my signs."

"Okay, now I really can't wait to meet this guy. But—" Jo pointed to Leah's bagel "—are you going to eat that?"

"No." Leah shook her head and pushed her plate away. "Feed it to the kid," she joked. "But what?"

"But?" Jo realized she'd fallen off track. "Oh, yeah. First things first is getting this construction project back up and running. You said I could get access to the main construction office when I got here?" She wanted to dive deep into the paperwork and employment records so she knew what and who she was working with.

"Sure." Leah dug into her purse and placed a set of keys on the counter. "Have at it. I've heard the place is a bit of a mess. Jed Bishop—"

"The foreman," Jo said. "I read what the mayor's office sent already," she explained, noting Leah's surprised expression.

"Right. Jed's a pretty self-sufficient guy. Competent and decent. Maybe a bit too trusting? He also isn't the neatest of individuals. No telling what you're going to find in there.

Don't get me wrong. Jed did what he could, but Gil was more of a looming shadow than you're used to and his opinion carries a lot of weight. The investigation did prove that it was the supplier who provided substandard materials. Jed didn't make the connection until after the accident."

Jo had read the reports and agreed it hadn't been easy to see. "In his statement, Jed said he was overruled on who their main supplier should be." She hesitated. "Any chance someone else had something to gain with the accident?"

Leah frowned. "If you mean the mayor, no. This project has been his baby from the start. As much as I disapprove of the job Gil's doing as mayor, I don't think he's crooked, Jo. Maybe shortsighted. He doesn't always see the big picture, but I know criminals. I've even defended some of them." Leah's eyes sharpened. "That's not Gil."

"All right." Jo took Leah's observation seriously. Jo's job was to move things forward, not to dig for dirt about the past. She wasn't, however, going to ignore any potentially important information she might come across while overseeing the project. Though she wouldn't run the day-to-day operation of the site, that task would still be the foreman's, she would be supervising the whole operation, from liaising with the foreman to maintaining safety standards, verifying permit applications, negotiating or, in this case, re-negotiating contracts and setting up a new schedule for construction and development. "Jed's going to be at the top of my list of people to talk to, so I'll hash out any doubts he has."

"You might have to do more than that. Jed hasn't committed to coming back." Leah hurried to explain. "The accident took a toll on him. Not just the broken arm, but mentally. He might not be anxious to step back onto a project that collapsed around his crew's heads. In spite of the fact that it wasn't technically his fault, I believe he blames himself."

"Huh." Jo absorbed that tidbit of information. "Okay." That could definitely put a kink in the schedule. She was on a tight enough timeline, having to hire a new foreman would set them back even further. Especially since most of her contacts in the area were, as far as she knew, committed to other long-term jobs. But she had a few extra days to sort that out. She scribbled a note to herself and stuck it on the edge of the counter so she'd see it later. There was always a solution no matter what the problem was. Finding it, even when it didn't readily present itself, was what she was known for: tightening the ship and bringing it safely into dock. "I've already reached out to some of my Bay Area connections in case we need more workers, but I'd really like to get a detailed look at the original plans before we get started again."

"I'm sure they're in the office somewhere, and if they aren't, Xander Costas is the architect. You can find him at Duskywing Farm. His wife owns it."

"I passed it on my way up the hill. Looked nice. By farm do you mean livestock that moo or…"

"Organic produce and homemade goods," Leah said on a laugh. "Jams, honey, syrups, that kind of thing. She got chickens last month and the eggs are incredible. She also hosts a neighborhood farmers market on the weekends. Everyone goes."

"Since this one won't let me sleep," Jo said, rubbing her stomach, "maybe I can walk there and back and lull the kid with exhaustion."

"Don't overdo it," Leah warned. "That little one's a miracle. And besides, I know you, Jo. Nothing slows you down. Don't forget, it isn't just you that you have to worry about now."

"The work can't stop because my circumstances have changed." She brushed off her hands and followed Leah to the door. "I'll get myself caught up and then call you. How about lunch next week at that diner place? Or maybe coffee at that bakery? Decaf, of course, for me."

Leah rolled her eyes. "You're going to eat your way through Butterfly Harbor, aren't you?"

"While I have a very good excuse to?" Jo's eyes went wide before she grinned. "You'd better believe it."

AFTER GETTING IN a good few hours of sleep along with a substantial run on the beach, Ozzy headed into town about the time school let out. The late-afternoon breeze kicked up as if welcoming him to his time off. Sure, he had chores he should be doing around the house, but he'd spent a lot of years wishing he had places to go rather than holing up in his house playing for a new high score on the latest video game. One of the positive changes he'd eventually made in his life was getting out more, and a walk around town was the perfect solution.

If only he could get Jo Bertoletti off his mind. Even now, he could feel that bubble of anticipation—or was it excitement—bounce in his chest. It wasn't the first time he'd seen his town through a newcomer's eyes, and it was her eyes he couldn't stop thinking about now. There was something appealing about the confidence she displayed, the way she'd readily dropped right in to get to work.

Being a keen observer most of his life meant he'd seen the underlying circus that went on in a small town. A sheriff's deputy, after all, bore witness to all sorts of zany antics and unpredictable events and tended to know the truth behind the gossip that swirled about.

He didn't see any in Jo's eyes, or in any part of her. What he did see piqued his interest, though. Far more than any photograph on his phone or first date he'd gone on.

"Don't get ahead of yourself, Oz," he muttered to himself. In part it was a warning. Jo had a lot going on in her life at the moment. No doubt the last thing she needed was his firmly settled self somehow developing a crush on her, an out-of-towner who literally lived on wheels no less.

The breeze kicked up and gave him a nice slap back into reality. He loved this time of year, when Butterfly Harbor was in between tourist seasons. The summer crowds had yet to descend and their few late-spring visitors were usually only in for the day. Steady trickles of customers along with smatterings of schoolkids on their way home or wandering over to the youth community center kept Butterfly Harbor buzzing.

At the end of the street he spotted two locals stringing up the music festival banner across Monarch Lane so newcomers would be sure to see it.

The weekend concerts in Skipper Park weren't scheduled to kick off for another couple of weeks, but the warming weather meant the beach barbecues and baseball games were in high demand. At least the ocean was still cool enough they didn't get too many adventurous swimmers. This would be his first official summer working water rescues, and truth be told, it wasn't something he was looking forward to. But one thing Ozzy had learned about himself in the last two years was that he could rise to a challenge.

Frankie and Roman, his bosses—co-fire chiefs who had gotten married a couple months back—were well aware of his trepidation, and Ozzy had been informed, they planned to start him and probie Jasper O'Neill on dedicated training sessions soon. Knowing how high a bar Frankie and Roman set, Ozzy would have his work cut out for him. All the more reason to keep up with his rigorous fitness routine.

"Whoops. Sorry, Ozzy!" Mandy Evans had spun out of her father's store, the Cat's Eye bookstore, her arms loaded with an extra large box with holes cut out on the sides.

Ozzy skidded to a stop before he plowed into the teenager. "You got that okay?" Ozzy automatically held out his hands to help, but Mandy shrugged him off.

"I'm good, thanks. Just running this batch of kittens up to Doc Campbell for a checkup. They're going to foster homes later today if they pass their medical." She eyed Ozzy.

"Don't suppose you're looking for a feline companion?"

"Uh-uh." Ozzy chuckled and quickly walked backward away from her. "Turn those hopeful eyes on someone else, kiddo. Besides, I help take care of Sparky, remember? That little black cat you pawned off on Roman and Frankie is a handful and a half."

"Aw, man. Everyone's onto me." She scrunched her face. "My mom and dad won't let me keep any more since I'm working now. Tribble and Zachariah need some youth to keep them going, you know?"

"I'm not taking sides in that argument." Ozzy shifted his attention across the street to where Harvey Mills sat in front of Harvey's Hardware, a catch-all store that also served as the town's postal annex and, in all honesty, gossip central, second only to the diner.

The older man had taken up backgammon again in the last few months after he'd tumbled off Mrs. Johanson's roof while cleaning her gutters. Harvey hadn't broken anything—a minor miracle—but it had been strongly suggested he take it easy and refrain from offering handyman services to single ladies of a certain age.

Now that the weather had cleared, he'd moved his old-fashioned table and chairs outside to get his daily dose of Vitamin D while he played. It had become a bit of entertainment about town, with many residents helping to occupy Harvey's time by challenging him to a game. Including, Ozzy's brows arched at the sight, their very own mayor.

Ozzy glanced at his watch. "You sure you're good carrying them as far as Doc Campbell's?"

"Yep," Mandy insisted. "Feels good to be outdoors. I've been stuck inside studying all week. You and Hunter still going fishing tomorrow morning?"

"Before the sun's up," Ozzy confirmed. "Phoebe's coming with us, too. Her idea," he added at Mandy's wide-eyed surprise. "I know. Who knew seven-year-old girls like to fish."

"Oh, well, I loved it." Mandy shifted the box as a little pink-tipped gray paw poked out of one of the holes. "But then my dad says I was born with flippers on my feet. I'll probably see you at the marina. I'm running one of the whale-watching tours for Monty."

"By yourself?"

"Uh-huh." Mandy beamed. "My first solo run and I got a raise. Monty actually pays me to be out on the water." She shook her head. "Best job ever. I need to get going. I'll see you tomorrow."

"Yeah, tomorrow." Ozzy watched her scoot across the street and head down Monarch Lane toward the vet's office. Curious, and deciding he had some time to kill, he jogged across the street to the hardware store.

"I was going to stop by and see if you were up for a game," he said to Harvey, who pushed his thin wire-rimmed glasses higher on his nose and gave him one of his cool smiles. "Guess you've found some new competitors, huh? Afternoon, Gil. Didn't know you played backgammon."

"I don't," Gil Hamilton said with a bit of a shake of his head as Harvey quickly moved two of his pieces closer to bearing off. "As you can see."

Ozzy did see and honestly, the image left him oddly amused. He'd known Gil Hamilton all his life, had trailed a few years behind him in school, and Ozzy, along with countless others, had ridden in the wake of the town's favorite son's successes. There wasn't anything Gil hadn't accomplished: class president, star quarterback, prom king. He'd also earned a nickname thanks to Frankie, Ozzy's boss. Gil "The Thrill" Hamilton had been the King Midas of Butterfly Harbor; everything he touched turned to gold. But just like Midas, the benefits came with their own particular curse.

The Hamilton touch had become tarnished in recent years. Whether the tarnish started with Gil's father or grandfather, the only remaining Hamilton offspring carried the brunt of it now. So far, Gil had managed to keep his reputation from completely crumbling, but given the number of "Elect Leah Ellis" signs in store windows and spiked into front yards, it was only a matter of time before Gil found himself in the unemployment line.

It wasn't that Gil was a bad guy. Living in the shadow of a father who had all but ruined the town couldn't be easy, but there were times Gil seemed to forget that his ideas and plans for Butterfly Harbor actually affected the people who live here, and not always for the better. That, at least for Ozzy, was what irritated him and would pretty much guarantee he'd be voting for Leah Ellis in November.

"Backgammon is a great equalizer," Harvey said, clearly catching Gil's sour expression. "And a great teacher of patience."

"Right now it's just teaching me that I'm terrible at it." Gil rolled a four and three, and without much of a glance at his pieces, reached for one. Ozzy coughed a little too loudly into his hand. Gil glanced up and Ozzy shook his head.

"Ozzy, wait your turn," Harvey admonished and stretched out his right leg with a bit of a wince. "The man needs to learn on his own."

Gil arched a brow, sat back and checked the board. "What aren't I seeing?"

"Opportunity." Ozzy casually lounged against the front of the hardware store. "Sometimes it's best to take the easy move while you can."

Gil frowned, his dark blond eyebrows Vee-ing. "I don't… Oh, wait. There it is." Gil clicked one checker straight into place. Harvey smiled, snatched up the die and rolled, before knocking Gil's blot into the center of the board.

"Hang on." Gil straightened in the low hardback chair. "I thought—"

"I said sometimes," Ozzy said. "It's luck and strategy, remember. You should be looking at his pieces just as much as you do your own. And now—"

"Game over," Harvey announced sweetly and moved his final checker into the winning spot.

Gil deflated, his shoulders slumping. The mayor sagged back in his seat.

"Sorry, kid." Harvey winked.

If Gil took offense to the moniker Harvey had tagged him with decades before, he didn't let on. Instead, Ozzy watched as irritation was quickly replaced by acceptance. "Obviously, I need more practice."

"Only one person in this town's ever bested me consistently," Harvey said.

"I'm guessing it wasn't my father," Gil said and got to his feet. Something in his tone caught Ozzy off guard. Not just Gil's tone. It wasn't often that Gil mentioned the former mayor and town patriarch, either by name or inference.

"Your father was never particularly interested in the game," Harvey confirmed. "He used the time as an excuse to smoke those cigars of his and drink Scotch."

"Given those cigars are part of what killed him, he should have paid closer attention to the board," Gil said. "So, who did beat you?"

"Who do you think?" Harvey jerked a thumb at Ozzy, who felt his face go hot. "Not every time, mind you. Boy had his own learning curve. You know he competed at the state level through high school, right?"

"I…" Gil frowned, as if this was indeed news to him.

Never mind the fact that Ozzy had made the town paper, as well as the ones in the surrounding areas. He'd even been interviewed for the Monterey news station. "Competed," Ozzy emphasized. "I didn't win."

"Winning isn't everything." Harvey began to reset the board and gave them a pointed look. "Don't you go downplaying your accomplishments, Oz. You made it to the state finals two years running. That's nothing to sneeze at."

"No one's sneezing," Ozzy replied. His mother still had his finalist trophies sitting on their own shelf in her living room.

"Seeing as I've been beat. Again." Gil moved to go. "I'll see you for another game next week, Harvey. Oz? Do you have a minute?"

This day was chock-full of surprises. "Yeah, sure. I'll take black this time, Harvey." Ozzy shoved his hands into his pockets and followed Gil a few feet away. When the mayor pivoted toward him, he had that familiar determined look in his eyes. "What's up?"

"I heard you went up to greet the new construction supervisor. It probably should have been me, but I wasn't expecting—"

"She was early. Wanted to get settled in before she got to work."

"She?" Gil was quick, but not quick enough that Ozzy didn't catch the flash of surprise— or was that shock—on his face. "Jo Bertoletti's a woman?"

Ozzy pressed his lips tight. If Gil didn't know Jo was a woman, he was really in for a surprise when he got a look at her. Still, it wasn't typical for Gil to be caught off guard. Clearly Gil wasn't at the top of his game—in more ways than one. "She is indeed. Looked ready to get down to work, if you ask me."

"It's funny, it never even occurred…" Gil scrubbed a hand across his forehead. "Okay, that'll make things interesting. How did you find her?"

"I drove straight up Monarch Lane."

Gil snort-laughed, which set Ozzy's nerves on edge. Since when did his jokes land with Gil? "I found her impressive, actually. If you really want my opinion."

"Of course I do. You're a good judge of character, Ozzy. It's not going to be an easy job, supervising this project. Especially if we're going to push to still get it done on schedule."

Ozzy knew what Gil was asking. He was wondering how much of a pushover Jo Bertoletti might be. Ozzy couldn't wait for Gil to find out the answer to that himself. "I think if you let her do her job everything's going to be fine. She doesn't strike me as someone who likes to be micromanaged." But Ozzy would bet good money Jo was used to people at least attempting it.

"I'll take that under advisement," Gil agreed as behind them, Harvey cleared his throat. "Wait. Before I go, Oz, there's something else I'd like to ask you. I didn't know you played backgammon."

"I also have my grandfather's old comic collection." They could play this game of "I didn't know" all day.

"I was thinking—could you maybe help

me learn to play? I mean, really play and not just pretend to know what I'm doing?"

"You want *me* to teach *you* to play a game?" Ozzy had the sudden urge to check for hidden cameras. His radar pinged and for a moment, he was back in high school, the geek who had just been asked to sit at the cool kids' table before becoming the victim of some prank. "Why?"

"I told you," Gil said. "And, to be honest, I kind of like the routine Harvey and I have gotten into. Taking a walk after lunch to come here. It's helping with my physical therapy, too." He pointed to the leg he'd seriously injured last Christmas during a fire at his office. A fire he'd almost died in partly because of his proposed cuts to the local fire department. If there was one thing Gil seemed to excel at, it was learning lessons the hard way.

"I guess I can give you a few pointers." Ozzy considered his schedule. "I'll be off next Monday afternoon and Tuesday. Either of those days work for you?"

"Tuesday would be great. Come by the office? I can order lunch in."

"How about I bring lunch. I'll be there around twelve thirty?"

"Perfect. Thanks, Oz. I appreciate it." Gil slapped a hand on Ozzy's arm and walked away, leaving Ozzy standing there, blinking.

"What just happened?" he asked aloud.

Harvey chuckled as Oz took Gil's vacated seat. "You've never seen someone try to make friends before?"

"Not since my playground days," Ozzy muttered.

"Take it for what it is. Gil's reaching out. Ah, thanks, Shelly." He accepted the can of soda one of his employees had brought out. "You're a peach."

"No problem. Hey, Ozzy."

"Hey." Ozzy didn't look up at first, but when he did, he found the twentysomething redhead watching him with one of those secret female smiles he could never interpret. Tight jeans, an equally tight green T-shirt with the hardware store logo, she also wore a black apron around her waist to keep her notepad, pencils, pens and tape measure handy. She was cute, with freckles dusting her nose and bright blue eyes that were clearly saying something. Instead of attempting to interpret that something, however, he found himself thinking of another pair of eyes he'd looked into early this morning. Gold-flecked amber eyes that carried humor and confidence. Teasing eyes.

Tempting eyes.

"Do you want a soda, Ozzy?" Shelly asked. "I can bring you one, no problem."

"Ah, no, thanks." He cleared his throat as images of Jo Bertoletti swam through his mind and, oddly, cleared his foggy brain.

"Water, then?" Shelly shoved her hands in her front pockets, rocked forward on her heels. "Or coffee? I could go get you one."

"Leave the man alone, Shelly," Harvey admonished. "Water would be fine, I'm sure. Right, Ozzy?"

"Yeah, sure, water's great. Thanks." Instead of smiling after her, he frowned across the board at the older man. "Am I missing something?"

"Yes. As usual."

"Does this have to do with that bet thing? About Monty and Sienna's upcoming wedding?"

He kept his tone casual, as if he wasn't fishing for details and focused his attention firmly on the board as he arranged the black pieces for a new game.

"Surprised you're so calm about the whole thing," Harvey said. "It's not every man in this town who has a price on his head."

"A price?" He'd almost squeaked.

"Last I heard there are four eligible females hoping for an invite to the wedding from you. Word is Ursula started a pool for betting on who you'll ask." Harvey shrugged. "That's just the rumor, though."

The very idea he was the focus of some feminine betting pool left him rather unsettled. That was the kind of thing that happened to other guys, not to Ozzy.

"I'm not saying anything," Harvey declared with far-too-innocent eyes. "But if I were to speculate, I'd say you aren't on the wrong track with Shelly." When Ozzy didn't respond, Harvey chortled. "You've transformed yourself, Ozzy. You're a new man. New and improved according to what I'm hearing. And you're a firefighter now. A hero, day in and day out. That's its own kind of feminine appeal."

That phrase *new and improved* didn't sit particularly well. "I'm the same Ozzy I've always been." The packaging was a bit different that was true, but on the inside he'd like to think he was still the decent, hardworking guy he'd always been. He felt like an idiot for even dwelling on it.

He was proud of what he'd accomplished. Because of the weight loss, he'd been able to go after dreams that had been out of reach for most of his life. But that didn't change who he was. His character, his principles... Why didn't people understand that?

"Fact is," Harvey said, "we're all proud of you, Ozzy. Making those changes really shows what you're made of. You can't hold it against some who maybe want to do more than just appreciate in silence. Something that might lead to even more changes in your life? Hint, hint."

When Shelly returned with his bottle of water, he accepted it with a friendly smile. "Thanks, Shelly."

"Anytime, Oz. I mean that." She turned and flipped her wavy hair over her shoulder.

Darn it! Harvey was right. Opportunity was walking away. "Hey, Shelly?" He pushed to his feet and nearly knocked the backgammon set over. "Sorry, Harvey." The older man grunted as Shelly turned expectant eyes on him. "Ah, Shelly, I was wondering, they're starting a retrospective of Bogart and Bacall films this weekend. Would you be interested in—"

"I'd love to," Shelly blurted. "I'm off tomorrow. You are, too, right?"

"Yes, I am." Was his work schedule common knowledge? "I'll meet you at the theater at six? We can get something to eat after. If you want."

"I'll want." Her smile took up most of her face. "Sounds great. I'll see you then."

"Huh." Ozzy watched her head back into the hardware store.

Harvey drank some of his soda and pointed at the board. "You ready to play?"

"Absolutely." Ozzy glanced over to where Shelly had vanished.

He had a date with a nice lady, the kind of woman he'd once never had the guts to ask out. This was good, he told himself as he waited for Harvey to make his first move. He was making progress.

Progress. A date with kind, sweet Shelly

who worked at the hardware store. It was exactly what he'd always wanted. Regret niggled at the back of his mind.

Wasn't it?

CHAPTER THREE

THERE WERE FEW certainties in life, but one thing Jo had never counted on was being kicked awake by a baby-to-be. Was it possible, she wondered, as she shifted in bed, that the kid could tell time?

Was *kicked* even the right word? The persistent fluttering going on in her stomach struck her as both reassuring and disconcerting. It just felt…weird. She reached behind her, yanked the pillow she'd shoved against the small of her back free and gave silent thanks that for the first time in ages she felt as if she'd finally slept. Except now she had to get out of bed. She flopped out an arm.

Ugh.

If she had to bet money, she'd say her baby was going to be a champion swimmer. Or more likely a kicker for the NFL. Jo pressed her palm against her belly, her lips curving in a sleepy smile before twinges of panic tickled her nerves. What did she know about kids' swimming or sports lessons? Or even school, for that matter?

Other than math and science, she'd barely paid attention when she'd been a student herself, and she certainly hadn't played sports. She'd much preferred spending time with her grandfather at construction sites or in his office. After he passed, she'd found her true home at the sites she worked. Some would say she had no roots, but she'd just made hers mobile. In a matter of months, she was going to have to start evaluating the education options for a brand-new life that would be utterly and completely relying on her.

"Stop it." She pressed her fingers into her temples. She'd only make herself sick staying on this endless carousel of uncertainty. She'd figure it out. She always did. This was just one more challenge to overcome.

"And with that, it's time to get another day started." Jo had never been one to lounge around in bed, not even on holidays and especially not on weekends. Once she was awake, she was full steam ahead, and as usual, she had a list of things to do that needed to get tackled if construction was going to resume next week.

She shoved herself up, sat on the edge of the bed for an extra few moments, waiting for the morning sickness that had finally abated to take another swipe at her. She'd been pretty lucky in that regard. The few weeks of discomfort and nausea hadn't hung around as long as the websites she'd visited had suggested. Of course, there were days Jo was convinced she'd willed it away. She didn't have time to feel sick.

That didn't mean, however, that she moved as efficiently as she used to. Not for the first time, it felt as if she had to readjust to whatever her body had done overnight. No two days felt the same. She hadn't anticipated feeling quite so out of control where her body was concerned, and for a control freak like Jo, it was not something she planned to get used to.

It took her a while to get showered and dressed and peruse the meager contents of her refrigerator to rustle up breakfast. She topped the last leftover slice of pizza she'd had delivered from town—hey, it had veggies on it—with hot sauce and grabbed a bottle of water and her cell before heading over to the construction office to finish the last bit of organizing she'd tackled after Leah left yesterday.

Once outside, Jo took a long, deep breath and released it. She could definitely get used to that sea-kissed air every time she exited her house. Tucking her sweater tighter around her, she took a beat to greet the day. She walked the short distance to the trailer office, but before she pulled open the door, she found herself drawn to the thin patch of dawn light peeking in through the grove of eucalyptus trees. Leah had been right to entice her here. It was time Jo expanded her horizons. Besides, as her grandfather had always advised, *You should see the space from every perspective.*

She shoved her cell into her back pocket. Munching on her pizza, she ducked under the remnants of yellow tape. The widened path had erased a significant swath of trees and shrubs, enough to provide the soon-to-be-built structure the perfect view of the cliffs and ocean. A nature walk would be created, one that would include a natural barrier of protection along the cliff's edge and a meticulously integrated path through and around the remaining flora and particularly the eucalyptus and redwoods.

A twig snapped. Jo swung around, heart jackhammering as she frantically scanned the tree line. The shadow that moved out from the thick trunks seemed oddly calm as the sun continued its rise beyond it.

"Sorry," the man said, offering a tight flash of a smile. She winced, tried to see through the playing shards of light. "Didn't mean to spook you."

She took in his lean frame, the shoulder length dark brown hair, and the way he shoved his hands in the pockets of his worn jeans, rocking back on his heels as he looked at her.

"The site is still closed," Jo said, planting her feet hard in the ground. "Any particular reason you're lurking?"

"Revisiting some ghosts," he said after a quick glance toward the ocean. "Didn't realize anyone would be up here."

"Jo Bertoletti." She didn't offer her hand. She had the feeling that maintaining her distance wasn't a bad idea. "I'm the new construction supervisor."

The man's eyebrows went up and after a moment, he nodded, ducked his chin. "So they're going ahead with the build even after the accident."

Jo could barely hear him, as if he was speaking more to himself than to her. "They are. Were you on the previous crew?"

"No." His answer did nothing to make her feel better. "Just passing through. Heard about the trouble and got curious. You should be careful." He gestured to the rocky ledge. "Cliffs like this can be dangerous."

It seemed an odd comment to make. Was it a threat? The man started to walk away.

"I didn't catch your name," Jo called after him.

"I didn't throw it." He shouted the joke over his shoulder before he disappeared into the trees.

"Well, that was very strange." Now Jo was the one muttering to herself as she shivered against a sudden chill. She shouldn't have expected to be completely alone up here, but the fact that she hadn't seen a sign of the man until she was well away from the main site had her nerves continuing to ping. She inhaled a calming breath, forcing the encounter out of her mind and her thoughts back to the task at hand: her job.

Having examined the designs, she could imagine the exterior of the sanctuary and education center butting right up to where nature refused to retreat, where butterflies would be drawn to during their migration season. She'd accepted this job because it came across as both a challenge and yet should be a fairly straightforward responsibility. That didn't mean she took the task any more lightly than she did other jobs. But given the information she had on the forthright foreman and the hardworking crew, she'd be surprised if her stress level increased any more than normal.

Jo put a hand on one of the thick trunks and looked up. She could swear she saw the faint flickering of dotted orange wings swaying in the morning breeze. The ocean waves crashed into the shoreline far below, and while she was too far from the cliff's edge to feel the spray of the water, she could smell the intoxicating freshness that only came from nature. For miles in each direction the trees spread, outlining the construction site with their own determined if not manicured formation. Looking back down the trail she'd taken, she could see the trees were less dense from this angle and that during the day, the view that visitors would have would be stunning.

Atmosphere, especially in regards to a project like this, was as important as the structure itself. It was a point of pride that she'd been entrusted with overseeing its completion. She had mere weeks to make a miracle of timing happen.

"Okay, Jo." She finished her breakfast, took one last lingering look at the ocean stretched out before her. There would be plenty of time to admire the view later. "Time to get to work."

Her sneakers crunched in the dirt and rocks as she returned to the construction trailer. When she pulled open the door, she inhaled the familiar dusty, warm air of a claustrophobic office that welcomed her at every job. Butterfly Harbor was no different inside these walls than Seattle had been. Or Dallas or Louisville or Charlotte.

She'd spent most of yesterday digging through the paperwork and files inside the trailer that was about the same size as her house on wheels, yet it felt smaller. The solitary desk had only one name plaque. "Gil Hamilton." Of course. Jo picked up the mayor's bronze nameplate and set it down again. Leah had warned her Mayor Hamilton was one of those hands-on politicians who needed—no, make that *expected*—to know precisely what was going on with whatever projects his office was responsible for.

Her friend had made it sound like a negative trait, but Jo wasn't so sure. It made sense, given that this project was the mayor's baby from day one, that he'd want to stay on top of things. Whether that made him deserving of the only desk in the compact office was another thing entirely.

Clearly this would warrant a discussion.

The second her pen finished scribbling a reminder note, she heard the sound of tires grinding over gravel. She stood up as quickly as she could, walked over to the window and twisted open the dusty venetian blinds. The classic black car with tinted windows possessed a shine that spoke of attention to detail and a whole lot of money. The driver climbed out, his sandy blond hair catching against the morning sunlight.

Jo took in the flashy car, the styled haircut, the pressed chinos and shirt, as well as the designer loafers that had no business being anywhere near a construction site, let alone on one. Only one person that could be.

She returned to the desk, flipped the notepad open, put a checkmark next to "contact the mayor" on her list, then went to the door.

"Mayor Hamilton?" she called.

He skidded to a halt and seemed to take a moment before he turned around, a polite expression on his face. "Ms. Bertoletti?"

Nuts. Jo kept her face passive. He'd known she was a woman. "Jo, please." She waved him over. "I had just made a note to call you. Come on in." She let the door drop closed behind her and headed to the anemic coffee machine wedged into a space on top of a metal file cabinet. "Coffee?" she asked when he joined her.

"Sure, thanks. Even if I am already over my quota for the day." He stood just inside the door. "I was surprised to hear you arrived early. Sorry I didn't stop by yesterday to welcome you to town." Jo turned to hand him a paper cup of pod-produced caffeine. "I was caught up—" His eyes scanned up and down, catching on her rounded stomach, before his gaze popped back up to her face. She could practically hear the questions screaming through his brain. "Ah. Congratulations." He accepted the cup and drank, winced, drank some more. "When's the baby due?"

"October. Don't worry," she said as if he had started to speak. "Being pregnant won't get in the way of my job. Let's sit, shall we?" She gestured to the desk.

If he was thrown off kilter by her moving to take a seat behind it, he didn't show it. Instead, he waited until she was settled, then emptied one of the straight back chairs, shifting the papers and folders, and sat across from her.

"I wasn't aware you were married."

"I'm not." If he was waiting for her to explain, he'd be waiting all day. "So. We've got a lot to do." She retrieved her notepad and pen. "Why don't we start by talking about our expectations for one another. I'll start." She plowed ahead before he could argue. "I'm going to make sure everything with this project runs smoothly from here on out. I'm not here to assign blame for what happened, but I will be looking into that situation as we move forward, if only to ensure the same mistakes aren't made again. This project is now my responsibility. The successes, the failures, it's all on my shoulders. That I'm sure will be a relief for you."

"I've got a lot riding on this butterfly sanctuary."

Honesty. That was a good start.

"Then I'll only have to ask you for one thing. Your trust." She kept her eyes locked on his. "I'm good at my job, Mr. Mayor."

"Gil," he said. "And I have no doubt that you are. Leah wouldn't have recommended you otherwise. She's…fastidious when it comes to the details."

Jo would bet that was grudging admiration she heard in his voice, and she appreciated the apt description of her friend. "I don't take her endorsement lightly. If anything, it makes me even more determined to do this job right. But we're starting from the ground up, so to speak. I understand there's some question about your foreman returning. What can you tell me about Jed Bishop?" She clicked open her pen, ready to take notes.

"You want my take on him?"

"I want your take on all the employees. You've been managing the project very closely, haven't you? I'd appreciate any insight you can give me." Names in a file were one thing. Personality, impressions, anecdotes added a whole other layer to her future relationship with these employees. "The more information I have from the jump, the better I can keep the ball rolling. And it will be rolling. If that means we take it to six days a week, we'll do it."

"Six days a…" Surprise jumped into his gaze, quickly followed by disbelief. "That's not possible. We're using a union crew. Six days—"

"Having negotiated on behalf of construction unions in the past, I can assure you I'm well aware of what we can make happen. We'd create two teams and give time and a half for Saturdays to those who want the positions. It'll be a choice, not an ultimatum, and this is merely a backup plan. If we don't get enough to cover both teams, then I'll be bringing in some workers I know from the Bay Area."

"If you need outside help, I've got contacts—"

"No offense, Mr. Mayor. Uh, Gil," she corrected and pounced on the opportunity to get the ground rules established. "But this isn't your project. The sanctuary might have been your idea, but that's where things should have stopped. It's the town's project and the town has hired me. Whatever position you held previously, honorary or otherwise, around here it's over. The hirings, firings, schedules, pay, union negotiations, you name it, that's all my job. You will not be signing another piece of paper or giving another order where the sanctuary and education center is concerned." She stood up, retrieved the name plaque and handed it to him. "That means you won't be needing a desk in this office any longer."

Gil looked at the metal plate in his hand, and for the first time, Jo found herself unable to decipher his expression. She'd done her homework; she knew he was a lifelong resident of Butterfly Harbor, and in reading his bio on the town website, she had no doubt he was used to getting his own way.

"Since you've requested my trust and you've led with it, I'm going to be honest with you, as well, Jo."

"Excellent." She sat and cracked open her water, drank to coat her dry mouth. "Go for it."

"Trust is earned. Especially with this project. I've sunk too much of the city funds into this sanctuary already, and to be honest, if it wouldn't cost a fortune to walk away from it, I would. To call it a *money pit* is an understatement."

"A *pit* is what you fall into when you approve contracts with substandard suppliers," Jo countered. She'd seen the invoices and paperwork. Jed Bishop hadn't signed off on anything more than his crew's paychecks. Gil had done all the final negotiations. But until she had proof Leah's gut was right—that Gil was unaware of the shoddy and shady deal he'd made—Jo wasn't ruling any nefarious activity out. "It's going to cost more to get us back up and running, and you're looking at what I'm estimating is a good twenty percent overage on the estimated cost of construction."

"Twenty—"

"Estimated," Jo said again. "My goal is to bring the project in as close to the original budget as possible. I've got a pretty good success streak going, and I'm not about to change that for anything. I'm good at my job, remember," she repeated. "Whether you trust me or not, you'll have to believe that. Now." She took a seat at Gil's former desk and grabbed one of the stacks of files she'd made yesterday. "How about we start with the employee files?"

BY THE TIME Gil left a few hours later, Jo was feeling much better about where things stood, not only with the mayor, but also with the project and her prospects for moving ahead.

Gil's optimism in regard to the crew initially came off as a bit unrealistic. At least until she'd reached out to the crew members herself. It took only a few conversations to feel her own positivity settle in. By the time she'd made her way through the list, she had a full crew ready to come in and begin construction first thing Wednesday morning. Her issuing a mandatory employee meeting Monday morning at 6:00 a.m. hadn't earned her many raves, but the occasional grumble had reaffirmed her original belief that this crew wasn't as perfect as she'd been led to believe and gave her a more familiar frame of mind.

She'd hope for the best, plan for and expect the worst, and be happy if reality landed somewhere solidly in between.

Feeling as if she'd made a good dent in her preparations, she gave herself the rest of the day off. Besides, it was half past noon, and with her fridge bordering on bare, she was ready to find something to eat. By going into town she could also scope out the bank so she'd know where to submit the paperwork to add herself as a signatory on the project's bank account.

She grabbed her cell and returned to her house for her keys. She considered taking her truck, but she was still feeling those kinks and tight muscles from the drive as well as the hours she'd spent hunched over the desk. Plus, the walk would justify whatever yummy food she decided to treat herself to.

There was, she discovered as she meandered through the residential streets, an unexpected calm that descended on her. She'd memorized the layout of the town and had a pretty good idea where she was going, but there was a world of difference between a map and an actual place. She soon learned there was no getting lost. All she had to do was follow the intoxicating, seductive scent of that wondrous ocean that seemed to reach up and roar protectively around the entire town, even from a distance.

Beneath the seagull cries and the breeze whipping against her ears, she could hear the telltale sounds of Saturday as she wandered past homes. People were catching up on the yard work or puttering around. She encountered more than a few garage sales that had better attendance than any she'd ever encountered before.

There was something a bit out of the past in this town, Jo realized as she admired the many homes with their manicured and sometimes very festive yards. Pinwheels spun and glinted against the early-afternoon sun. Thick color-topped bushes of poppies and snapdragons dotted fence lines and divided properties. One yard in particular was filled with a collection of metal animal statuary that made it look as if they'd broken out of their storybook zoo to take up residence at the almost cottage-like house. Most homes displayed stone bird baths, landing places for bees and butterflies to take a break and drink beneath the sun.

She'd often heard but never understood the phrase *charming* when it came to places like this, but she did now. The way the neighbors moved fluidly between homes, the way kids rode their bikes and skateboards in the street under the watchful eyes of family and friends made more than an impression. It gave her a glimpse of what she, as someone who had grown up in and around some of the biggest cities in the country, had missed out on.

She stopped at the corner of each block, taking in the various architectural details, getting her bearings, and memorizing street names and landmarks. She was going to be here at least until October. Best she get her bearings sooner than later.

After a half mile she stopped to admire the scene. It didn't take her much more than getting another glimpse of waves lapping against the shore down the hill and beyond the stone retaining wall to understand why Leah had decided to make her home here. There was something soothing about this almost laid-back rhythm of life. She wondered how long it would take for boredom and frustration to set in. It was as if she'd stepped into an old

TV sitcom where everything and everyone were…well, simply weren't possible.

As she reached town, her attention shifted. Storefronts filled the first floors of two-story buildings. Cute little antiques and home-made-goods stores. A comic book shop. An art gallery, photography studio. A music shop with a display of multicolored ukuleles caught her attention. Her musical abilities had never been tested, but that didn't mean she hadn't longed to learn to play an instrument.

"I'll give you fifty for it right now."

Jo's ears perked at the sound of a familiar male voice. She scanned the street for the owner of the voice and caught sight of Ozzy's dark SUV parked in front of On a Wing, the town thrift store.

"Fifty? Ozzy, seriously, this piece of junk isn't worth half that."

"It is to me."

Intrigued, Jo crossed the street in time to see a middle-aged man hauling a rusted, dinged-up bicycle out of the back of his truck. "Don't know what you think you can do with it," the man grumbled as he handed it over. "I was just going to toss it in the trash."

"I'm going to restore it," Ozzy announced

as he pulled out his wallet. His face brightened when he caught sight of Jo. "Hi. Out and about today, then?"

"Thought I'd see this town Leah's been bragging about." Jo cast a wary glance at the bike. "Couldn't help overhear. I'm Jo Bertoletti," she introduced herself to Ozzy's disbelieving salesman.

"Irving Drummond." The silver-haired man offered his hand. He wore faded jeans and a large red flannel shirt over his white tee. Big, bushy brows made a vee over narrowed eyes. "Bertoletti? You'd be the new foreman up at the construction site."

"Supervisor." She didn't want anyone getting the wrong idea. She wasn't here to take anyone's job. Just to make sure everyone was doing theirs. "I've been walking around a bit, getting the feel for things. Thought maybe I'd have lunch down at the beach."

"Perfect day for it. Hang on a second." Ozzy handed Irving some cash. "Here's fifty."

Irving turned his suspicious gray eyes on Ozzy. "Never known you to ride a bike, Oz. You branching out to repair work?"

"Nah." He looked almost longingly at the

bike listing against the wall as if desperately trying to stay upright. "It's for Charlie."

"Little Charlie Bradley?" Irving's back went ramrod straight. "Well, why didn't you say so?" He held up his hands and backed away from the money. "I'm not taking that. Especially not for a hunk of junk."

"You hauled it off the old Pickering place, didn't you? I recognize that rusted-out wagon back there, not to mention that picnic table and old porch furniture."

Jo was curious, so she stepped around to peer into the back of the pickup truck. It was packed so tight she could barely make out what was what. "Is all this for sale?" she asked.

"Some of it will be. Still have to go through it. And this is just the first load."

She spotted a few pieces that caught her attention. "I'll buy whatever outdoor furniture you have."

Irving's brows knit. "You two working some kind of double-team action?"

Jo smiled. "Happy coincidence. The weather's supposed to be pretty amazing for the foreseeable future. I'd like to set up an outdoor eating area for the construction crew.

I hear a food truck comes by every day, is that right?"

"True. Alethea Costas with Flutterby Wheels," Ozzy told her. "It's part of Jason Corwin's restaurant, Flutterby Dreams, up at the inn. It's casual gourmet."

She'd seen mention of the truck in the office notes. "A crew needs someplace to sit." She did a quick estimation and threw out a number to Irving for the outdoor furniture that was well below the budget she'd set. It would cost three times as much to rent what she'd first planned. This way the money went back into the community, and when the project was finished, they could pass the pieces along to people who wanted them. "How much extra to deliver?"

"For that price, I'll throw it in for free." Irving looked as if he'd hit the jackpot. "You want it today?"

"I wouldn't say no." She could spend tomorrow cleaning it all up and figuring out where to arrange the pieces. Something to add to her Monday list of things for her crew to do. "Just leave it by my house and I'll sort through it when I get home."

"You mean *the* house?" Irving said with a

glint of interest. "I heard a rumor it's pretty snazzy."

"I was going for snazzy," Jo teased.

"I'm going to call my son to help me lug everything over. Already made my daily quota thanks to you two. I'd best tell the wife she's on her own in the store a while longer." He was pulling out his cell phone as he went into the thrift store.

"Wait, hang on!" Ozzy started after him, but the door closed in his face. He looked down at the cash Irving had refused. "I'll stop by later and give this to his wife." He stuffed the money in his pocket and came over to Jo. "So you're going to open a cantina at the construction site, huh?"

"Minus the alcohol." Jo's fingers itched to dig into that load of junk in Irving's truckbed. "I guess I lucked out today. Who did you say this all belonged to?"

"Winston Pickering. Man was old when I was a kid. He died last summer and his kids are only now selling his property." Ozzy grabbed the bike and hauled it over to his own vehicle. "No telling what the old man had stashed away. Though you realize you're probably going to end up with a lot of old dingy furniture?"

"But there will be treasure among it." If there was one thing Jo couldn't pass up, it was a bargain. Or an opportunity. "You know, the original plans for the sanctuary included a children's playground."

"That idea got scrapped when the budget exploded." Ozzy's mouth twisted. "Any hope we had of saving it disappeared when the frame collapsed. It's too bad, too, but there might be a way to get it further down the road."

"Shouldn't have to wait." If there was a means to work the budget, she'd find it. "Um, what's the story with the bike?"

"My friend's daughter had an accident last week and totaled hers. She's being quite selective about what she wants as a replacement." He ran his hand down the line of the bike. "It's just the right size for her. Bigger than the one she'd outgrown, but not quite full-size. I'll fix it up like her old one and hopefully she'll approve."

Jo's heart tilted at the wistful smile on his face. "I'm surprised you don't give people cavities, Ozzy. That's one of the sweetest things I've ever heard."

Ozzy's cheeks went that adorable shade of pink before he glanced away and shut the back of his car. "Charlie's a good kid. And it doesn't seem right not seeing her zipping around town on two wheels."

"So you like kids?" Now where had that question come from?

"Sure." Ozzy shrugged. "They're just miniature adults, right? Except for the brats," he added with a chuckle. "I'll walk with you to the beach. I need to stop in at Cat's Eye for a book on bicycle repair."

"You can walk with me any time if you want." She eyed him. "You don't need an excuse."

"Was that an excuse?" He pocketed his keys and fell into step beside her.

"Whatever information you need for the bike you can find on the internet. It'd be cheaper and quicker." At his cool shrug, warmth crept into her cheeks. So much for thinking he was flirting.

"True, but I have to pick up an order, anyway." He slipped his hands into the pockets of his olive green cargo pants. That smile of his was back, and this time it came with a teasing glint in his dark eyes. "It's nice to know I don't need an excuse to walk with you, though."

That odd shiver raced up her spine when he smiled at her. She tugged her sweater tighter around her, crossed her arms and felt her nerves jingle in a most unwelcome way. It wasn't that his attention and friendliness were unwelcome. It was flattering to have an attractive man like Ozzy notice her. Despite his being younger, she sensed a maturity in him that she appreciated and that appealed to her. But she'd done her time with good-looking, superficial charmers. One charmer in particular, but Leah was right. Comparing Ozzy to Greg was useless. The two were nothing alike. Besides, she didn't care for the afterburn one had left around her heart.

"Company would be nice." She considered a diplomatic, inoffensive tack to steer him off any romantic route he might be walking. "Aside from Leah and you, I don't have any other friends in town."

Ozzy's chin tilted up and he glanced away. "Ask anyone in town, and they'll tell you," he said, "I do excel at being a friend."

She bit the inside of her cheek. Clearly she'd hit a nerve. "I'm sure you do. You strike me as a great guy, Ozzy. Great guys need friends, too."

"Yes, they do." He shook his head as if to clear it. "So do nice women."

"I'm not sure your mayor would agree with your description of me." She couldn't help but grin. "We had a nice long chat this morning."

"Set your ground rules, did you?"

"Who tattled?"

"No one." Ozzy smiled. "I know Gil and I met you. You didn't strike me as the type of woman who'd be wanting him to hang around and stick his nose in."

"He took it better than I thought he would. Of course…" She turned the corner and kept the pace, made note of a cute little candle shop that offered original made-to-order items. "He might have still been a bit shocked when he saw I was pregnant. I'm surprised that tidbit of information hadn't made the rounds." She eyed him.

"Like you said, other than me or Leah, you hadn't met anyone yet. And neither one of us is a gossip."

She'd bet he considered that a badge of

honor. And he should. "Hmm, in any case, I appreciated surprising him. Kind of leveled the playing field a bit. Do you think it'll become an issue?"

"You being pregnant? Not in the way you expect." Ozzy glanced at her. "People will be curious. They're going to be nosy. And there will be advice."

"About the baby?"

"Sure." Ozzy's lips twitched. "About that, too." When she didn't respond, he gave her a gentle nudge with his arm. "See? You are nice. You just used your filter. And for the record, I am an excellent judge of people. You want proof? I bet I can tell you three things about yourself you don't think I could possibly know."

Oh, yeah. He was definitely flirting. Not as well or effectively as she might have anticipated, but enough to keep a smile on her face as they continued walking. "All right. I'll take that bet. But the obvious is off the table," she countered, pointing to her stomach.

"Fair enough." He gestured to a store across the street on the next block. "Let's cross over. Observation one. You don't have a lot of friends, but you're incredibly loyal to the ones you have."

"I suppose that's true."

"You accepted the job because your friend asked you to," Ozzy clarified. "You drove your entire house across state lines because Leah needed your help. That's loyalty."

"It's also selfish." She flashed him a smile. "If I do my job right, it puts me in line for a possible partnership. Taking the job here in Butterfly Harbor isn't particularly altruistic on my part."

"That doesn't negate the loyalty. She trusts you. You trust her. But you don't trust everyone. That would be observation two."

"Only fools and hopeless romantics trust everyone." She considered him and the somewhat starry expression she'd caught in his eyes when they'd first met. "I'd ask which you are, but I already know I wouldn't call you a fool."

"I like to think of myself as a hope*ful* romantic. Despite getting shot down by a beautiful woman only a few moments ago."

She groaned, rolled her eyes and laughed. "I can't believe you just said that."

Ozzy chuckled. "Desperate times…"

There wasn't anything desperate about the man that she could see. "Fine, that's two things you've gotten right. Ready to take a stab at number three?"

He pointed up to the sign above the store's wood-and-beveled-glass door. The hand-carved sign showed a big-eyed cat curled atop a book. Ozzy reached around her and clicked open the door. His hand brushed the small of her back as he escorted her inside. "You're lonely."

CHAPTER FOUR

OZZY HAD ALWAYS wondered what it would be like to stun a woman into silence. Of course, in his imagination the circumstances would have been different. A perfect compliment, a life-altering good-night kiss. Presenting her with the ideal gift that left her speechless.

Declaring a woman lonely really shouldn't have been on the list. But she was. He'd seen it on her face when she'd approached him outside the thrift store. She'd been curious, sure, but he'd also identified a flash of relief in her eyes when she'd seen him. Someone she already knew. Someone she could talk to. Like always recognized like.

"Hey, Ozzy. Figured you'd be by today." Sebastian Evans, owner of the Cat's Eye bookstore, zipped past him with his arms loaded with stock. "Just give me a second and I'll grab your book."

"No rush. I have something else to look

for." Only now did he dare glance at Jo, who appeared caught between shock and consideration. "I shouldn't be too long."

"Take your time." Jo waved him off, stepping back and lifting her chin to scan the upper perimeter of the store. "There are cats on the walls." She pointed up at the maze of platforms and ledges. "Actual cats."

"That's Zachariah." Ozzy indicated the fluffy gray cat with bright blue eyes. "And the smaller gray one is Tribble. Do you like cats?"

"In theory." Jo looked confused by the question. "I've never had one as a pet, though."

"Dog person?"

"Never had one of those, either. Isn't that dangerous?"

"Cats always land on their feet," Sebastian chimed in as Tribble took a gravity-defying leap up a level. "Trust me, they won't fall. We had a cat named Rowena for a while who used to leap down on male customers' heads. Thankfully, she got adopted out pretty quick."

"Sebastian, this is Jo Bertoletti. Jo, this is Sebastian's store. Well, his and his family's."

"It's nice to meet you, Sebastian." Jo, still

looking somewhat distracted, shook his hand. "Interesting combination…books and cats."

"My daughter, Mandy, takes in cats and kittens to foster while they wait for adoption. Thankfully, not as many as she used to. Putting the two together made sense for us."

Ozzy thought about asking about the box of kittens Mandy had been lugging over to the vet's office yesterday, then decided not to. He didn't want to give the impression he was in the market for one. It wasn't just Mandy who had a tendency of pawning off cute little fur balls on unsuspecting customers.

Ozzy wandered off to the home repair section, passing a few familiar faces as he went. The wooden shelves that filled the store had always brought him a sense of peace.

He'd spent countless hours perusing the stacks in this place over the years; he knew every inch of Cat's Eye by memory, and why wouldn't he? Ozzy's escape, even when he was a kid, had always been books, all kinds. Fiction, nonfiction, informative, instructional. Between this store and the town library, his imagination had been busy even as his social life had been empty. Friday nights would often find him curled up in one of the reading corners getting his fix. Books had been his best friends, never judging, always accepting and always there when he needed them. Books, he'd learned early in life, were something he could trust. Now, with his job, the only time he had to read was during his downtime at the station.

Plucking a few books out, he finally found one on restoring vintage toys that had a good section on bicycles and old-fashioned wagons. Flipping through the pages, he headed up to the counter, where he found Jo and Sebastian deep in conversation over a familiar title.

"Sebastian was just showing me Hunter MacBride's book on the Liberty Lighthouse." Jo indicated one of Mayor Gil's pet projects, which had brought the well-known photojournalist to town last year. "I have to add that place to my list of things to see. The architecture and restoration look amazing."

"Kendall did a fabulous job," Ozzy confirmed.

Sebastian retrieved a book from the special-order shelf behind him. "Here's the book you ordered, Oz."

"Thanks." Ozzy tried not to notice Jo's curiosity as she examined the cover.

"I think I can now guess three things about you, too," Jo teased. "You play D&D?"

"Not as well as I used to," Ozzy admitted as he thumbed through the character encyclopedia for Dungeons and Dragons. "I've been getting back into it. One of the guys I work with is starting a group. I need a refresher course."

"Has to be Jasper," Sebastian observed. "Roman wouldn't have the patience."

"We've almost got our co-chief to commit to giving it a try," Ozzy said. "Jasper and Kyle are super into it. Not that Jasper has a lot of extra time, but Kyle has more than his share these days while his leg heals."

"Are you talking about Kyle Knight?" Jo asked. "I need to speak to him, actually. In person if possible."

"Kyle's been helping out at the sheriff's office with his dad on the weekends. Office stuff while he recovers." Ozzy paid the bill after Sebastian rang him up. "We can head over there now if you're up for it."

"Sounds like a plan. I'll also take this." She paid for the book on the town's lighthouse and accepted her Cat's Eye reusable bag. "How cute."

"You get ten percent off your purchase if you bring it back," Sebastian said. "It was nice to meet you, Jo."

"You, too."

"Look at that. You're up to four friends now," Ozzy teased when they left the store.

"I'm not lonely." It was the way she said it, with that knife's edge sharpness, that had him regretting his previous cocky observation.

"All right."

"Being alone doesn't mean you're lonely. And I'm not alone, remember?" She tugged her sweater over her stomach. "I don't need anyone feeling sorry for me, Ozzy. I'm perfectly happy with my life and circumstance."

"Message received." He could see the muscle in her cheek pulse, as if she were grinding her teeth. "Being lonely isn't a crime, just so you know. I mean, if you were."

Judging by the sour expression on her face, she certainly considered it one. "You got two out of three."

"I'm not out of guesses yet." They came to the corner of Monarch Lane, just a couple of blocks away from the Butterfly Diner. He stopped and waited, not for her to continue the conversation, but for her to notice they were standing in the best part of this town. He'd lived here long enough to recognize that moment of realization, of accepting that what lay before you didn't exist anywhere else on earth.

The waist-high stone retaining wall meandered along the length of the main thoroughfare of Butterfly Harbor. With the ocean stretching out in front of them and the town standing tall at their backs, this particular spot was where Ozzy came to reconnect and remind himself why he would never leave.

He leaned forward, just enough to watch the haughtiness evaporate from her gaze, replaced by the same wonder and awe he still felt whenever he walked the streets of his home. "I've got my third guess," he said. "You, Jo Bertoletti, just fell in love."

Jo blinked in shock, her gaze locked on his. For a moment, everything around them faded into the distance. He scanned her face, looking beneath the surprise and beautiful wide eyes. When he lifted his hand to brush hers, she stepped back and turned away.

She checked both directions of the road

and waited for two cars to pass before heading across the street. He followed, a bit behind, giving her the space she needed to absorb the sight in front of her.

"I knew it would be beautiful," she breathed when he joined her at the wall. "I mean, it's the ocean. I've seen it before, of course. Just… not like this."

Even from a distance Ozzy could almost feel the sand under his feet. The desire to kick off his shoes and sink ankle deep never dulled. To one side the beach stretched out and around outcroppings of rocks that peeked and played their way into the distant shore. Looking in the opposite direction, the Flutterby Inn stood proud on the commanding cliffs. Its yellow and white paint, glistening like a beacon, highlighted its classic Victorian structure. At the inn's base far below, he could envision the path leading to the "secret" caves where he'd played as a child and where, only a few years ago, his life had changed.

"There's a history here," Jo said. "I can feel it. The ocean on its own is a powerful force, but it's what it brings to the town." She glanced up as a bright orange butterfly fluttered toward her on the wind. "Together it's… I don't know." Jo reached up a hand and the butterfly skimmed over her finger. "It's magic."

"I've always thought so." His heart did this odd little jump as the butterfly circled Jo's head a few more times before flitting off toward the cliffs. "And with the butterfly sanctuary and education center, even more people are going to come here and be witness to it."

Jo nodded, as if she'd only realized that herself. "How do people not just stand or sit here for hours?"

"Who says we don't? Let's go talk to Kyle. Then I'll take you where you'll get the best patty melt you've ever had in your life."

"Now that would be a tall order," Jo said as she walked beside him, keeping her eyes on the beach and water. "My grandfather used to make the best burgers. I have quite the critical palate when it comes to food like that."

"Noted. And challenge accepted." Ozzy kept the conversation light, and as they strolled to the sheriff's office, he pointed out the entrance to the marina as well as the recently razed property where a new corner building would be built.

"That's where you had the fire last Christmas, right?" Jo asked.

"It is. The town council's supposed to vote on approving new construction to happen next year. Maybe," he hedged.

"You guys take on a project at a time, then," Jo said.

They veered off to the right and started the trek up the hill. Soon they found themselves on the other side of a thick patch of redwoods that offered privacy and shade.

"We don't like to stretch our funds into too many areas at one time. At least that's the city council's argument. Turns out it was a good decision considering what happened with the sanctuary site. We wouldn't have had the funds to jump right back into it if we'd had other projects going, too. That would have pushed its completion well into next year."

She pulled open the police station's door before he could. When he followed her in, his gaze went immediately to the spot where, for more than eight years, his desk had been perched in front of the window. The clip-clip of four paws alerted him to Cacius, Sheriff Luke Saxon's devoted golden retriever. The dog abandoned his department mascot duties to greet them with a gentle *woof.*

"Hey there, boy." Ozzy bent down to snuggle the dog and ruffle his thick coat. "Haven't seen you in a while. How're you doing?"

Cacius let out a solitary bark, tail wagging as he licked Ozzy's face, then turned his attention to additional affection.

"Jo, Cacius. Cacius, this is Jo."

Woof.

"Hello there." Jo held out her hand to let him get a good sniff. Cacius left Ozzy and planted his fuzzy butt on the floor beside Jo and leaned his head up into her stroking hand. "You're a sweet guy, aren't you?"

"Yeah," Ozzy said. "The town's full of them."

"Don't spill all our secrets at once, Oz." Deputy Matt Knight popped up from around the corner and opened the pass-through portion of the scarred wooden counter. "What brings you by?"

"You did, actually." Ozzy waited for Jo to move through to the offices. "We're looking for Kyle. Heard he was filling in around here while he recoups. Jo, this is Matt Knight."

"Kyle's father." Jo held out her hand. "Jo Bertoletti. I'm the new—"

"Supervisor up at the sanctuary site," Matt finished for her. But rather than smile at the information, he looked slightly resigned. "Kyle's been waiting for this."

"Waiting for what?" Jo asked.

Matt sighed. "Let me get him for you." Matt ducked into Luke's office and they could hear muffled voices.

"He has a limp," Jo murmured. "Was he injured on the job?"

"Lost his leg in Afghanistan," Ozzy explained. "I'm surprised you noticed. It's a lot better than it used to be."

"I make my living watching and managing people who do a physically demanding job. I notice things like that." Jo kept her voice low. "Sometimes men don't own up when they're hurting."

"I'll plead the fifth."

When Matt reemerged, it was with Luke Saxon, and bringing up the rear was Kyle on crutches.

"Ms. Bertoletti. Sheriff Saxon." The taller man offered his hand. "Luke. It's a pleasure to meet you."

"Hi, Luke. It's Jo, please." Jo returned the greeting without the expected googly eyes

Ozzy had often witnessed whenever the good-looking lawman was around. These days if you were searching for the definition of a devoted family man, Luke would be exhibit A.

Ozzy had rarely gone a day when he'd not been impressed with his former boss. The sheriff was, as far as Ozzy was concerned, as good a man as they made. When Luke had taken over the sheriff's job a few years back, Ozzy hadn't been convinced it was a good fit. He also hadn't appreciated Gil hiring someone from outside Butterfly Harbor. Well. Partially outside. Luke had grown up in Butterfly Harbor. But it had been his reason for leaving and then coming back that had caused a pretty big stir.

Luke's predecessor, who also happened to be Luke's now father-in-law, hadn't placed much faith in Ozzy to do more than maintain the office equipment and man the phones. In hindsight, he'd had good reason to think that. Luke's mentorship and guidance were a big reason why Ozzy had taken the chance to improve as a cop and then achieve his dream of becoming a firefighter. Luke still gave him a hard time for abandoning them at the sheriff's department, but the sheriff had also, on multiple occasions, told Ozzy how proud he was of him.

"How much longer are you on the crutches for, kid?" Ozzy asked and earned a crooked smile from Kyle. Funny how that nickname meant different things to different people. Hearing Harvey use it on Gil didn't have nearly the same affectionate reaction as it did when aimed at Kyle.

That said, it wasn't so long ago that Ozzy had been called by the same moniker, and he'd been more than happy to pass it along. Especially to a young man who, until Matt Knight had adopted him, had been one of Butterfly Harbor's worst juvenile troublemakers.

"Doctor thinks I can switch the cast out for a brace next week," Kyle said. "And then I'll start physical therapy."

"That's a maybe for next week," Matt corrected his son. "His head's healed okay, but the rest of him is taking some extra time."

"Stop, Dad." Kyle spoke out of the corner of his mouth. "She's my boss. For now, at least."

Jo didn't miss a beat. "Kyle, I was wondering if you and I could speak privately for a few minutes?"

"Sure thing." Kyle shrugged, but the look he sent his father betrayed his nerves. "How about we go outside?"

"Perfect. Lead the way." Jo stepped back so he could pass, then hurried around him to open the door for him. "Be back in a bit."

"THANKS FOR NOT doing this in there." Kyle walked beside Jo toward the stone table and benches situated among a thick grove of redwoods next to the station.

"No problem." She knew the young man was just shy of his nineteenth birthday and appeared to be caught in that post-growth-spurt, pre-fit young male build. She wondered if it was her growing maternal instincts that had her thinking he needed a haircut, but she'd bet the too-long bangs and brown hair nearly to his shoulders earned him his fair share of swooning sighs.

"My dad worries I'm going to take bad news the wrong way." His grin struck her as sheepish. "I haven't always had the best coping mechanisms."

"Oh?" Jo feigned innocence. She'd read

his file and the fact that it had made note of his difficult childhood right here in Butterfly Harbor told her a lot of people hadn't forgotten. Nor would they try to sweep something under the carpet. She also knew he had a juvenile record, but she wasn't interested in who he had been, only in who he was now. "From what I've heard, you've done a lot of great things around here. You were working for Kendall MacBride for a while, too, right? The woman who refurbished the Liberty Lighthouse?"

"Yeah. She worked construction in the army so she knows a lot about a lot of stuff. Until the accident I was able to do both jobs." To say the young man looked miserable about his situation was an understatement.

"Kendall anxious to have you back?"

"I haven't asked her." That sheepish grin returned. "I'm a little worried about the answer. Kind of like with you now."

Jo sat across from him, giving herself a solid view both of the young man and the captivating ocean that lay just beyond.

Pulling her attention back to what was important, she watched Kyle arrange himself into some sort of comfortable position. He winced, no doubt still in pain from the severe fracture and the metal rod they'd had to put in his leg.

"I thought it best this conversation be had one-on-one." She set her bag down, attempted to cross her legs, then realized that wasn't going to be happening and instead rested her arms on the table. "Kyle—"

"If you're going to fire me—"

"That's not what this is about." And here she'd attributed his distanced, almost sullen mood to being in pain. "I'm sorry for the misunderstanding or if I've misled you. I have no intention of letting you go. Quite the contrary, I'm in need of your help."

"My help?" Kyle's brow furrowed. "With what?"

"Your boss, Jed Bishop. I take it you liked working for him?"

"Jed's great." Kyle's head bobbed and Jo could see him start to relax. "I've learned a lot from him, too. He's the one who encouraged me to start working toward my contractor's license."

"I bet you've had lots of time to study these past few weeks." She needed to find a way to get to her idea and hopefully him being receptive to it. She might have a knack for reading people, but she also had a tendency to be a bit of a bulldozer when it came to marking things off her list. People, she reminded herself, needed more care and patience than inanimate objects. "You going to stick with it?"

"Yeah. And it keeps my mind off other stuff. Leo, he's my brother, he helps me sometimes, but he's only seven. Quizzes me and stuff." The affection that slid across Kyle's cute young face tweaked at Jo's heart. "He's a fun kid."

"Word is Jed isn't sold on coming back," Jo said. "I think he might be dealing with some things as a result of the accident. He feels responsible, you know? Maybe a little scared it could happen again."

Kyle nodded.

"How do you feel about coming back?" she asked.

"All right, I guess. Now, anyway."

"You didn't always?"

"No. No, I was ready to quit. But the day I got released from the hospital, my dad drove me up to the site. I told him I didn't want to go, but he said it was the only way to move beyond it. He was in Afghanistan with Kendall," Kyle added. "They were both hurt. Kendall got burned real bad and my dad lost his leg. He said he couldn't go back and face the accident head-on, but that he wished he had. That's why he made me do it. Made me face what had happened to me head-on, make it a part of me that I could live with. Every week we'd take a drive up there, I'd walk around or just sit in the car until the fear went away."

"And has it gone away?" Jo pressed.

"Mostly." Kyle frowned. "I still get nightmares sometimes. Not about the accident, but about being trapped in the dark. Not as often, though. I was lucky."

Very lucky, from what Jo had read. Kyle had the worst injuries of the bunch, but he'd gotten them trying to save his fellow construction workers. And that, to her, was the true testament of who he was. And why she wanted him back on the job if he felt safe about it.

"Nightmares are perfectly normal. I remember being on a work site with my grandfather when there was a collapse. I think I was about ten? It was like watching an erector set just fold in on itself and the people caught in it." She took a deep breath, grateful for the pristine ocean air. "I can still hear them crying out, and sometimes I get pulled right back to that day and it's been…" She did the mental math. "Wow. That's twenty-five years ago now. But if you're facing it head-on, if you want to get back to work—"

"I do. I have to." Kyle frowned. "I never thought I'd find something I'm good at. Something I like doing."

"Find something you love to do and you'll never work a day in your life." Jo recited one of the affirmations her grandfather had imparted.

"My mom says that." Kyle smiled, but it didn't quite reach his eyes. "My new mom. Lori. She and Matt adopted me a couple of years ago."

"Family is what you make of it." Boy, she was just full of platitudes today, wasn't she? "So, about Jed. I know you can't work with the crew yet. Both of us know that won't happen for a while."

"My doctor says maybe six months if I'm lucky."

"If I can convince Jed to come back, how would you feel about being our administrative assistant? It would be office work, but you could shadow him on the site once you're more mobile, see how things really operate, get a feel for the business end of construction. I'm betting that if Jed knows he'd be helping you reacclimate and move forward, he'd be more likely to return." She was taking a chance on both these men, but with what was at stake, for herself and the project, and for them, it was worth the gamble. "What do you think?"

Kyle nodded. "Yeah, I can do that."

"Great. We're officially starting on Wednesday, but I've got the crew on call to be in at six Monday morning. We'll talk over the details then."

"Thanks, Ms. Bert—"

"Boss when we're on the job. Otherwise it's Jo." She reached her hand across the table. "I look forward to working with you, Kyle."

They slowly made their way back to the office, Kyle with a bit more enthusiasm in his voice. The conversation inside the station stopped the second they opened the door.

"Everything okay?" Matt came around the counter, the concern on his face tugging at a piece of Jo's heart she forgot she had. Her father had been gone long before he may have looked at her that way: protective, proud and hopeful.

"Everything's fine," Jo said. "Kyle's agreed to come back to the crew. He's going to be our administrative assistant, which will give him the time he needs for any doctors' appointments or physical therapy." At Kyle's wide eyes, she shrugged. "It won't be a problem. Your main task is to get better. We need you at a hundred percent. And don't worry," she assured Matt when she saw the concern shadowing his gaze, "I'll make sure he doesn't overdo it."

Kyle was immediately swept into a circle of male revelry and as the guys, joined by a barking, excited Cacius, slapped backs and congratulated their younger charge, Jo wandered away, giving them their privacy.

Odd, she thought as she admired the almost homey atmosphere of the sheriff's office. The dark walls should have made the space feel closed in, but the color, along with the polished wood counter, took away a lot of the stodgy feel she'd expected. Photographs and commendations were neatly framed and arranged so they were seen almost the moment you walked in. A smile curving her lips, she moved closer, scanned the images of what was clearly a timeline of Butterfly Harbor law enforcement. Some of the faces she didn't recognize, at least not from the older photographs. But there was one in particular that caught her attention.

The group of men was standing right where she stood now, in front of the wall of memories. She recognized Luke Saxon, of course, along with his canine companion. Next to him was Matt Knight and two other deputies, one who would have given a Hollywood action star a run for his money, and another who... She peered closer, narrowed her gaze.

The man's frame was completely unfamiliar, but those eyes...oh, she was all too familiar with those dark green eyes.

She glanced over her shoulder, caught Ozzy in midlaugh at something Kyle had said, then looked back at the picture.

She touched her fingers to her mouth, trying to reconcile the significantly heavier man who was clearly Ozzy Lakeman with the man she'd met only a few days before.

But there was no mistake. They were one and the same.

The transformation was amazing, and for a moment, she wondered what was behind it, but it wasn't any of her business, nor did it matter to her task at hand. She had no doubt the Ozzy in the pictures was, at heart, no different than the man she knew.

CHAPTER FIVE

"THAT WAS REALLY nice what you did. For Kyle," Ozzy said when they were back outside and headed to the diner to pick up lunch. Walking with her, being with her, felt so…natural. As if it was where he was meant to be. He wasn't, however, under any illusions that Jo felt the same. He'd seen her look at the pictures in the sheriff's station. The fact she hadn't asked him about them said either she hadn't made the connection or she didn't care. Personally, he was hoping it was the former.

Experience suggested otherwise.

"I didn't do it for Kyle. I did it for me. He's a good employee." How the sunlight caught her hair made it seem to glow like gold. "A good crew member. I can't have too many of them if I'm going to meet my deadlines. But moving Kyle to administrative assistant is only half the plan."

"And what plan is that?"

She arched a brow and looked him straight in the eye. "I'm sure you'll understand I'd like to keep a few secrets to myself."

The bubble of hope that she hadn't connected him to the image in those photographs burst. But there was something else along with the teasing glint in her eye that had his gaze shifting across her pink cheeks and full lips.

He couldn't help it. He had the strangest urge to kiss that smile from her lips. The very idea was so bold, so utterly contrary to Ozzy that he found himself both grateful and nervous at the prospect. And oddly determined.

With all the dates he'd been on, all the women he'd met in the last year, women who offered everything he should want, rarely had the impulse to kiss one of them ever hit him with the force it did now.

Friends, he reminded himself. She'd made it clear she was interested in being friends. There was a reason for that, one he could only hope she'd share down the line. Her immediately shutting him down when he'd asked about her baby's father told him she'd been burned and that the wound was still raw. Now was not the time to push. So, friends it would be. Friends was a good place to start. Beginning now.

"Secrets, huh?" Ozzy said, his usual expression of good will back in place. "I won't promise not to try to wheedle it out of you over lunch. You and the kidlet must be starving."

"Beyond. Leah told me you used to be a deputy." She seemed to notice he wanted her to set the pace downhill to Monarch Lane. "Seems like a good place to work. What made you change to being a firefighter?"

"Writing speeding tickets and answering lost pet calls got tedious after a few years." Ozzy shoved his hands in his pockets.

"Ozzy." It was the way she said it, part disbelief, part daring that had him admitting what he'd only recently been able to see for himself.

"I guess I wanted to be in a position to help, rather than dealing with the aftermath." It sounded sappy when he said it. "Firefighters and deputies, we see people on their difficult days. If I can make that day easier for them to deal with, then that's what I want to do."

She touched his arm. "I think that's very noble of you."

Noble. Ozzy's lips twitched. Not a word he'd ever associated with himself before.

"The opportunity to switch over presented itself. There were new openings at the station house and we had more than enough deputies. Too many, actually. Matt and Fletcher belong there."

"From what I could see, you do, too."

"The job works well for them and I didn't want to get in the way of that. Besides—" now he finally grinned "—being a firefighter means every day is a different adventure. We never know what's going to come across as a call."

"Butterfly Harbor isn't a hub of criminal activity, then? Good to know."

"Let's say being a sheriff's deputy got a bit predictable, routine, that sort of thing."

"You like playing the hero?"

The words caught him off guard. "No." Was that what she really thought? That he was in this for some kind of hero worship thing? "That's not what it's about."

"Bad joke," she apologized. "Of course it isn't. It's about doing the right thing at the right time. Sometimes the thing others aren't capable of doing."

The tension knotting in his stomach eased. Maybe she did understand, after all.

"I'm sorry if I offended you. But in my defense, firefighters are pretty darn heroic. It's not everyone who runs into the flames. And I'd be lying if I didn't say the idea of you doing something like that scares me a little. Forgive me?"

"That depends." He narrowed his eyes. "Will you have dinner with me?" The request caught him off guard. But it had felt so natural, so…right. Not clumsy at all, if he did say so himself. "If you want to, I mean. Friends have dinner together, right?" Ah, there he went again.

"Let's say we do lunch first and go from there." She inclined her chin toward the diner across the street. "Like you said, the kidlet is hungry."

ACCOMPLISHING TASKS KICKED her appetite into overdrive, and as she was almost done with her to-do list for the day, she was beginning to feel like she could plow through the diner's entire menu.

Jo shouldn't have been surprised that when they reached the Butterfly Diner Ozzy pulled the door open for her. She'd caught his uncertainty back at the sheriff's station when she'd reached for the door first. As if he hadn't considered a woman could open the door for herself. It had amused her to set him off-kilter.

He'd readjusted now, seemed to have found his footing, even if he had literally tripped a bit getting to the diner door first.

When she stepped inside, however, all other thoughts were obliterated by the instant feeling of...well, of home.

"Did I just walk through a time portal?" Save for the surprising color combination of black, orange and white—an ode, she instantly realized, to the town's monarch namesake—the eatery definitely had that old-fashioned diner feel. Add in the distinct, excellent, growling-stomach-inducing aroma of grilling burgers, cooked onions and the promise of caloric enhancement, and she could understand why the diner was considered a town hub.

"Hey, Ozzy. Wherever you can grab a seat, go for it." The tall, curvy brunette with plates balanced with practiced ease on her arms swept past them with a quick smile.

"We're getting to go, actually." Ozzy mo-

tioned toward a pair of empty orange upholstered stools at the counter. "Let's sit so you
can peruse the menu."

At the far end of the counter a taller, thin-
ner young woman flitted between customers, topping off coffee cups and clearing
plates. Her straight black hair was tied back
in a high ponytail and displayed a neon blue
streak through its length. A hint of tattoos
peeked out from the short sleeves of her black
T-shirt carrying the diner's logo on the front.
She glanced their way, her gaze landing first
on Ozzy with an unsurprising smile, then
flicked curiously to Jo. "You ordering to go,
Oz?"

"Thanks, Twyla. We are." Ozzy remained
on his feet rather than sitting and handed Jo
a menu. "Twyla, this is Jo Bertoletti. She's
the new supervisor—"

"For the construction project." Twyla
let out an all-too-identifiable sigh of relief.
"Okay. That explains it. Coffee?" Twyla held
up the coffeepot.

"No, thanks." Jo was never going to get
used to having to kick caffeine. "It's nice to
meet you, Twyla."

"You, too." Twyla eyed Ozzy in a way that

should have amused Jo. Ah, to be twenty-something again with a massive crush on the hot single firefighter. Twyla may as well have it tattooed on her forehead. How many times had Jo herself issued that same lash-fluttering, cartoon heart–hammering expression over the years? Except… Jo frowned. She really should have found Twyla's attention more amusing than she did.

Ridiculous. Jo tried to focus on her menu. She had no cause or right to be jealous of anyone. Though Ozzy would tick most, if not all, the boxes for perfect boyfriend material anywhere. He was a good-looking, fit, sweet-natured firefighter. Heck, they'd probably broken the mold with him, and if what she suspected was true and he was sporting a new version of himself, Twyla's rapt attention made even more sense. That gnawing in Jo's insides was just hunger. Yep. That's all it was. Anything else was simply unacceptable.

"You sure I can't tempt you with a mocha shake, Oz?" Twyla kicked out a hip and tapped her fingers against her very flat apron-topped stomach. "It's been a while since you've had one."

"No, thanks, Twyla." Ozzy just gave her

one of those smiles Jo had come to expect. "How about it, Jo? You going with that patty melt, or do you see something else you want?"

"Huh?" Jo blinked, her confusion lasting for a moment before she cleared her throat and focused. "Oh, yeah." Wow. Now who sounded like a teenager with a crush? "I'll take the patty melt. Can I get that with hot sauce on the side?"

"Sure." Twyla scribbled on her pad. "I can have Ursula add some jalapeños to the onions if you want to give it more of a kick."

"That sounds great, thanks." Okay, *now* her stomach was rumbling with anticipation.

"Should be about ten minutes," Twyla said. "You want anything to drink?"

"Just water for me," Ozzy said.

"Same," Jo agreed, then leaned her chin on her hand as Twyla darted off to deliver their orders. She caught Ozzy scanning the filled booths behind them. He gave a few waves, then his eyes sharpened. "What?"

"Kyle said you wanted to reach out to Jed Bishop." He inclined his head. "That's him there. Unless you wanted to do what you need to over the phone?"

Jo shifted so she could see the man. The middle-aged guy with distinguished gray at his temples was eating his lunch and reading on his phone. "I'm all about the personal touch." Hesitating, she wondered if it was best to approach him in the middle of what she assumed was gossip central for the town. But why waste time and a special trip to track the foreman down? Opportunity, she reminded herself. "Thanks, Oz. I'll be back in a few."

She slid off the stool and approached Jed. "Mr. Bishop? Sorry to bother you. I'm Jo Bertoletti."

Jed's bright blue eyes sparked with recognition as he wiped his mouth then held out his hand. "Good to put a face to the name." That glint of humor in his eyes eased some of the nerves knotting in her stomach. Every project had a guardian at the gate. Whether Jed had committed to coming back or not, he was still the main person she needed on her side if they were going to bring this project to completion. "I heard you hit town ahead of schedule."

"Do you mind if I sit for a minute?"

"Not at all." He gestured to the bench

across from him, then let out a chuckle when she had to sort of back in and turn before facing him. "Kind of like operating a forklift, huh? My wife's joke," he added at Jo's arched brow. "We have three kids. Mostly grown now, but I do remember those days. And so does she, believe me."

Jo wasn't entirely sure how to respond to that comment. "Mr. Bishop—"

"Jed."

"Great. Jed. I've spoken with each of your crew members and they'll be back on the job Wednesday morning."

"Yep." Jed took a drink of his coffee. "Word got around."

"Right." Jo pressed her lips into a thin line. With Jed Bishop there was a physicality about him, beneath the polite tenor and neat appearance. *Sturdy*, she thought. And, judging by his record, dependable. "The word I hear is that you aren't sure you want to come back."

He toasted her with his mug. "Word is rarely wrong."

"I've spent my entire life in construction," Jo said to break the ice. "And I wouldn't be lying if I said I understood your reluctance.

I've been witness to a number of accidents, but I've never been involved in something as devastating as I'm sure this was."

"Watching your crew get trapped beneath steel and concrete isn't something I'd recommend." Even now she could see the ghosts hovering around him. "For the record, the supplier we used was not my first choice. But then my recommendation—"

"Was twenty percent above what most other bids came in on and money was the deciding factor." Now this was something Jo understood. "You and I both know that money, at least in this situation, can buy a certain level of security and confidence. I read the original bids and your recommendation. I would have agreed with you." Something she'd conveyed to the mayor during their conversation this morning. "That's something I've already rectified. The new supplies will be arriving late next week. I'd very much like you to be there to accept them."

Jed tilted his head. "I'm used to being the boss. I'm not used to working with a supervisor looking over my shoulder, and to be honest, the one time I did, disaster struck."

Jo waved off his concern. "I'm a damage

control specialist and supervisor who only wants to get this project back on track. To do that I need the best people for the job. That's you. And to be honest, you're the only person on my list."

"Chuck Elington's a good man. If I were recommending someone—"

"Chuck isn't you." She feigned struggling for words. "Okay, I'm just going to be honest. I spoke with Kyle Knight a while ago."

"How's he doing?" Guilt was a difficult emotion to hide, especially for someone who clearly cared about his crew the way she suspected Jed did. "I saw him in the hospital, but not since he got out."

Guilt and avoidance, Jo knew, often went hand in hand.

"He's doing okay, actually. I made him an offer to come back, but like you, he's hesitant." A white lie here or there wasn't going to hurt. Especially since she wouldn't be here long enough for it to matter after a few months. "I offered him an office job, being an administrative assistant, but also thought, considering his plans for the future, he could work closely with you."

"With me?"

"He needs guidance. He wants to learn. And he needs to feel safe while he's doing it. He feels safe with you, Jed. He trusts you. That tells me a lot about both of you. If it would help him get back on his feet—"

"So to speak?" Jed asked.

"Yeah." Relief washed through her. She liked Jed. He got it. And, if she wasn't mistaken, he was leaning in her favor. "If coming back will help him get over the rough patches, maybe it's something you can think about?"

He pushed his plate away, sat back and folded his arms over his chest. "How much oversight is there going to be? I understand the need for caution and I even understand the need for a special supervisor. But I need to know I have the final say with my crew."

It was a logical concern. She'd have been surprised if he hadn't brought it up. "I can promise you this. If I don't agree with something, I'll address it with you in private. We will work together on a plan of action, and unless I get the feeling you're going completely off the rails, you'll have free rein. I'll be signing off on the paperwork and orders until completion, which means most of that just got lifted off your shoulders. That also means if you want back on the crew yourself, I've got no problem with that. But we'd be a partnership, Jed. And you'd have to be okay with that from the jump."

He considered her for a good long moment, offered the brunette server a quick smile when she set his bill on the edge of the table. "I need to talk it over with my wife. She hasn't been entirely unhappy that I've been home more. That's what she *says*, anyway."

"While work will officially begin on Wednesday, I've called for a crew meeting Monday morning. Six a.m.," she told him. "I'll expect to see you at the same time."

Jed frowned, the creases in his slightly tanned forehead showing a bit of his age. "I haven't said yes yet."

"No, you haven't." She scooted to the edge of the booth. "But you will. I'm a good judge of people, Jed. The second I said Kyle needed your help you were in." Once she managed to get to her feet, she smiled at his befuddled expression. "I look forward to working with you."

Before he could respond, she returned to the counter where Ozzy was skimming through his phone. She peeked over his shoulder, saw the collection of feminine faces smiling up from his screen and recognized the layout of a popular dating app. She grimaced, thinking about her own disastrous experience with online dating. She wouldn't wish that on anyone, let alone a sweetheart of a guy like Ozzy. Swallowing that uncomfortable and unwanted lump in her throat, she gave a discreet cough before sliding back onto the stool.

Ozzy clicked his phone off so fast she might have imagined it was there in the first place.

"How'd it go?" he asked.

"About as I expected." She sipped her water and watched Twyla bop back and forth behind the counter. "I'll know for sure in a few minutes. So—" she chewed an ice cube "—you two ever gone out?"

"Me and Jed?"

"No." Jo gestured toward Twyla.

Ozzy scoffed. "Me and Twyla? No." His tone would not, Jo thought, have gone over well with their server. "No, I've known Twyla since we were kids. She was a few years behind me in school."

"So? She's cute," Jo said. "And she likes you," she whispered conspiratorially. "You should think about doing something about it." Why was she pushing so hard?

"Mama mama mama mama!" The shrill cry of a little one's voice had Jo swiveling on her stool toward the back corner booth. The server who had greeted them earlier detoured and quickly bent down to scoop up a toddler scooting out from under the table. After a quick conversation with two boys—one significantly older with thick round glasses and a faded superhero T-shirt—she gestured to the stack of coloring books on the closest windowsill. The older boy grabbed one and handed a crayon to the other boy sitting beside him.

Without missing a beat, the woman pivoted and headed around the counter, the little girl with short dark pigtails sticking out of the sides of her head perched on one hip. "Sometimes no one other than Mama will do," she said with a smile. "Enjoying your day off, Oz?"

"You know it," Ozzy confirmed. "Holly, this is Jo—"

"Bertoletti," Holly finished for him and offered Jo a quick welcoming nod. "Luke called and said you were heading over. That's so great of you to offer Kyle a job. How are you finding things, Jo?"

"Interesting." Jo couldn't bring herself to stop looking at the little girl in Holly's arms. In just a few months this would be her, juggling her job and a little demanding life that clung to her. The reality of it hit her like a sledgehammer. "Hello there, little one."

"Hi!" The girl's round face lit up and she grinned before turning her face into her mother's shoulder.

"This is Zoe." Holly rubbed Zoe's back. "She and her brother Jake over there take turns being the loud ones."

"Their brother Simon's a good distraction," Ozzy added.

"That's an apt description," Holly laughed. "Most of the time he loves being a big brother. Other times?"

"Other times he's trying to take over the world," Ozzy muttered and earned appreciative nods of agreement from other diners who overheard. "Remind me to tell you about the time Simon hacked into his neighbor's Wi-Fi—"

"Oh, for heaven's sake, Oz," Holly snapped

good-naturedly. "That was a bazillion years ago. He doesn't do that anymore."

"He was an eight-year-old bored computer genius," Ozzy clarified for Jo. "But his actions are also partially responsible for Holly marrying Luke. She had to marry the town sheriff to keep her son out of trouble."

"He's oversimplifying things," Holly argued as Jo found herself enjoying the playful banter and retrospective town gossip. "Mostly. Oh, coming, Penny!" Holly gestured over Jo's head at one of her customers. "Here, sweetheart. Go with your uncle Ozzy for a few minutes, okay?"

"Zee!" Zoe let out a squeal of delight and practically dived out of her mother's arms.

Ozzy stood up and reached out as Holly handed Zoe over the counter. "There's my girl. Hey, there, Zoe. How ya doing?" He settled back down with Zoe in his lap. Jo watched, amazed, as the toddler settled against him and let out what was a definitive sigh of contentment. "You using that playground we built for you yet?"

"The swings at least," Holly said as she grabbed the coffeepot and headed out for a round of refills, no doubt. "That reminds me—Luke's got a new grill on order, so be on standby for a barbecue." She glanced at Jo, at Ozzy, then back to Jo. "You should come, too, Jo. Nothing fancy. Just friends hanging out watching my husband blow up our backyard. It'll be a great time to meet more people from town."

"I'll play it by ear," Jo said. She appreciated the polite invitation but wasn't looking to make connections. She just wanted to do her work and move on. "But thanks."

"She's only kidding about the grill exploding," Ozzy said. "That's more Hunter MacBride's area of disaster."

"Too true," Holly agreed.

"Total lie," Ozzy said when Holly was out of earshot. "Our sheriff was responsible for a lot of my emergency training. By default," he added. "I'll be sure to put an extra extinguisher in my SUV just in case."

"Jo?" Jo glanced up at Jed Bishop. "Hey, Oz," Jed said and gave Zoe a quick wink. "I just spoke with my wife."

"And?" Anticipation bubbled in her blood. "What's the verdict?"

"I'll see you on-site Monday morning."

"Excellent." She couldn't stop beaming as

Jed paid his bill and headed out. Just like that, her to-do list for the day was done.

"Hi." Zoe's hand shot into the air as she grinned again at Jo.

"Hi." Jo laughed but the smile faded from her face when Zoe held out her arms and leaned forward. "Oh, no. You don't want me, sweetheart."

"Up." Zoe scooted forward and nearly toppled off Ozzy's lap before he caught her and, much to Jo's shock, plopped the little girl right in her arms.

"Not up, Zoe. You're too heavy for her. But you can sit."

"'Kay." Zoe twisted her mouth as if contemplating Ozzy's words. "Hi." She tilted her head back and let out a laugh that would have made even the curmudgeonliest person break out a smile. "Hi hi hi."

"Hello to you, too." Jo winced, shifting the little girl around her belly. "You're a cutie, aren't you? I'm Jo."

"Doe!" Zoe cried. "Doe doe doe."

"Um. Okay."

"She has fun with new words," Ozzy chuckled.

Jo tweaked a finger under Zoe's chin. Uncertainty flooded through her. She hadn't spent a lot of time around kids. Even when she'd been one, she'd felt far more comfortable around adults. When she'd learned she wouldn't be having any children of her own, she'd tended to go out of her way to avoid them. She didn't want to be reminded of or shown what she'd never have. Tears burned the back of her throat, confusing and embarrassing her. She swiped a hand across her cheek, but it was too late.

"Sad?" Zoe's bright and cheerful face darkened. She scrambled up and linked her chubby arms around Jo's neck. "No sad, Doe. No cry." She patted her little hand against Jo's back.

"You okay?" Ozzy asked, reaching out to press his hand against Zoe's back to keep her from falling. But Jo only nodded and wrapped her arms around little Zoe and held on.

"She's a big bundle of love, isn't she?" Jo blinked again and felt the tears escape. "Sorry," she whispered. "Hormones." Her hand brushed Ozzy's. Jo started, unable to process the spark that jumped between them. This town, or maybe it was this man, definitely lent itself to sensory overload. "You think maybe Holly would let me practice on her for a while?"

"If you mean would Holly accept free babysitting, I can attest that she gratefully would," Ozzy replied. His fingers touched hers again, as if he, too, felt what she did.

Twyla dropped two paper sacks on the counter. Jo and Ozzy jumped and Ozzy pulled his hand back. "Here're your orders."

"Thanks, Twyla." Ozzy stood up and reached for his wallet.

"You bet. Have a good time with Shelly tonight."

Jo wasn't an idiot. That little zinger of information was purely for her benefit.

"Shelly?" Ozzy looked honestly baffled for a second, then said, "Right. The movies. Thanks. I'd almost forgotten."

"Got yourself a movie date, huh?" Jo teased and ignored that pang of envy when it chimed once more. "What are you going to see?"

"*The Big Sleep*. It's classics night at the theater. Have you seen it?"

"Classics aren't my thing. Don't," she ordered when he went to pay for her lunch. "I've got it. It's the least I owe you for playing welcoming committee and tour guide. Please," she added at Ozzy's reluctance.

Deciding that Jo had had enough comfort, Zoe kicked out her feet and made to escape. "Oh! Careful!" Jo almost lost her hold as the tiny body slipped away.

"I've got her." Ozzy caught Zoe like an expert and hauled her over his shoulder. The ensuing squeals and laughter had even the sour-looking Twyla smiling. He turned and scanned the restaurant. After a quick gesture to Holly, he beelined to a table filled with senior citizens. Zoe's ensuing cries of "Mya! Okar! Arold!" told Jo this group of customers were also regulars. "Quick. Let's make a run for it." Ozzy returned to grab for the bags and dashed for the door. When Jo stood up, Twyla was back to glaring, but one glance down at Jo's stomach had the hostility in her eyes fading and the color rising in her cheeks. "Sorry. I didn't realize—"

"I'm not standing in your way, Twyla," Jo said quietly as she set money down and added a tip. "Believe me, I have enough going on. I'm not looking to get involved with anyone."

"Oh." Twyla let out a sigh of relief Jo suspected she'd been holding onto for months.

"Okay. Good. I mean, not good, but good to know. You know?"

"I do know." Jo moved off, then turned back to the younger woman. "Maybe stop waiting for him to notice. If you're interested, tell Ozzy. From what I've seen, he doesn't pick up on signals very well."

"That's what I suggested," Holly muttered as she crossed behind Twyla. "Excellent advice nonetheless. We'll be seeing you around, I'm sure, Jo."

"I have no doubt." She'd have to play that by ear. As nice as the warm welcome had been, she wasn't here to do anything but work hard enough so she could move on. She liked Ozzy. She liked his friends. She liked this little town. But she'd learned the hard way the second she let her guard down, the second she started to settle in and trust others, life took its own opportunity to slap her down.

Better for everyone, especially herself, if she kept her distance, focused on the sanctuary site, and moved on to the new life she had planned for herself and her child when the time came.

"You ready to hit the beach?" Ozzy asked when Jo finally emerged from the diner. His bright look of expectation bolstered her re-solve as Jo reached for her bag.

"Actually, I'm going to head back." This was a practical decision. One that had noth-ing, absolutely nothing to do with how she'd felt when he'd touched her. Twice. "I'll save the beach for another time."

"Oh." He frowned and, after a quick check, handed over her lunch. "But I thought—"

"I appreciate the personal tour." She cut him off and backed away. "But I've got a lot of work to do to get ready for next week and I'm not here to play. I'll see you around, Oz."

"At least let me drive you home."

"I'd rather walk." A lie. She was more tired than she thought, but the idea of being in a confined space with Ozzy Lakeman unsettled her more than the prospect of heading home under her own steam.

She liked him enough already. Any more and she'd just be asking for trouble. "Have a good time on your date tonight." She offered him her brightest smile before she headed off for home.

Alone.

CHAPTER SIX

As was his routine, before heading in for his 8:00 a.m. shift at the station house on Sunday, Ozzy pulled his SUV into the driveway of the pale blue bungalow cottage and parked behind his father's hybrid. Located nearly dead center of Butterfly Harbor, the house was on Clover Path Drive, one of the few streets where the homes had remained occupied and well-tended to despite the rough patch the town had endured the past few years.

Ozzy was greeted by the familiar roar of the lawn mower before his father rounded the corner in his quest to maintain the perfect landscaping display for the entire town to admire. Lyle Lakeman, retired city registrar, was second only to florist Lori Knight in the horticulture department. His father could just look at a plant and it would grow to its fullest, most colorful potential.

"Morning, Dad!" Ozzy hauled out the two

bags containing the fish he'd caught yesterday morning as well as leftover produce he'd picked up from Duskywing Farm. He'd spent the hours before his date last night meal planning and prepping for the week. Handing over the leftover produce was, as Ozzy had learned in the last couple of years, the best way to ensure his mother at least got some healthy food into her. His father was from the generation of meat and potatoes, with potatoes qualifying as their main vegetable. Baked, broiled, fried or covered in cheesy cream sauce. How his father wasn't on cholesterol medication was a mystery for the ages.

Lyle flipped off the engine as Ozzy closed the back of his vehicle. "Your mother's waiting for you. Something about the coffee maker being on the fritz again."

"Right." Ozzy nodded. "I'll get on it." His days as tech support were never going to be behind him.

"Heard you and Shelly Tate had a date to the movies." Lyle pulled off his Dodgers baseball cap, a reminder that his father was that team's sole supporter in all of Butterfly Harbor. It had become the family—and town—joke, made all the funnier by Ozzy's lifelong devotion to the San Francisco Giants. "How'd it go?"

"Fine." Not remotely close to the truth. Shelly, it turned out, was a screen talker. The running commentary before, during and after the film had pushed Ozzy so far down in his seat he could barely see the screen. She'd been shushed so many times Ozzy spent most of the film waiting for the theater manager to kick them out. There wasn't anything Shelly didn't have an opinion on large or small, and the judgements had continued throughout the rest of their evening. It probably hadn't helped that Ozzy had spent most of the night wishing he'd taken someone else to the movies instead.

"Going to see her again, then?" Lyle asked.

"Shelly? No." He eyed his father. "Why?"

"Just wondering when you're going to get serious about someone is all. Your mother worries."

That was something Ozzy knew, but then his mother had never understood why he hadn't been more popular in high school or college. Ozzy could have told her, but he doubted she'd have believed him. How could she when she'd never seen his weight as anything other than more of him to love? "I'm not even thirty yet, Dad. I've got plenty of time."

"Uh-huh." Lyle slapped his cap against his jean-clad thigh and put it back on his head, covering the hair that had started going stark white more than a decade before. "By your age I was married with you on the way."

"Times change, Dad. I need to go my own way, not yours." It had taken Ozzy longer than it should have to offer that crumb of knowledge to his father. It was almost funny how much stronger he'd gotten when the weight had come off. "I need to get the food inside before I get to work."

"Go on, then." Lyle flipped the mower back on and pivoted in the opposite direction.

Ozzy shifted the bags into one hand and opened the front door. He immediately inhaled the aroma of fresh baked pie and hot sugar. Typical. His mother did most of her weekly baking on Sunday mornings before the sun began to rise. He didn't call out. Instead, he walked down the hallway and past his father's study and straight into the kitchen.

The mocha-colored walls were covered

in photographs Ozzy would prefer to forget existed. Like he needed photographic evidence of his weight struggle, yet his mother refused to take down a single picture. At least she'd added the one he'd had taken when he'd passed his firefighter physical exam. Ozzy had been the one who had it framed and placed on the mantel for her. In some ways, his mother liked to pretend he was still the homebody teenager she used to dote on.

"Hey, Ma." Ozzy set the reusable bags on the counter by the refrigerator. "Dad said the coffee machine's busted again?"

"Ozzy, you're early." Bea, her faded brown hair tied into a knot at the base of her neck, smiled over her shoulder at him from where she stood at the sink. "I'm in the middle of baking your favorite. And I dragged out the old machine from the garage." She pointed to the box by the back door. "You can take that home and fix it."

"Great, thanks. Let me guess." Ozzy tried not to cringe as the familiar intoxicating scent grabbed him by the nose. "Blueberry crumb-cake pie?"

"You know it." Bea toweled off her hands and faced him. "With my special ingredient."

His mother's special ingredient—a combination of lard and shortening—had been a major contributor to Ozzy's lifelong battle with the scale. "I'll take it to the station house with me. Roman and Jasper will be thrilled."

"My son, the fireman." Bea reached up and touched his cheek. "I can hardly believe it. You know, my bridge group says the same thing. Who can believe my pudgy little Ozzy's a town hero now."

"I'm no one's hero, Ma." He'd preferred the way Jo used the word, despite her meaning it as a joke. Her changing her mind about lunch with him yesterday had bothered him more than he wanted to admit. But he also wasn't one to push where someone else didn't want to go, and it was obvious Jo Bertoletti didn't want to spend more time with him. It must have been those pictures, he reminded himself. Those stupid pictures that wouldn't let anyone forget what he had been.

To distract himself from the desire to dive headfirst into his mother's baking, he started unloading the produce. "Sounds to me like your bridge group needs a new topic of conversation."

"Oh, don't worry, we have one." Bea came

over and crossed her arms over her flower-print shirt. "Did you know the new foreman for the construction project is a *woman*!"

"Supervisor," he corrected. "You don't have to whisper, Ma. It's not a secret. It's also not a big deal."

"She's not just a woman. She's pregnant! You could have knocked me over with a feather when I heard. Can you imagine?"

"That a grown woman can get pregnant? Sure." He could imagine it quite easily. Ozzy had to stop himself from slamming the crisper drawer closed. "Her name is Jo Bertoletti, and from what I've seen, she's more than up to the job."

"You've met her, then? What's her story? Is she married? Is he going to join her here?"

"I have met her. She's very nice. I don't know her life story, but I do know she isn't married, so I'm thinking no, he, whoever he is or was, won't be joining her." It didn't help that Ozzy wanted the answer to those questions himself, but Jo had made it clear she preferred to be left alone.

"It's just so…odd. A pregnant woman working construction."

"Not just construction." Ozzy decided he

could have some fun with this. "She's the boss. What's wrong with that, Ma? I thought you were all for equality for women."

"Well, yes, certainly I am." Bea's green eyes shifted away from his. "It came as a surprise is all. I can only imagine what Gil's going to think."

"From what I heard, he handled the situation with his usual aplomb and sensitivity." The words nearly caught in his throat. "The buzzer's buzzing."

"What? Oh!" Bea spun toward the oven and pulled out not one, but two golden-crusted pies. "We'll let these cool a bit and you can have a slice before work."

"Actually, I can't. I need to get in earlier than usual to help Jasper with something." He couldn't think of what at the moment, but he knew what would happen the second his mother got a plate of anything in front of him. He'd have to eat every crumb before she let him out of the house.

Food, at least as far as his mother was concerned, was love. It was how Bea Lakeman showed she cared. It was also how she dealt with her own emotions, by burying them in whatever she cooked or baked. Guilt over wanting to make his mother happy had had Ozzy scarfing down pretty much anything she put in his sight. The more he'd eaten, the bigger he'd gotten and the happier she'd become. Until finally, he'd had enough. In more ways than one.

"Well, that's disappointing." Without missing a beat she retrieved a pie caddy from a cabinet and got it ready for transport. "I'll keep one for your father for dinner tonight. I'm making a nectarine and blueberry pie next. There were tons of blueberries at Calliope's Friday morning. Maybe I'll take it up to the construction site to welcome our new worker bee."

Worker bee? Ozzy could only imagine how Jo would react to that title. "She's still settling in, Ma. Maybe give her a few days to get used to us before we smother her with comfort food."

"Hmm."

Normally he'd just stay out of it and let his mother do what she was going to do, but he felt oddly protective about Jo. Not because she was fragile or that she couldn't handle herself. She could. Any woman who lugged her entire home with her around the country was more than capable of taking care of herself and her baby.

But he'd gotten the distinct impression Jo wasn't quite sure how to handle a community like Butterfly Harbor. It also appeared as if she didn't have much experience with kids. It would take subtlety, something his mother was not known for, to ease her into the reality of this place. And possibly whatever the future had in store for her.

"Since I've already met her—" Ozzy scrambled to come up with a solution "—how about you bake the pie and write a nice note and I'll take it to her. I'll stop by tomorrow night and get it."

Bea turned, narrowed her eyes at him as if she was waiting for the punch line. "Will you come for dinner?"

"I will if you promise to leave Jo alone for the time being." Nothing like blackmailing his own mother.

Bea's mouth twisted as if she were debating. He hadn't eaten at his parents' for over a year. He'd never come right out and said why, that he couldn't trust his mother to respect the changes he'd made in his eating habits, but it had, at the time, been the only way he could reach his goal. "All right. Six o'clock sharp. You know how your father likes to eat—"

"At the same time every night. Yes, I remember, Ma." He walked over and kissed her cheek. "And I've even brought you fresh fish you can cook up. I need to get going. You letting me take one of those?"

She had a pie wrapped up and in his hands before he could blink. "We'll see you tomorrow night for dinner. Be safe, Ozzy."

"Always, Ma." He lugged the pie out with him, gave his father a goodbye wave before climbing into his SUV. He stayed there for a long moment, a slow smile spreading across his mouth as he glanced down at the pie.

Blackmail did work. He'd just found an excuse to see Jo again.

IF THERE WAS one constant in Jo's universe, it seemed as soon as she started settling in, trouble found her.

Something had woken her up. Jo touched a hand against her stomach, felt the familiar kick, but didn't think the cause was baby related. An odd rustling sounded in the distance, but she chalked it up to the wind and tried to go back to sleep.

Less than a minute later she stared wide-eyed at her bedroom wall. Nope. Despite her plan to get an extra hour, it wasn't going to happen. Time to get up and see what the day had in store for her.

She'd expected trouble to come at her fast and furious on Monday, but apparently it had been delayed.

The crew had turned up on time yesterday morning for her inaugural meeting. When she'd laid out their rather exhaustive and expansive work schedule for the next month, the seventeen-man and two-woman crew had seemed both relieved to be back at work and guardedly optimistic about the plans she had in place for all of them.

When they'd asked her about the pile of outdoor furniture that had been taking up a significant amount of space, she'd told them what she had in mind, and mere moments later, they'd gotten to work and within a few hours had their eating area set up and ready to use. Normally there were at least two or three grumpy Guses who pushed back or gave her attitude, but nothing so far ticked her frustration radar.

She'd thought trouble had turned up at

lunchtime when Gil Hamilton pulled into the parking lot. But rather than him approaching her, he'd merely gotten in line at the food truck and left as soon as he received his lunch, giving her an absent wave as he drove off.

No sooner did she think perhaps she'd lucked out for the rest of the day than her cell phone rang and, well, trouble was on the other end.

Said trouble turned out to be almost good news. The new supplier called to say that due to a shortage of transport vehicles, the cement, rebar and sand she was expecting on Wednesday would be delayed at least two days. Add to that the heavy equipment she'd rented would also be coming later, on Wednesday morning, but after a quick schedule adjustment, she decided they'd tackle the rest of the nature path they'd been clearing near the cliff's edge. Problem—and trouble—solved.

Now Tuesday morning dawned and with it came Jo's determination that nothing was going to throw her off-kilter. That was before she swung her legs over the edge of the bed and sat up. Five o'clock. Despite being an early bird, there were days she would give anything to be able to sleep five more minutes.

Jo scooted forward, her feet dangling until they touched the wood floor. Her toes felt funny. She looked down, and unable to believe what she saw, her mouth dropped open.

Her swollen ankles bulged, and her toes were now crammed together like all those little piggies after their visit to market. She pressed her hands against her cheeks, as if that would give her an explanation as to what was happening.

"What the heck is this?" She pushed herself up and made her way quickly to the bathroom, a trip she'd already taken twice during the night. Her stomach seemed to be demanding its own space, and as she dragged herself into the kitchen afterward, she was torn between vomiting and hoovering up whatever she had in the refrigerator. "How can I be hungry and sick at the same time?" She still couldn't feel her feet.

She opened her laptop, clicked on her search engine and typed in *pregnancy symptoms*. What she found certainly didn't do much to alleviate her concerns that she had, in the space of one night, lost the last bit of control over her body. Swollen feet were typical for expectant mothers. She attempted to tug her robe tighter, but there was a significant and possibly permanent gap between the edges. "Kid, you and I need to have a serious conversation."

Headlights swung across and through the windows and the sound of tires over gravel had her hurrying forward, praying this wasn't an earlier than expected delivery. She'd given the crew a 7:00 a.m. call, mainly because she'd been too tired yesterday to finish her initial sketch for the children's playground that she planned to break ground on while they had the time.

She flipped open the blinds and spotted Ozzy's SUV pulling to a stop outside her door.

"Ah, jeez." She yanked the tie out of her hair, fluffed her fingers through it and scrubbed her hands hard against her eyes. She was barely awake and certainly not functioning, but there was no mistaking the jolt of excitement that zinged through her at the thought of seeing him. "Cool your jets, Jo." She wanted to dissuade him, right? What better way to do that than to just open the door as she was?

Which was precisely what she did. "Morning, Ozzy." Her overly cheerful, chirpy tone had her wincing as he jumped back, whatever he had in his hands nearly toppling free. "Oh, sorry."

"I've got it." Even in the barely-there light she could tell he was blushing again.

"Got what?" He really was fun to tease.

"Ah, a welcome-to-town gift from my mother. She calls it blueberry crumbcake pie. It's kind of her specialty."

"You had me at *pie*." Not wanting to be an ungracious hostess, she stood back and held open the door. "Come on in."

"Thanks." He looked tired, if not exhausted, as he walked past her and set the carrier on the counter. "A gift from my mom. I wanted to drop this off to you before I went home to crash."

She should send him on his way, but she hadn't realized until she'd recognized his vehicle that she'd missed seeing him. She didn't even want to know how that was possible after only knowing him a few days. "Rough time at work?"

"Four car accidents on the highway just out of town. No fatalities, thank goodness, but there were kids and, well, chaos. Ended up working an extra eight hours." He inclined his chin. "What happened to the security cameras?"

"Gil had them removed after the accident. It was an unneeded expense when things were shut down and now that I'm living on-site, I don't see the need. Is everyone okay? From the accident," she added at his blank stare.

"Minor injuries. You're out here alone without any protection?"

"Yes." Jo kept her tone pleasant. "Wasn't it you who said Butterfly Harbor isn't a hub of criminal activity?"

"Actually, you said it and I didn't argue. I don't think—"

"No thinking allowed. I invited you in because you look wiped out and you have pie."

"But—"

"I'm a grown woman who can take care of herself. No one's going to come messing around with a construction zone that's in limbo," she said. "There's nothing here worth stealing or messing with."

"You're here."

Jo took a deep breath. Contrary to his protestations the other day, obviously Ozzy Lakeman suffered from a severe case of hero complex. "I have my cell and I have a satellite phone for backup. I'm fine." She narrowed her eyes. "I mean it, Ozzy. I appreciate the concern, but I don't need it. Now—" Jo crossed her arms over her chest "—are you dropping off and running, or would you like to stay for coffee?"

"I wouldn't say no to decaf." He hesitated, clearly evaluating his options. "No need to wait on me, though, I can get it. If that's okay."

"Sure. Help yourself. Top left cabinet," she said, grateful for the offer, and headed over to a stool at the counter. "Mugs are in the one next to it."

"Thanks." That grin of his flashed and she felt that warm fluttering sensation sliding through her. He made himself right at home, sorted through her single-cup pods and popped one into the machine. It was something she could get used to, welcoming him home at the end of his shift. She cleared her throat, shook her head. Time to start a new conversation before she melted into a puddle on her kitchen floor.

"So, were you busy at the station?" Wait. She'd already asked that, hadn't she?

"Interesting." He chose a mug, set it in place and started the coffee machine. "We were on our way back after the accident when we got a call from Roman's mom, Ezzie. She's kind of a caretaker for the Cocoon Club—"

"What's a Cocoon Club?"

"Right, sorry." With his fingers, he rubbed at his eyes. "Everything here needs its own disclaimer. The Cocoon Club is a group of older residents here in town. They pooled their resources and moved into this refurbished old Victorian. Made it a kind of seniors' residence rather than getting stuck in one elsewhere. Oscar took a fall."

"Okar?" Jo remembered baby Zoe calling his name. "Stooped stoic bald man? Uses a walker?"

"That's him. He decided to go rummaging around in the garage for his old croquet set. At two in the morning," he added. "As Ezzie said—she keeps an eye on the club— sometimes those seniors are worse than teenagers. We eventually convinced him to go for

X-rays to make sure nothing's broken. Last I heard he's still in the hospital."

She could sense his ready sympathy for the older man and admired him for it.

"I really did just plan on leaving the pie for you outside." He pulled his cup free of the machine and took a tentative sip. "Have an early start this morning?"

"Late, actually. Kidlet was done sleeping." She lifted her feet, which were still looking like mutant appendages. "I think it's got me in early training for midnight feedings."

"What's going on with these feet?" He came over, glanced down before she could lower her legs. "Oh. Huh. That new?"

"It is indeed." She sighed. "I was probably on my feet too much yesterday, but we got so much done." She rested her cheek in her hand. "We might even have a shot at catching up in the schedule. Provided we don't have any problems today."

"Just because you have a lot to do doesn't mean you should ignore what your body's telling you. And before you get mad, I'm saying that as a friend." He offered a flash of a smile that had her catching her breath. "And a trained EMT."

While it irritated her that he didn't think she'd come to these conclusions on her own, they might as well get it all out at once. "Do you have any thoughts on the matter?"

He should carry a permit for that smile of his. "Why do I have the feeling you're humoring me?"

"Because you're a smart man who knows when he's crossing into danger."

"Or maybe I'm someone who recognizes someone who needs a confidant or sturdy presence in her life."

She could imagine him being that in her life. Far too easily. Which was why she needed to keep him at arms' length and any conversation between them as impersonal as possible. "Let's stick with the advice for my feet for now."

A flash of disappointment crossed his face, but not enough to dim the flirtatious light in his green eyes. "First, I'd say we get these up and off the floor." He leaned down and caught both her feet and lifted them up onto the second stool beside her. She had to catch her balance and readjust her position, grabbing hold of his shoulder to steady herself.

"They've been off the floor all night," she grumbled.

"I know Abby over at the Flutterby Inn drank a particular herbal tea when she was pregnant with her son, David. Her OB recommended it to help flush toxins out of her system. What did yours say?"

She grimaced. "I've actually been meaning to make an appointment with one."

Rather than lecturing her or acting surprised that she didn't currently have a doctor, he pulled out his phone. "Do you have one in mind? If you don't—"

"Leah recommended one. I wrote the name down and put it over there." She gestured to the notepad behind her. "I've been meaning to give her a call." Jo pointed to her desk. "Could you grab my calendar?"

"Sure. Still stuck on a print one?"

"It's my backup in case I don't have my phone." Or if she had to stand up to get it. Five months into this pregnancy and she was beginning to wonder if she'd make it another four. "I don't need a keeper, Oz, I promise you."

"Oh, Cheyenne." He found the note with

the doctor's name. "Great. That's who I was going to suggest you call."

"Recommending OBs now, are you?" He was chock-full of information, wasn't he?

"With the baby boom we've had in this town the last few years, believe me, everyone knows who to call. Cheyenne does a lot with holistic and natural remedies and treatments. She and Calliope Costas are developing a line of products together, so whatever she recommends, you can probably find at Duskywing Farm."

"I meant to get there over the weekend and didn't manage it." Instead, she'd made a quick stop at the market to stock up on necessities. "What are their hours?"

"Calliope has an open gate policy. Just don't be surprised if it seems as though she's waiting for you." That secretive little smile of his had her spidey senses tingling.

"Why would she be waiting for me?"

Ozzy just shook his head and sipped his coffee while she copied the doctor's phone number onto her calendar.

She found, however, her attention was drawn to the pie caddy he'd set on her counter. "What kind of pie did you say that is?"

"Blueberry crumbcake." Before she knew it, he was rummaging around for a plate and cutting her a slice. "It's my mother's special combination of coffeecake, crumble and pie." The blueberries and their thick glaze glistened as he transferred the slice to a plate. "Breakfast of champions."

She grabbed a fork out of the canister on the counter as he moved to her fridge. "Aren't you having any?"

"No." He poured a glass of milk, emptying the carton, then slid that in front of her. "Drink up."

She was about to say again that she didn't need a keeper, but right now? All she could think about was that amazing-looking pie. After her first bite she was nearly swooning. "Oh, wow." She covered her mouth as the sweet brown sugar mingled with the tart berries. "That is amazing. I don't know how you don't scarf down the whole thing in one sitting."

"I've done that plenty of times, believe me." He leaned back against her counter, coffee in hand, and eyed her. "I should give you a heads-up. Bringing that by was actually me saving you."

"Saving me from what?" She couldn't remember being this hungry before.

"My mother turning up. She considers you a bit of a curiosity."

Jo smirked. "What's she most curious about? My job or my single mom-to-be status?"

"Both." He eyed her over the rim of the mug. "She means well. And she's determined, so she might very well pop up at some point. You might want to be prepared."

"Don't worry." Jo had dealt with more than her share of busybodies. She instantly regretted the thought. Not a nice thing to think about someone's mother. "Are you sure you won't have some?" She pointed at the pie. "Seriously, I shouldn't eat that whole thing myself." But she could. Far more easily than she cared to admit.

"I try to curtail the sugar when I can and I've had more than enough lately." He went back to the coffee cabinet and took out a stack of plates. Within seconds he had the pie divided into neat slices, covered in plastic, then foil and stuck all but one slice into the freezer. "There. Out of sight, out of mind. You get one a day," he ordered.

"Not bad." Even now as she finished her piece, she could feel the temptation ebb. "Is that one of the tricks you learned to lose weight?"

His hand hesitated when he lifted his mug again.

"I saw the pictures at the station," she explained. "If it's a touchy subject…"

"It's fine." But some of the light faded from his eyes. "I had to learn a lot of tricks to take the weight off. Tricks I still have to use."

"It's not easy, what you did. It's commendable."

He shook his head. "It was necessary."

"It does make you uncomfortable, I mean, to talk about it." She pushed her empty plate away and sat back. "Why? If I were in your shoes I'd be—"

"You'd be what? Shouting it from the rooftops? Celebrating? Believe me, it's not that easy to do when everyone you've ever known remembers you as you were. There's only so many times I can hear 'you look great, Ozzy' or 'you should have done this years ago' or, my particular favorite, 'look what you've been hiding.'" The fact that he met her gaze directly as he spoke told her how much she really didn't understand about him. "Lives are complicated. My weight was always the first thing people saw. Before my abilities, before my sense of humor, and for a long time, I let myself be defined by it. You know a little about first impressions, I'm sure."

"More than I care to." She considered her next words carefully. "I have to admit to being guilty of preconceptions. For instance, when I first saw you, I assumed you were a flirtatious, play-around firefighter with more female attention than you knew what to do with."

His teasing smile returned. "You're partially correct. I don't know what to do with it all."

She rolled her eyes. "So that's why you had a whole gallery of potential dates displayed on your phone the other day?"

"How did you—"

"I'm always curious—you should know that about me. I saw you scrolling at the diner. That's quite a selection of pretty ladies you have to choose from."

That blush she was so fond of rose up his cheeks. "I'm taking the spontaneous approach to dating these days. Choosing randomly and seeing what sticks."

"Has it worked?" She was dying to inquire about how his date had gone on Saturday, but she bit back the thought. It wasn't any of her business, and a hint of interest could send the wrong message.

"I've discovered I have a lot more deal breakers than I could have imagined possible."

She grinned. "Interesting. Having failed spectacularly in my own choice of potential mates, I could lie and say it only gets better, but I'll go with 'you'll know when you find her' instead." It was the extent of her romantic advice.

"A mistress of clichés and platitudes." He toasted her with his mug. "Well played. And since you've brought it up—"

"Only for comparison and connection of understanding," she warned.

"I can't let something like that dangle without comment." He reached for her plate and glass and, to her astonishment, began to wash up. "I won't tell anyone if that's what you're worried about."

"It's not." Funny. It had never occurred to

her that she couldn't trust him. That was odd in itself. "It's not that unique a story. Girl meets boy at work, girl and boy hit it off, boy decides it's time for him to get married, girl agrees and they get engaged. Girl gets pregnant shortly before the wedding. Boy doesn't want kids so he left."

"Seems to me, being engaged and almost married would up the chances of that happening. The getting pregnant part, that is."

Not willing to get into the particulars, she shrugged.

"So he knows about the baby?"

"Yes." She didn't think she'd ever forget the look of abject horror that appeared on Greg's face when she'd told him the "good news."

"Maybe it was only taking him time to get used to the idea." Ozzy's hands slowed under the running water.

"It wasn't supposed to happen." She sat back, rubbed her stomach. "Me, having kids. Doctors told me I couldn't, and then when I found out I was pregnant, Greg said it wasn't what he had signed on for. No pity, now," she added with a warning glare. "Things work out how they're meant to, and besides, I have him to thank for reminding me of what I'd obviously forgotten."

"What's that?"

"That the only person I can rely on is myself."

Ozzy reached for a towel to dry the dishes. "That's a pretty solitary line of thinking."

"I speak as I find." One of her favorite literary phrases. "Based on my own personal experience, it's true. Men, people don't stay. Particularly when things get rough or take an unexpected turn. It's like they're looking for an escape hatch and the second they find one, they're gone." And those who left her in other ways... Jo's luck keeping people she cared about close seemed to be temporary at best.

"I believe a therapist would say that particular emotional wound stems from further back than a few months."

"Said therapist would be correct." Unable to get comfortable, she lowered her legs and stood up, stretching a bit before she went to the two-seater pullout sofa against the wall. "If this conversation continues, we're going to end up sharing along those lines." She curled one leg under her and looked directly at him, leaning her cheek on her hand. "You up for that?"

"I will take that as my cue to leave." He gathered up the empty pie carrier, pushed open the door, but glanced over his shoulder. "We aren't all bad, you know. Men. Some of us stick it out. Good times and bad. You never know, Greg might realize the mistakes he's made."

"That's a nice sentiment, Ozzy." Jo wanted to believe him, wished she could. "Even if he did, there's no going backward. This is a reality I accepted a long time ago." She checked her foot and saw the swelling had gone down, but not much.

"You'll call the doctor and make an appointment?" he asked.

She rolled her eyes. "Yes, Ozzy. I'll call the doctor. Now shoo. I've got to figure out a way to get dressed."

His smile lit up his entire handsome face and lightened her heart. "If you need help with that—"

"Go!" She pushed herself off the sofa and shoved him playfully out the door.

CHAPTER SEVEN

NEVER IN HIS wildest imagination would Ozzy have ever pictured himself having lunch with Gil Hamilton in his mayoral office while teaching him to play backgammon. His quiet, introvert teenage self wouldn't have believed it—hanging out with the most popular kid in town. He would have accused present-day Ozzy of having delusions of grandeur. Nevertheless, that was precisely how he was spending his afternoon.

"You aren't looking at the entire board." Ozzy pointed to the exposed solitary piece ripe for the taking.

"Right," Gil murmured with an absent nod and seemed to rethink his position. He reached for the remnants of his lunch, plucking up a salt and vinegar chip and popping it into his mouth. The ensuing crunch echoed in the massive office. "I've seen kids play this game effortlessly. Why does it seem so hard?"

"Because you're trying too hard to win." One of Ozzy's early lessons. Sometimes you need to focus on staying in the game until an opportunity presents itself to seize a victory.

"Every game is going to be different. You can't beat Harvey, or anyone, with a predictable, memorized strategy. Besides…" Ozzy finished his iced tea and dropped the empty cup into the trash. "Harvey's been playing longer than either of us has been alive. The only way to compete with that is to play and practice as much as you can."

"I'm confused. Are you saying you play the player or the game?"

"In poker you play the player." Something Ozzy had learned when he'd joined in on Sheriff Saxon's Thursday night poker games. Since he'd been working as a firefighter, he was frequently on shift Thursday nights, which meant he missed out. One of the trade-offs he'd had to make. "In backgammon, whatever you want to do is at the mercy of the die."

"Maybe I should have taken up something easier, like chess."

Ozzy chuckled. He wasn't about to admit to having earned trophies playing that game too. Backgammon was enough of a challenge for Gil. "In chess, you focus on creating your own method using logical thinking. Planning a few moves ahead, depending on what you anticipate your opponent might do, keeps you sharp and focused." He hesitated. "Couldn't hurt to do that in real life, too."

Ozzy was so distracted giving advice he was caught off guard when Gil knocked one of Ozzy's pieces into the center of the board.

"Good catch," Ozzy said and rolled himself free with double sixes. "Sorry."

"Don't be." Gil waved off his concern. "Even a false bump of confidence is a bump. Something specific on your mind, Oz?"

So much, Ozzy thought. "Are you planning on reinstalling the security cameras up at the construction site?"

Whatever Gil had been expecting Ozzy to say, obviously that wasn't it. "I had planned to, but it was one of the first things Jo nixed when we spoke. Why?" Gil frowned. "You think it's necessary?"

"I think if it was necessary before she got here, then it's no different now. Maybe it's more necessary, since she's up there all alone."

"All right." Gil nodded. "I'll tell her I've reconsidered. Better to be safe than sorry."

An unexpected weight lifted off Ozzy's shoulders, even as he reminded himself to be cautious about possibly pushing too much where Jo was concerned. "She won't be happy about it."

"Fortunately, that's one area with respect to folks that I have vast experience with." Gil's gaze shifted back to the board. "Anything else you want to talk about?"

"Not really."

"How about asking me what my ulterior motive is?"

"With Jo?"

It must have been the way he'd said it, unintentionally, with a warning edge that had Gil arching a brow. "With these backgammon lessons. Ah, now that's better." Rolling a double four had Gil shifting pieces out of danger. "Lucky roll." But that was part of the game. Ozzy quickly countered, knocked not one, but two of Gil's pieces off the board, and slid his last piece into place.

Earlier, Gil would have visibly resented his

defeat, now, he steepled his fingers below his chin and examined the final arrangement of pieces. "Well, it wasn't quite the bloodbath it could have been. Thanks, Oz."

"No problem." Ozzy got to his feet and gathered up the last of his trash. "Trust me, you can hold your own against Harvey. Not letting him intimidate you is step one."

"Do I intimidate people?"

Ozzy didn't answer right away.

"I read the polls, Oz. And I have ears. What do I have to do to get people back on my side?"

Ah, here it is. The real reason Gil had asked him to come to the office. He wanted inside information. "That depends. Do you mean vote for you?"

Gil's expression didn't shift. "I'd appreciate someone telling me the truth as opposed to saying something they think I want to hear."

Ozzy nearly quoted a certain military trial movie, but refrained. "It's only my opinion, but it's difficult to maintain a positive connection with people you seem incapable of seeing."

"Is that what people think? That I don't

see them? That I'm only in this for myself? Is that what you think?"

"Yes, frankly." Because Gil remained where he was, Ozzy kept standing, shoved his hands into his pockets and rocked on his heels. "I've watched you from a few perspectives. First as schoolmate and then as a sheriff's deputy and now as a firefighter. I've also seen you from the point of view of a son of a city worker who was forced to take early retirement because of your cutbacks." The wall of control Ozzy kept in place threatened to crumble.

"You govern from a distance, exactly how you existed when we were younger. You were the banker's kid, the mayor's son. The chosen one who had everything handed to him and could never relate to the difficulties anyone else was going through. You never asked what anyone thought or what anyone wanted, but rather made decisions based on what you heard or what you were told and whatever improved the bottom line. Cutting budgets, eliminating jobs, making things more difficult when you didn't have to? Without asking people for alternatives that would cause less damage? That isn't seeing people, Gil. That's bulldozing right over them." Ozzy cleared his throat. "Sorry if that sounds harsh, but you did ask."

"I suppose that's clear enough." Gil's voice was tight, about as tight and taut as his jaw as he flicked his gaze from Ozzy to the desk. "One might argue that people's perspectives could be a bit skewed. Contrary to how you see things, I can promise you not everything on my side of the desk has been easy or that cut-and-dry. But I appreciate the honesty."

"If I might add one more thing?" Ozzy didn't have anything to lose at this point. "A massive pivot in the opposite direction isn't going to win you votes, Gil. It would be seen as a panic move with you doing whatever you think you need to in order to stay mayor. And I doubt there are many who will trust you mean what you say, anyway."

"So I've already lost?"

Ozzy could easily twist the knife by telling Gil that he didn't know anyone who planned to vote for the mayor, but that wasn't who he was. "If you want a chance at winning, it's time for you to climb out of the ivory tower your father placed you in the day you were born and get to know how the people in your town really live. Be a better human being, Gil. But don't shine a light on it. Just do it. It might provide a softer landing at the end however the election turns out."

"In another life you would have made an excellent campaign manager, Ozzy." Gil took a deep breath. "Gives me a lot to consider. Again, I appreciate your time." He pointed to the board. "Would you be up for another game?"

"But I thought the backgammon—"

"Was a ruse? Oh, it was." Gil's all-charm, no-harm smile was back in place. "But I also enjoyed this more than I expected. Same time next week?"

"Sure." Ozzy shrugged. "Why not."

"TIME FOR LUNCH!"

Jo glanced up from her computer screen when the trailer door popped open and Jed stuck his head in, his brow raised. "You go on," she told Kyle, who was already reaching for his crutches. She returned her attention to the pavement stones that would double as donation markers in the meditation garden. "I want to finish this before—"

"Paperwork can wait," Jed said without missing a beat. "It's Thursday."

"Thursday's gyro day on the food truck." Kyle's pronouncement made it seem as though that explained everything.

Jo waved them on. "You guys go ahead. I'll grab something late—oh." Jed was suddenly standing in front of her, holding the plug to her computer in his hand, threatening to pull it out of the socket.

"Gyro day is a treat, and besides, you've been holed up in here all week. The crew's beginning to think you're more a mirage than a sentient life-form."

That was by design. She didn't need anyone getting attached to her. And she certainly didn't want to be doing any attaching herself. But she appreciated the sentiment. What interaction she did have with the crew had been professional and agreeable. She was beginning to think the issues they'd had here had been a major fluke of the universe. "If lunch is that important you can just bring me—"

"The crew's chomping at the bit to get their hands on those excavators and backhoes that are sitting there waiting for action," Jed said. "Put them to work already. After lunch. Which you should have with them if only to check out the job they've done with the playground."

Jo set her pen down. "They're finished already?"

"When you give them the go, they go," Jed confirmed. "I told you, they're bored. My crew likes to work, Jo. You need to let them."

Jo angled a look at her foreman. "What else did you have in mind?"

"Let's discuss it over lunch." He held up the still-connected cord. "Don't make me pull the plug."

Kyle chuckled and slowly made his way outside.

"Fine." It would take less time to agree and eat than it would to argue. She spun her chair and scooted her feet out, grimacing at the sight of the laces she'd been unable to tie the last few mornings. She bent over as far as she could and stuffed the ends into the top of her steel-toed work boots, reminding herself once again she needed to shop for some new comfortable work shoes. She stood up and stretched and nearly sighed in relief as Jed released the cord. "These better be some pretty good gyros."

"Best you'll find around here."

She grabbed her yellow hard hat from the hook by the door and stuck it on her head.

"Mario's asked for Saturday and Monday off," Jed told her as she exited the trailer. Feeling a bit like a vampire being lured from her lair, Jo shielded her eyes from the sun. "His wife has a conference in San Francisco this weekend and their sitter had to cancel."

"Shouldn't be an issue." After only a few days of working with Jed, she knew the foreman wouldn't be implying his approval if he didn't have the shift covered. They'd be getting down to serious work come Monday when all the deliveries she was expecting arrived. "Cement truck's on schedule last I heard. We have someone to cover?"

"Nestor and Carl have offered to fill in. It'll mean overtime for both of them."

"Consider it approved." So far she hadn't needed to send out an SOS to her Bay Area people, and that was good news. "We get that cement poured and the pylons in before Monday, we have a good chance of getting ahead next week."

After taking a quick look at the playground area, which had been neatly framed out with

planks cut from the trees that had been removed for the sanctuary, she wondered again
if she was being too optimistic about getting
that completed along with the main structure. It had to be doable; she just needed to
find the funds to make it happen. She'd already noticed the tendency of some of the
schoolkids to stop by the site on their way
home. It was only a matter of time before
they got more curious and probably adventurous. They needed a distraction or at least
someplace to hang out while they observed
the construction process.

"We were able to expand the framing out
by another eight cubic feet," Jed told her.
"Hope that's okay."

"Should be fine." The plans had allowed
for that kind of wiggle room. She sniffed the
air and felt herself start to swoon. "Is that
lunch?"

"That is Thursday's heaven on a plate," Jed
confirmed with a grin. "This is also me not
saying I told you so."

"Glad you're holding yourself back," Jo
laughed and joined the lineup of workers
waiting for their serving of roasted beef and
lamb served in soft, hot fresh-baked pitas.

Having gotten a look at Flutterby Wheels, the food truck painted with bright flowers and multicolored butterflies, earlier in the week, she'd been inspired to buy out Harvey's hardware store of their spray paint on clearance.

The now repainted yard furniture, which lay scattered about the area, was exactly what the site needed and gave the workers a sense of their own space outside the project itself. So much of the last few days had been arranging and managing and planning, getting everyone up to speed on the schedule and plans.

There had been a method to her madness, from where she'd parked her house (the future location of an expansive concessions stand for the sanctuary and education center) to where the eating spot would be (situated close to the playground) and the fenced-in temporary storage containers parked on what would become the main parking lot. She liked to see as much open space around a project as possible, but particularly on this job. Jo was so used to being crammed in among cement and city streets that she was taking every advantage of enjoying the natural setting.

Standing at the end of the lunch line, she half-listened to the conversations around her and assessed the team's progress. She shifted, pressed a hand against the small of her back as the tables were filled and food was consumed. By the time she got to the truck's window, she was ready to order ten of the darn things.

"Hey, it's the boss lady." The young woman beaming down at her was impossible not to like at first glance. The wide friendly smile on a round face framed with springy black curls haphazardly tied back seemed permanently on display. "I was beginning to think you didn't really exist. You want the lunch special?"

"Please. You're Alethea, right?"

"Sure am." Her voice echoed kindness and confidence as she turned to work on the order. "Xander said to let you know he'd be back this weekend. He'll touch base with you as soon as he catches up at home."

Jo reminded herself of the connection. Xander, the project architect, was Alethea's older brother. The cook popped back into view, quickly got Jed's and the last two orders going, and returned to the window.

"Love the new setup," Alethea said. "Makes me feel like it's my own special parking place."

"Well, in a way it is. It's great of you to come up here every day."

"I do the breakfast thing down by the beach. I catch a lot of people who don't have time to hang out at the diner." She pointed to the group of people heading up the hill. "Knowing I'm here most days brings people by to check up on the project, too."

Jo noticed, and she couldn't help but worry about their safety. Construction zones weren't the best place for people to hang out, but if it kept interest focused on the sanctuary, it couldn't be a bad thing, right?

"Why don't you grab a table and I'll bring your lunch out to you," Alethea offered.

Normally she wouldn't have accepted the special treatment, but standing in the surprisingly warm sun for as long as she had left her anxious to sit. "Do you have a…water." She chuckled as Alethea shot out a hand holding a frosty dripping bottle. "Thanks."

"Give me a few and I'll be right out. Hi!" She greeted the approaching group of visitors. "Menu's right down there and we've got the special…"

Jo wandered over to one of the few empty tables, an old metal set with an umbrella that had been spray-painted a neon blue. Once she sat down, she noticed Alethea had added her own touches of a plastic utensil caddy that also held paper straws, napkins, salt, pepper and other condiments. Jo cracked open the bottle of water just as Jed joined her.

"So what is it we can get a jump on?" she asked him as he got settled. She had to admit, his steaming pita piled high with thinly shaved meat, red onions, tomato and drizzled with a white sauce had her hoping Alethea would deliver her lunch quickly.

"Always on the clock," Jed teased. "I was taking another look at the plans for the nature trail."

"The one that'll track around the main structure and go by the cliffs?"

Jed bit into his lunch, nodded. "I'm not convinced that survey's right. I believe we should take the line back another ten feet from the edge. Just to be safe."

Recalling the plans, Jo considered the request. "How many more trees would have to come down?" If she remembered correctly, the removal of healthy trees had been a major point of contention among the residents and had earned its own council meeting so everyone could have their say. The last thing she wanted was to rile tempers in the town.

"I talked it over with one of our guys, Kenny, who works part time for a tree service. He thinks we could get those ten feet by removing only four of the largest trees. We'd have to be surgical about it, and it would take some deft maneuvering in the area, but in the long run, it's a good solution."

If it meant making the nature path safer, Jed was right. It would be worth it. "Show me the area after we eat, walk me through the options and we'll go from there. I want Kenny there, too."

"Can do." Jed nodded. "I'm also going to pull the last of the fencing out of storage and haul it up here so we can fence off the cement work when we're done."

"You are reading my mind," Jo said. "Does Flutterby Wheels really draw this big a crowd every day?"

"Today's kind of slow to be honest," Jed said. "Alethea will move on to other locations if business slows too much. Oh, hey, Alethea. We were just talking about you." He toasted her with his sandwich. "Excellent as always."

"Sorry yours took so long." She set Jo's gyro in front of her. "Just got a call from Jason. As soon as my last few orders are done, I'm heading to the inn. Need to cover at the restaurant for a few hours."

"Everything okay?" Jed asked.

"Oh, yeah. Abby's taking David in for his first round of baby photos and Jason wants to go. I keep telling Jason it might be time to hire more help, both in the restaurant and in the truck. Or maybe add another truck." Alethea narrowed her eyes as if considering. "Maybe I need to work up a business plan. Guess I shouldn't have dropped out of college so early."

"There are good online tutorials you could take," Jo suggested.

"But the good ones cost money." Alethea grimaced. "I'm saving up everything I can for my own place. Living with my brother and his wife has been good, but I'd like my independence again."

Jo took a healthy bite of her lunch, and after her brain processed the incredible tastes exploding in her mouth, she held up a finger. "I could walk you through the basics for a business plan. Would only take a couple of hours."

"Seriously?" Alethea's blue eyes brightened. "Oh, wow, that would be awesome. I thought about asking Calliope, but she's got so much going on. Gotta check my schedule. I'll let you know as soon as I can. Thanks!"

"Sure." Jo was smiling as she checked her buzzing cell phone. "Excuse me. I've been waiting for this call. Hi, Dr. Miakoda. Thanks for getting back to me."

"Sorry it took me so long, Jo," replied Dr. Cheyenne Miakoda, the OB who Leah and Ozzy had recommended. "I had a last-minute cancellation and thought I'd get you squeezed into the schedule."

"Oh, um. Okay." She mentally went through her calendar. "I figured you'd want to wait for my medical records to arrive."

"They got here this morning and I've already read through them." Her tone didn't give anything away, but Jo did feel a bit apprehensive and even nervous. "How's three sound?"

"Today?" She looked at Jed, who was chatting with Alethea. She still had a lot of work to do, and while everything had been running smoothly… "I'm not sure I can get away on such short notice."

"Sure you can." Dr. Miakoda's voice was gentle and firm. "You've already missed two prenatal appointments, Jo. Given your medical history, it's best if we get you caught up as soon as possible."

Jo winced. "All right." She rubbed her forehead wearily. "I'll be there at three."

"Excellent. And come with a full bladder. We're going to need to run some tests."

"No problem on that front," Jo joked. "It's always full." She disconnected and attempted to swallow the worry.

"Everything okay?" Jed asked.

"Fine. I'll need to take a few hours this afternoon. Baby appointment." She'd become well enough acquainted with the town in the last few days to know where she was going.

"No problem," Jed assured her. "You finish lunch and we'll do that walk through to assess the trail. Everything's been going great, and if something does happen, you'll be the first to hear about it."

CHAPTER EIGHT

"Sparky, you are not a dog. Get off the darned truck already." Ozzy held the fire hose in his hands and watched the soap cascade off the side of the bright red paneling. The jet-black cat with big yellow eyes merely blinked at him and leaned down to bat away droplets of water. "How did nature come up with that menace?" he asked his boss. Co-chief Roman Salazar had just rounded the corner. "Cats are supposed to hate water. Can we retrain him?"

Roman, who stood a good three inches taller than Ozzy and could have given a pantheon of gods a run for their money, grinned up at the furball and shrugged. "That cat and my wife were made for each other. He's started dive-bombing us in the shower now." His smile faded. "Come to think of it, maybe you're right. *Menace* is definitely the right word. Frankie was asking how'd the call go at Well Springs."

"Straightforward. Panic attack," Ozzy said. "I let Jasper take the lead. He's going to do fine on his EMT exams."

"Great." Roman gave an approving nod. "Thanks for taking an extra twelve today. Callahan'll be on next shift. Volunteer sheet is full, so your schedule won't change after all. I've got to run my mom into town for big box shopping, but Frankie'll be here, Jasper, too. You've got the next two days off."

"Great." It was definitely good news considering his plans for Friday afternoon. Luck was clearly on his side. Now all he had to do was stop feeling guilty for not using this extra time to respond to the many thumbs-up he'd been getting on his dating app.

After his disastrous movie night with Shelly, who had apparently bragged to everyone within hearing distance about how well their date had supposedly gone, he'd been putting off any more social interactions.

His reluctance to respond had absolutely nothing to do with his increasing fondness for a construction supervisor with a penchant for his mother's baking, he told himself. Or the surprise he had planned for her.

"We still doing the water-rescue training next week?"

"Five a.m. Tuesday morning. Rain or shine," Roman added, knowing Ozzy's penchant for praying for a rain delay. "Four-mile swim followed by a two-mile run. Timed. Be ready for it because you know Frankie's going to make you suffer if you fail." His boss chuckled.

Oh, he knew. Roman might be a walking example of testosterone and pinup-calendar-inspiring goodlooks, but his wife—Ozzy's other boss—wielded her own special talent when it came to motivating her team. Expectations weren't merely high, they were hovering in the stratosphere. There were times Ozzy appreciated the challenge. But there were other times when…

"Hey, you hear about Luke and Holly's barbecue?" Roman asked. "Are you planning on going?"

"As long as there are no emergencies," Ozzy said. "Have to. I've got a water fight title to defend." Simon Saxon and Charlie Bradley had already emailed him to make sure he was coming and had informed him that Simon had applied his special brand of knowledge to their neon plastic weaponry. The idea of Simon souping up water guns was only one of the worries keeping Ozzy up at night.

Getting Charlie's bike finished and presentable was another. His free weekend should help with that.

"And don't forget, you've got the extra day off next week."

"I'd meant to talk to you about that. I probably won't need the extra day—"

"Doesn't have to do with need or want, Oz. Those days give us the flexibility to keep everyone on a fair rotation of shifts. One of us goes off and it screws everything else up." Roman leaned his shoulder against the truck, crossed his arms. The second he made contact with the vehicle, Sparky the cat slid his front paws down until he could drop securely onto Roman's shoulder. "What's going on? Why are you fighting days off?"

"I just like to work," Ozzy said. "I know you and Frankie took a big chance taking me on here."

"Only chance we took was ticking Sheriff Saxon off," Roman half-joked. When Ozzy didn't laugh, he cleared his throat. "You've proven yourself, Oz. More than you needed to. We know we can rely on you."

Ozzy hoped that was true. He wasn't entirely sure where this crisis of confidence was coming from, but he needed to get over it and fast. He had a lot of people relying on him—from his co-workers straight to Jo, whether she acknowledged it or not.

"It's not like we're giving you special days off, Oz," Roman continued.

"Meaning?"

"Meaning we aren't purposely scheduling you more free time than you're due. Take advantage of the extra day. Heaven knows I plan to." He smacked Ozzy on the arm, then plucked Sparky off his shoulder and carried him to the SUV. "There must be something you want to do," he called out the window as he started up the car. "Something fun and unexpected. Just do it."

"Right." Ozzy nodded and returned to hosing off the engine, meanwhile, Roman drove off. Funny that the only thing he really wanted to do was head up to the construction site and check in on Jo. He wasn't looking for an argument, though. He needed another reason to visit her, something he could actually get by her without raising her suspicions. But nothing leapt to mind except…

The station alarm blared, quickly followed by the booming voice over the speaker system. First thing Ozzy did was check his watch, just as he'd been trained to do. Three fifteen. Frankie and Jasper popped out of nowhere and sprinted for their lockers and gear.

His stomach clutched as he heard the location blare over the intercom. It was the construction site.

"Not again." He cast a cautious eye to Frankie, who had been one of the first on the scene when the structure collapsed back in March. "Details?" he called as he yanked his gear free and threw it on. The engine was moving while he was pulling the passenger door shut.

"Nothing yet." Frankie dragged the steering wheel to the right and hit the sirens as she gunned the vehicle down the hill. "Check in with dispatch, see if they can put you through to someone on-site. Jasper?"

"Chief?"

"You stick close to me, you hear? You watch, you listen, you learn and you don't get creative." She glanced up at him in the rearview mirror. "I mean it this time."

"Understood, Chief."

Ozzy couldn't blame Frankie. Two weeks ago, Jasper had attempted to rescue a young woman who had been trapped in her car after an accident with a big rig that was leaking fuel. While Roman and Ozzy had assessed the situation with the EMTs, Jasper had taken it upon himself to get her out on his own. In the end, it had turned out all right, but it did erode a lot of the trust the probie had built up with the team. They needed to move, to think, to function as one, despite the overwhelming desire to help. Those extra moments could have made the rescue less harrowing and less stressful on everyone. Jasper had learned his lesson, which had come with a three-day suspension and a full eight hours of retraining on group dynamics.

As they roared through town and sped past the shoreline, Ozzy tapped on the keys of the onboard computer and attempted to access more information on the scene. Twice he nearly pulled out his cell to call Jo, just to make certain she was all right, but she'd have been the first to remind him that she wasn't his personal concern.

His heart was still hammering as they reached the site. He dropped out of the truck and beelined for Jed standing at the entrance to the hollowed-out section of trees leading to the cliff edge.

"Talk to me, Jed," Frankie ordered.

"Kenny Vogelman." Jed led them through the trees and to the edge of the cliffs. "He was guiding one of the excavators through the treeline in order for us to do some removing. Darn machine's brakes went out and the driver couldn't stop. Kenny dived and rolled out of the way but went right over the edge. Then he just dropped." Jed's face was ash gray, but he was maintaining control. "Lucky a ledge caught him. We tried to get a rope down to him, but he's kind of out of it."

"Driver okay?"

Jed nodded. "Seriously shaken, though. He managed to steer away from the edge and into the trees before he cut the engine."

"He didn't panic," Ozzy muttered to Frankie, who agreed.

"Give me a few to assess the situation." Frankie patted his arm, then gave orders for the rest of the construction crew to step back. She turned to Ozzy. "Have Jasper call for an EMT backup with transport to the hospital. We'll probably need the stretcher and a neck brace to be safe if there's a delay with the ambulance. Jed, I want you and your crew to remain back, all right? We've got this."

"He just dropped." Jed shook his head. "One second he was there and the next—"

"I can hear him!" One of the other men shouted as he pushed off his knees. "He's mad, but he's okay."

"All right. My turn." Frankie moved in and sank to her knees, crawled forward until she was peering over the ledge. Her long red hair was tied into a tight ponytail and glinted against the afternoon sun. She shouted down, and Ozzy heard a response despite the ocean wind.

"Where's Jo?" Ozzy asked Jed.

"Doctor's appointment." Jed shook his head. "I told her nothing was going to happen. This was all my idea. I know this wasn't on the schedule today, but I thought we could get a jump—"

"This wasn't your fault, Jed." Ozzy squeezed

his shoulder. "If she'd been here, she couldn't have stopped it any more than you could have."

"All right, he landed about fifteen feet down on this weird outcropping." Frankie brushed off her hands as she approached them. "The ground feels stable enough for us to get a line down to him, but he whacked his head pretty good and might not be able to secure it safely. He'll need help." She looked to Ozzy. "You up for it?"

"Yes." Ozzy nodded, adrenaline surging.

"Great. Let's go back to the truck and get you ready. Jed, I want you to keep Kenny talking, all right? But remember to stay at least two feet from the ledge. Looks like that heavy machine of yours might have begun to loosen the stability of the soil."

"That sucker was out of control," Jed muttered. "I'm going to have my mechanics take a look at it."

"Good idea," Frankie said with a nod. "Come on, Ozzy. Time for you to go for a ride."

"ALL RIGHT, JO." Dr. Miakoda's soothing voice drifted over her. "Here we go."

Jo took a deep breath and closed her eyes,

willed her racing pulse to slow as the doctor squirted the cold gel on Jo's rounded stomach. She had the oddest desire to squeeze someone's hand or at least look to find a face of comfort beyond the friendly, understanding one that belonged to the ob-gyn she'd liked immediately. Only one face came to mind, though, but the image of Ozzy Lakeman standing at her side only made her blood pressure rise. What on earth was the matter with her? And where had all these nerves come from? It didn't make sense.

The fact that Dr. Miakoda, Cheyenne, had insisted on an extensive conversation before she'd examined Jo should have put Jo at ease, but she hadn't been able to push the thought of work aside. She didn't like being away from the site, being away from her charges, her crew. Not that she didn't trust them, because so far they'd given her no reason to be cautious, but that job was her responsibility now. She'd hammered that home to everyone involved. Being away and out of the loop, even for a few hours, did not set well with her at all.

Her previous doctor had been satisfactory, but he hadn't exactly had much of a great bedside manner. In-and-out appointments. Test results, advice, vitamin prescriptions and move on. It hadn't struck Jo as being cold since it more than suited her "get back to work as soon as possible" mentality.

That fast-moving efficiency was not, in any way, a part of Cheyenne's small-town practice, located a block up from the light hustle and bustle of Monarch Lane. The office was even located in a small single-story cottage decorated in pretty pastels. The landscaped garden and collection of hanging baskets filled with various kinds of flowers along the front porch offered pops of color. One had to look pretty closely at the wooden sign attached to the porch post to identify this as a doctor's office. Whatever the outside lacked in identification, walking into the waiting room lined with dozens of happy new-baby, new-family photos certainly got the point across. Would the kidlet's picture join them?

Jo shivered. *Kidlet*. When had she started using Ozzy's nickname for her baby?

"I keep telling myself I need to invent some kind of instant gel warmer," Cheyenne said easily as she retrieved the ultrasound monitor. "Nancy, would you close the curtains a bit? We're getting a glare on the screen." She spoke to one of the two nurses who worked in the office. "Okay, Jo. I need you to relax." Cheyenne rested a hand on Jo's shoulder. "Just breathe. Nothing's going to hurt, I promise."

Jo released the breath she hadn't realized she'd been holding. "Sorry. Nervous, I guess."

"Not every day you get to meet your baby-to-be." Cheyenne's reassuring smile helped relieve the tension. Jo was grateful. "I know we discussed this, but if you've changed your mind about knowing the baby's gender—"

"I haven't." Jo was adamant. It wasn't practical, she knew. But there were so few real surprises in life. She wanted to experience at least one of them.

"Then we'll just make sure everything is as it should be," Cheyenne said.

"Works for me."

Try as she might, Jo couldn't clear her head. She had at least three calls she needed to return once she got back to the trailer. One in particular she anticipated being a problem. She'd already gotten pushback from the supplier of the sustainable wood flooring they'd be using for the main building. Jed had suspended the original order due to the project being delayed as a result of the accident. The supplier had since then tacked on a surcharge to the delivery fee, and while it wasn't a break-the-bank amount, it was large enough for Jo to assume he was trying to make a buck off their misfortune. If there was one thing Jo couldn't stand, it was an opportunist.

"Jo."

"Hmm?" She rested an arm behind her head. "Yeah, I'm here."

"Just making sure." Cheyenne shifted the scanner across her stomach. "Because it's showtime."

Jo stared at the screen, tried to make out the weird grayish squiggles and lines on the monitor. "I don't... I can't..." She frowned, narrowed her eyes and did her best. "Where—"

"Don't look," Cheyenne said softly. "Listen."

It took Jo a moment to focus. As she did, a gentle *womp womp womp* echoed from the machine. Jo gasped, catching the blipping on the monitor pulsing in time with the sound. "Is that the heartbeat?"

"It sure is. Healthy and strong." Cheyenne motioned Nancy over, murmured something to her. "Here's the umbilical cord. Everything looks okay there. No twists and turns. We've got the hands and feet. And a baby who's a bit shy." Cheyenne chuckled. "Good thing you want to be surprised because they aren't showing off."

Jo laughed or thought she did. The sound came out more like a half sob as her vision blurred. "It's really in there, isn't it?" Seemed strange to call her baby *it*.

"You had doubts?"

"Well, I had some idea considering he or she likes to play kickball with my bladder." She wiped her eyes. "They're really okay?"

"Everything looks normal, Jo." After a few more minutes, the scan ended and Cheyenne wiped a cloth across her stomach. "How about you head back into my office and I'll join you in a minute."

Jo nodded and pushed herself up, tugged her shirt over her still-cold belly. In the not so far distance, a siren blared. It was there and gone, fading into oblivion as she adjusted her top.

Her legs were a bit wobbly as she left the exam room. In the hallway, she stopped, braced a hand against the wall as her head went light. This was real. This was really happening.

She was going to be a mom. And in only a few months!

All this time, all these weeks, she'd understood the idea of being pregnant, but to see those tiny hands, to hear her baby's heart beating…

Emotions flashed through her, as if she were on a speeding train and couldn't see them long enough to grab hold. Excitement, fear, anxiety. Joy. There was so much to think about, so much to consider and dream of. *And so much, so much*, she thought, *to regret*.

Not on her part, but on Greg's.

She'd misjudged the type of man she thought him to be. Whatever anger she might have felt was quickly couched by pity. To think the father of this child hadn't taken more than a few seconds to comprehend its existence before he'd dismissed it and, along with it, her. She'd convinced herself she hadn't been surprised, that being disappointed in someone she'd had faith in was a given part of life, but Greg hadn't just walked away from Jo and their future together.

He'd walked away from their child. As difficult as betrayal was to accept for herself, she would never be able to comprehend it on behalf of her baby girl or boy. A child who had done nothing to deserve anything other than the absolute best Jo could give it. That best was clearly not Greg.

"Jo?" Cheyenne stood beside her, rested a hand on her shoulder. "Are you all right?"

"Just having one of those 'reality knocked me sideways' moments." She let Cheyenne guide her into the office. "I'll be fine once I process." She sat in the chair she'd occupied earlier and dragged her purse into her lap, automatically reaching for her cell, which she'd turned off.

"Before you leave, there are things I'd like to address."

"Oh?" Phone in hand, Jo glanced up. The stoic expression on the doctor's face had her putting her purse back on the floor. "Is something wrong?"

"*Wrong* is perhaps a strong word for it. I'm going to wait for your lab work to come back before I speculate, but to be safe, I want to get out ahead of a few points. That swelling in your feet to start with."

She scrunched her toes in her too-tight shoes. "I thought swelling is normal."

"It is. To a point. Your blood pressure is also a bit elevated, and you said you've been getting headaches. Taking into account your previous diagnosis—"

"The PCOS?"

"Polycystic ovarian syndrome can affect women in different ways. Some exhibit only a sample of the symptoms, but most do have a higher risk of miscarriage. We want to mitigate that possibility as thoroughly as we can. There's also your age. Thirty-five doesn't put you at high risk but you're still up there." She pulled a small stack of paper from her printer. "I'm more concerned about your blood pressure than anything. I've got a list of foods for you. What to eat, what to avoid. I'd like you to get at least an hour of walking in every day. Not exercise, not work, just walking, maybe on the beach, for a good chunk of time. From what you've told me, your job has a high level of stress."

"I oversee thirty construction workers under a time crunch and a budget with severe limitations." Jo tried to smile. "What do you think?"

"I think you're a woman capable of doing whatever she puts her mind to. I am also certain we can find a way to bring your baby to term with you still being able to do your job. And that's what we want. To get you to full-term."

Jo sat back in her chair. If she was looking at an either-or proposition, there was no doubt which she'd choose, but if she didn't have to... "You don't sound entirely convinced. Will I have to stop working? To make sure the baby is safe?"

Cheyenne folded her hands on top of her desk. "Let's get the lab results back in a couple of days and see what they say, all right? There's no point in worrying before there's something to worry about. In the meantime—" She stood up when a knock sounded on the door.

"Here you go." Nancy handed over a small manila envelope.

"Thanks, Nancy." Cheyenne passed the envelope to Jo. "And there you are. Your first bragging photo." She walked around and sat on the edge of her desk. "I've got a yoga class Monday and Saturday mornings at the youth center followed by a meditation session. There's a number of moms-to-be who attend, and I recommend you join us. Ten a.m."

"I'll take a look at my—" She stopped at Cheyenne's look. "Right. Ten a.m. Youth center. I can make Monday work, but Saturday'll be a toss-up." *Yoga?* "I hope there's an easy learning curve."

"You'll fit right in," Cheyenne assured her. "I've adjusted your prenatal vitamin regimen. The drugstore in town should have everything on this list. I also want you drinking more water and keeping your feet up when you can. It's not a sign of weakness," Cheyenne added when Jo opened her mouth. "And for the record, a lot of the men on your crew are fathers. If any of them give you a bad time, you let me know. Their wives are my patients. If they need a refresher course on the important things in life, I can make that happen."

"I appreciate that." Jo forced a laugh. "But I don't play that way. I'll just remind them that they can't birth a human being, let alone grow one." It would be a learning experience for all of them. "I'll make it work. Thank you." She stood up. "For everything."

"Great. I'll call you with the lab results,

and if all is well, I'll see you in about three weeks. Now go find someone to share those pictures with. That's half of the fun."

Jo walked back to her truck, in a bit of a daze, but also on a bit of a cloud.

Her baby was healthy and so was she. She had a lot of reading and planning to do, and if the glance she'd taken at that recommended food list was any indication, she'd finally be visiting Duskywing Farm. While she'd kept her future schedule fluid, including her eventual move to Montana, this visit solidified her decision to stick around here, at least until after the baby was born. Cheyenne brought her some peace of mind and these days she needed that most of all. Just as she'd already stated, she would make this work, not just for herself, but for her child.

She slipped the truck into Drive, was about to pull out and paused. She sat back and pressed a hand against the odd pressure in the center of her chest. It took a few minutes to sort through the emotions, but joy and pride rose up.

Jo did want to share her good news.

And she knew just who to share it with.

She put her hands back on the wheel just

as another siren blasted behind her. She took her foot off the gas and twisted in her seat as an ambulance shot down Monarch Lane and up the hill.

Dread pooled in her stomach. In the few days she'd been here, she'd only heard sirens from a distance, and not very often at that. Not to mention there was little up that hill save for Duskywing Farm and…

Jo swore, hit the gas and made a tight U-turn. A few seconds later she was on the ambulance's tail, heading straight for the construction site.

CHAPTER NINE

THE CALM, SMOOTH-RUNNING construction site she'd managed the past few days was now overrun by emergency vehicles and tense, worried workers. Jo pulled her truck into a spot at the edge of the site, left her bag behind and dropped out of the vehicle to hurry to the crowd that had gathered near the outline of trees leading to the cliffs.

She spotted Jed standing a good head above most of the rest of her crew, giving orders to Kyle, who went off to the trailer, and then to a group of others who began roping off the just-poured cement foundation.

"Jed?" Jo glanced to the fire truck as she approached her foreman, who was already on his way to her. "What's going on? Is someone hurt?" What had she missed? What precaution hadn't she taken? "Fill me in."

"Freak accident," Jed told her and stuck two fingers in his mouth. His shrill whistle had Jo wincing, but a second later, Jed caught a hard hat and immediately passed it to her. "Brakes went out on the excavator. Kenny tried to get out of its path and didn't quite make it. He's okay." He rushed on at Jo's gasp. "But he's caught on a ledge about fifteen or twenty feet down. Frankie's assessed the situation and we have Bill and Pax keeping him talking. They're going to go down and get him."

"Who's going to go down where?" Even as she asked, she shifted her attention to the fire truck, where Ozzy was being strapped into a harness by a tall redhead. There was a rolled-up rope and a stack of carabiners on the ground, along with a hip pack that was soon locked around Ozzy's waist. "Kenny went over the cliff? Jed—"

"I know." His face went hard as granite. "Believe me, I'm right there with you. One of those freak accidents we couldn't have seen coming."

One freak accident she might have understood, but this made two.

"We'll figure out what went wrong once Kenny's back on safe ground. Give me a second." She walked toward the truck. "Ozzy?"

She didn't like the uneasy sensation circling through her as he harnessed up and double-checked the knots on the ropes.

"Hey, Jo." He barely gave her a glance. "Jed fill you in?"

"As much as he could." In other circumstances she'd consider this sight inspiring, if not a bit thrilling. "Jo Bertoletti." She looked to the redhead.

"Frankie Bet...darn it. Salazar." She winced. "Why can't I get used to that?" She gave Jo an absent smile. "I'm going to make use of a few of your team if that's okay with you? I'll need them watching the line."

"Whatever you need," Jo assured her. "How is Kenny?"

Frankie glanced at Ozzy.

"The truth, please," Jo insisted.

"He's conscious," Frankie said. "That's all I can say for certain right now."

"Twenty feet max. Quick up and down." Ozzy hitched a last hook onto his belt. "Nothing to it."

He was about to go dangling off the side of a cliff and there was nothing to it? Jo swallowed the sourness in her throat. "You know what you're doing. But be careful," she added, trying to sound confident.

He hefted the rope Frankie handed to him and slung it over one shoulder. When she moved to follow him, Ozzy stopped. "Where do you think you're going?"

"That's my guy down there. He's my responsibility."

"Not at the moment he's not," Ozzy said, holding up a hand when Frankie opened her mouth. "You stay here."

"Excuse me?" She blinked. She had not just heard him *order* her to stay put.

"We don't know what kind of damage the vehicle's done to the cliff edge. You shouldn't be out there. It's not safe."

"You've had two of my guys talking over the ledge at him since before I got here. If it's safe for them—"

"They're well away from the ledge. It's not safe for you." He moved in front of her and pointed at her stomach. "There's nothing you can do except be a distraction. We need to focus on getting Kenny safe, not keeping an eye on you."

Jo balked, heat rising in her cheeks. "Since when do you—"

"Okay, whatever this is? Stop." Frankie stepped between them, a somewhat befuddled look on her face as she glanced over her shoulder at Ozzy. "Argue about this later when it's over, please. Besides—" she pointed toward the sound of a car plowing up the road "—you're about to have your hands full."

"What?" Jo spun around as Gil Hamilton screeched to a dust-raising stop. "Oh, for…" She bit her tongue to stop from saying what she was thinking.

"I'm beginning to think this place is cursed," Gil said as he climbed out. "What's happened now?"

She filled Gil in on the accident. Even as she ran through the details, she couldn't help but wonder if she'd made a mistake somewhere. "I used your recommendation for the heavy machinery."

"And?" Gil frowned. "The city's used the firm for years. They're a top-five supplier in the construction business throughout the state."

"Yet something went wrong."

"And until we know what that was, maybe we shouldn't jump to conclusions."

Jo pinched her lips together. He was probably right, but that left her frustration with no place to go.

"If a mistake's been made—" Gil went on.

"Then it's on me," Jo assured him. "The good and the bad, remember? Let's get through this and see where we are."

Needing to do something positive, she hustled back to the trailer. She saw Kyle visibly react, sitting behind his added desk, when she came through the door. Jo was rifling through contracts and insurance documents as Gil entered the office. She nearly ripped the report on heavy machinery in two when she found it.

"I went online for the company's safety record," Kyle said and handed her a printout. "There's nothing there, Jo. No red flags or signals of any issues. They're gold standard."

"Brake lines don't just go out," she muttered. "I suppose we should be grateful this happened now and not when the initial removal was being done." Given the trees that had been removed previously, if this same thing had happened, the entire vehicle could have gone over, along with the driver. She shuddered to think how bad this really could have been.

Although, until Kenny was back on solid ground and not dangling above a cliff's rocky base, there was no telling how bad it really was. But Kenny wasn't the only one out there. Ozzy was, too. She hoped things didn't get any worse.

Someone knocked on the office door. "Boss?" Kayleigh Prince, one of the welders, poked her head in. Her blue-gray eyes shone with concern. "Jed wants you to see something."

"Okay." Jo gestured for Gil to follow. "You might as well stick close. Lead on, Kayleigh."

She ended up precisely where Ozzy had told her not to go, where the excavator had backed into one of the massive redwoods. The tree had a giant gash in it. Just on the other side, she saw the thick rope, secured around the thickest tree. The line, curving and straining over the cliff's ledge, was being eased down slowly by four of her workers, with Frankie giving verbal commands.

Sirens blared in the distance as the ambulance made its approach. The remaining crew thinned and shifted, making room for a young man in black BHFD cargo pants and T-shirt.

The impact had tilted the excavator and exposed its underbelly. She found Jed and another of their crew wedged underneath, examining the inner workings. "Jed?" Jo crouched as much as she could and tried to see what the foreman was checking. "What did you find?"

"Not sure," Jed said as he shifted onto his back and shined a flashlight up and into the workings. "This here?" He pointed to the puddle of liquid darkening the soil "That's brake fluid. And it trails for quite a while."

"Couldn't rocks or debris have done that?" Gil asked.

Jo turned her head and frowned. The mayor had a point. "Jed?"

"Normally I'd consider that." Jed nodded. "But the cut in the line's smooth. Wear and tear would make it jagged if it wasn't well maintained, and this vehicle's pristine otherwise. I'm no expert." Jed shoved himself up and looked at the two of them. "But if I had to say?"

"Spit it out, Jed," Jo ordered.

"I don't think this was an accident," Jed told them. "This brake line was cut on purpose."

"Ozzy? You got him?"

Frankie's shout faded on the wind as Ozzy's booted feet hit the ledge. *More than a ledge*, he thought, with a flash of relief as he was able to pivot and adjust his stance beside Kenny Vogelman. But only barely. He tugged on his line to get some slack. "Hey, Kenny. Long time no see." Personally, Ozzy could have gone the rest of his life without seeing his former high school classmate. "What are you doing hanging out here?"

"Oh, you know." Kenny let out a weak laugh, swiped a hand across the side of his head that was caked with blood. "Thanks for the assist." He shifted, and as he drew in a breath, his face lost most of its color.

"It was a boring day, anyway." Keep them entertained and the mood light. It was something Ozzy had learned early on in his training. He couldn't let his own emotions show through; his concern would only make things worse for the people he was trying to help. "You lucked out big-time with this ledge, man." He shifted, ignored the gravel that broke away and dropped the hundred or so feet beneath them. "You having trouble breathing?"

"Mmm." Kenny nodded, his jet-black hair falling over one eye. "I've got this pressure building in my chest." He tilted his head up. "What's that mean?"

"It means you have pressure building in your chest." Ozzy wasn't about to speculate, but he had a pretty good idea one of Kenny's lungs was probably punctured. "Let's get you up and worry about the rest later, all right? No, don't move." He didn't want Kenny doing anything to make things worse. "I need you to stay as you are. Just give me a second." He unlatched his radio and clicked for Frankie.

"Yeah, Oz. Talk to me."

Ozzy would have turned away to keep this from Kenny, but there was nowhere for him to go. "I need you to send the stretcher down. We need as smooth a ride up for him as possible, understand?"

The hesitation was slight, but Frankie's "understood" had him breathing a bit easier.

"Okay, Kenny. We've got your ride coming. I'm going to need a little help from you when it gets here. You up for that?"

Kenny nodded. "So stupid."

"What?"

"Not you." Kenny winced. "Karma, man.

She came calling for me today. Payback for treating you like crap in high school. Good thing for me you're half your size now."

"High school was a long time ago." Ozzy never thought he'd feel sorry for one of his high school tormentors, but life had a way of doling out what you needed to see. "The past is the past."

"If I were you, I'd be trying to figure out a way to chuck me over the ledge."

"There's still time for that." The joke was slight and earned a quick smile. "But if you really want to have this discussion here and now, can I finally say I didn't appreciate you trying to stuff me in my gym locker."

"Sprained my wrist in the attempt." Kenny cringed. "Both times." Fear shining bright in his eyes, he met Ozzy's far-from-amused gaze. "I'm sorry, man."

"Apology accepted." It would have been easy to hold onto a grudge or the resentment he felt for the individuals who had made his teen years far from pleasant, but he knew he hadn't had it nearly as rough as a lot of other people. "How about when this is all over you buy me a beer and we can forget you beat me up for not doing your algebra homework?"

Kenny snort-laughed, then groaned. "No fair making me laugh."

"Right." Ozzy nodded. He saw the bright orange stretcher being lowered, and he stepped back to grab the end. "Okay, Kenny. This is going to go against your nature, but from here on, you're going to do everything I say, no argument. Do you hear me?"

Apparently out of breath and words, Kenny only nodded.

"I'm going to get this as solid as I can against the cliff wall. After I do, you're going to have to stand up so I can lash you in." Ozzy gave another look at the ledge, which suddenly seemed more narrow than it had moments before. "You lean on me, Kenny, as hard and as tight as you need to, and you let me do the maneuvering."

Another nod.

"Ozzy? Update, please." Frankie's voice crackled over the radio.

"I'm working on it." Ozzy clicked off, then considered the circumstances. "Give me three minutes, then start pulling him back up."

"As soon as we've got him, we'll pull you up."

"Understood." He hesitated, the thought of

Jo and how he'd left things with her sitting heavily in his gut. But now wasn't the time. "Standby."

"Copy that."

Ozzy clipped the radio back onto his belt and shoved the stretcher hard into the cliff wall. He rearranged it a few times, made sure it was steady, then braced his hand on the wall as he leaned over Kenny. "You ready?"

"Yeah." Ozzy could hear the wheezing in his lungs.

"You're going to reach up and lock your hands around my neck." Ozzy kicked his boots hard into the rock, partly to test its stability, partly to lock himself in place. "I'll do the lifting, Kenny. I'll get you where you need to go. Just push up with your legs for a few seconds. It's going to hurt like anything, so be prepared."

"Just tell me when." Kenny pushed the words out through gritted teeth.

Ozzy leaned down to give Kenny the space and time he needed to raise his arms. The moment he felt Kenny's hands lock at the back of his neck, Ozzy slid his arms under and hauled him up to his feet.

He felt it the second Kenny passed out.

Instant deadweight. His arms dropped and his head fell to the side. Ozzy was ready for it. His legs and thighs burned as he kept his feet in place. He pivoted slightly and pushed Kenny into the stretcher, moving one of his own feet back so he could shift the base of the stretcher out slightly. Kenny's body slid into place. With brutal efficiency, Ozzy connected the harness and strapped him in, waist, then chest, then thighs.

"Frankie?"

"Here."

"Bring him up. He's out cold. Possible punctured lung. Have a neck brace standing by."

"Got it ready and waiting. EMTs are here, as well."

Ozzy double-checked the straps, then reached up and gave a hard tug on the line. Slowly but as smoothly as he'd advised, the stretcher made its way up and over the ledge. When it was clear, Ozzy ducked his head and let out a breath. His arms and legs throbbed as the adrenaline leeched out of his system.

He turned, kicked a few rocks aside, and as he moved to lean back against the cliff face, he heard—no, he felt—the ledge crack beneath his feet. While he had no doubt the rope was secure, he was about to become dead weight for those ready to haul him up.

He grabbed for his radio. "Frankie! Drop another rope." He wanted something to brace himself against the rock face with. "The ledge is—"

"Oz? You—"

"Now, Frankie!" The ledge crackled and crumbled. "Drop one now!"

He looked up as a second rope came flying out and down. Ozzy reached for it, twisted one gloved hand tight and high as the pressure holding the ledge released. He hoisted himself up as the rest of the ledge dropped away.

Ozzy was jolted upward, the ragged cliff stone cutting through his shirt. He could hear Frankie shouting even as he felt himself being dragged, far faster than the stretcher had gone. He tightened his grip, shifted and pivoted, though he knew it would make it more difficult for the people pulling him up. At last he was able to get his boots into the stone and walk up the final stretch.

Hands locked around his wrists as he was hauled forward and collapsed on his stomach, face in the dirt. He panted, coughed, and spit out soil and gravel. "Okay." He shoved himself onto his back and stared up at the faces crouched around him. He gave them a thumbs-up. "It's okay. All good."

"You sure?" Frankie pressed a hand against his chest. "I can have the EMTs—"

Pride had him rising up. The roar of applause and cheers barely registered. He bent over, planted his hands on his thighs and drew in long, steady, painful breaths. "I'm fine," he said again as Frankie bent over to meet his gaze. "Thanks, boss."

She caught his face in her hands. "You did good, Oz. You did really, really good."

He offered her a smile, and then his gaze caught Jo's as she stood by the construction vehicle, her brown eyes wide with shock and relief. His impulse was to go to her, but he had work to do first. "How's Kenny?" he asked Frankie.

"En route to the hospital. Battered and bruised. The EMT agreed with you about the punctured lung. They've got him on oxygen."

"Pure dumb luck he hit that ledge," he told Frankie. Even more luck Ozzy himself hadn't dropped like a stone.

"We all know there's a bit of luck and magic around these cliffs." She slapped a hand on his back. At his wince, she shifted into chief mode. "Okay, Oz, I want you to get checked out at the hospital."

Ozzy shook his head. "It's just a few scrapes. Nothing—"

"That wasn't a suggestion, Oz. I'll meet you back at the truck." She walked away, then said over her shoulder, "Jasper will drive you to the ER."

"All right." Arguing with Frankie Salazar was a master class in futility. He glanced back at Jo, but she was gone.

"Jed?" Ozzy made his way through the group of workers, who were filtering through the trees, returning to the site. "Where'd Jo go?"

"She and Gil headed back to the office. I'm meeting her at the trailer in fifteen." The relief Ozzy expected Jed to display was nowhere to be found. In its place, he saw uncertainty and more than a bit of anger.

"What?"

Jed's eyes took on that steely, determined gleam. "This wasn't an accident."

"Who was driving the machine?" Ozzy

rounded the excavator. "Kenny rile some-one up?" Even as he said it, he realized what a ridiculous notion it was. Kenny may have been a bully years ago, and sure, there were times he drank too much and did his share of pain-in-the-butt foolishness, but a deliberate attack by someone?

"Steve Plunket." Jed waved off Ozzy's second question. "They're thick as thieves. I don't think any particular person was the tar-get. I bet the site was." He gestured for Ozzy to come closer and lowered his voice. "You did your time with the sheriff's department. Luke got you up to speed on basic scene ex-amination, right? What does this look like to you?" He clicked his cell phone app and shone a light into the shadows.

Ozzy pulled off his gloves, checked the line Jed pointed to. "It looks like a line's been cut. Smooth edges. That's not wear and tear."

"Exactly. But these machines weren't even supposed to be used until next week. This work we were doing? It was spur-of-the-moment."

"Not to mention that by the time we did use this vehicle, all the brake fluid would have been gone. Someone did this on purpose."

"But what does this get anyone?"

"Delays? That's all that's going to happen while Jo arranges for a replacement, not to mention the state's going to be sending someone in to investigate."

"They'll be quicker due to the last accident," Ozzy said. "Or they should be. Might reduce the delay getting back to it?"

"You think?"

"I do. I'll call Luke about the cut line. Or maybe Jo should—"

"Already took pictures," Jed said. "Jo insisted."

Of course she did. "Okay. We're going to need to get this entire area roped off. It'll be quicker to make a call to Gil, tell him you want those security cameras back in place. Immediately."

"No need," Jed said. "That's what he and Jo were talking about before Gil left."

"Well, that's good news, then." Apparently his conversation with Gil the other day hadn't fallen on deaf ears.

He left Jed and moved toward the trailer to talk to Jo, who was giving instructions to the rest of the crew. "Ozzy!" Frankie called. "Let's go! Hospital!"

"Give me five." He picked up the pace and jogged to the construction trailer just as Jo opened the front door. "Jo, hang on."

She slammed the door in his face.

"Oh, for heaven's sake." He swung the door open and stepped inside. He found Kyle sitting behind his desk. The young man's gaze darted from Ozzy to Jo, who stood beside her own desk looking only slightly less furious than she had before he'd dropped down the side of the cliff. "Kyle, I'm sorry to have to ask, give us a second, would you?"

"Uh, sure." He scooped up his crutches and made his way toward the door. "I'll go check in with Jed."

When the door closed behind him, the trailer dropped into silence.

"Okay," Ozzy began. "I know you're ticked—"

"Ticked?" Jo gaped, then snapped her mouth shut and waited. "Okay, we can go with ticked." She tossed her cell onto her desk and planted her hands on her hips. "I have work to do."

He didn't like the idea of her being irritated with him, but he wasn't going to apologize for doing his job. He wanted her to understand. "Jo, what I said back there—"

"I don't need a replay, thanks." Anger sparked in those amber-tinted eyes of hers. "Don't you ever do something like that to me again. Not in front of other people and especially not in front of my crew. You weren't the only one doing their job."

"Your job was not on that cliff, mine was." When he took a step forward, she held her ground and inched her chin up. "There wasn't anything you could do except get in the way."

"So you said." She crossed her arms over her chest. "Message received, Ozzy. You stay in your lane, I'll stay in mine."

"Jo." His voice softened. "I'm sorry if I hurt your feelings."

"My feelings?" She balked. "My feelings don't have anything to do with this."

"Don't they? If Frankie had told you to stay back, would you have bristled?"

She pinched her lips shut. "I know how to stay out of the way. That was my employee out there. That crew is my responsibility. I wasn't going to be some kind of distraction."

"Yes. You were."

"What?" She shook her head as if she

hadn't heard him correctly. "What are you talking about?"

"You distract me." He smoothed his hands down her tense arms as he pulled her toward him. "Entirely too much."

He kissed her, catching her gasp of surprise with his mouth. He could feel, taste her frustration and the adrenaline that came close to rivaling his own. He didn't overthink it, didn't worry about what he was doing—he just surrendered to the pull she had on him and let himself feel.

Her entire body seemed to react, and when her fingers clutched the front of his shirt, a surge of triumph had him lifting her more solidly against him. This, he thought almost dazedly, this was what he'd been waiting a lifetime for. This moment, this feeling.

This woman.

"Ozzy?" she murmured when he ended the kiss.

"I can barely think when you're around," he whispered, pressing his forehead to hers as he lifted a hand to her cheek. "I had a job to do and all I could focus on was you. I needed you safe and out of sight."

"That's...slightly disturbing," she said with

a laugh. She hadn't moved, seemed completely content standing here in his arms. "And very sweet."

He groaned. *Sweet.* "They're going to put that word on my tombstone."

She lifted one of his hands with hers, pressed a kiss into his palm. A sharp knock rapped on the door. "Hey, Oz!" Frankie's voice belted. "We've got reports to write and you have an appointment at the ER. Let's go!"

Ozzy broke the connection between them. "I have to go."

"You're hurt?" She squeezed his hands.

"Not remotely." The concern in her voice soothed his heart like a balm. "Just a precaution."

"Right." She stepped back and his mind began to clear. "I'll see you—"

"Soon." Ozzy nodded. "You'll see me soon, Jo." He smiled at her and closed the door behind him.

CHAPTER TEN

"WHAT'S GOING ON?" Jo had no sooner finished up her phone call to the local inspector's office to request an on-site visit ASAP
when she heard two trucks pulling up in
front of the construction office. Grabbing
her nearly empty bottle of water, she headed
outside and found Jed greeting an unfamiliar
crew of five grabbing equipment and tools
out of their respective trucks. "Jed?"

"Security system installers," he said as if
he'd been practicing what to say for a while.
"Gil put a rush on it."

"Wow. That was fast." She sighed, admit-
tedly welcoming the help.

"Guy's got power when he chooses to use
it. I'll stick around while they do the instal-
lation. Gil upped the service package and
added in remote video monitoring. There will
be three screens installed in the office, and

you and I can download the app. We can log into the feed anytime we want."

"Some fun after-hours viewing, then." A security system wasn't going to tell them who was responsible, though. Unless whoever it was made a return visit. "How much is all this going to cost?"

"I didn't ask because I don't care." Jed handed her a new bottle of water, motioned toward the lunch tables. "I gave the crew the rest of the day off, told them not to come back until Monday."

She groaned, dropped into a chair and leaned her head back. "We were finally starting to make headway." A headache pricked behind her eyes, and she instantly tried to relax. She thought about prying off her boots, but she'd never get them back on. "I guess now I don't have an excuse not to go to that yoga class Saturday."

"Afraid not. Look, about Ozzy."

She would not blush. She would *not* blush. Heat rose up the sides of her neck. She'd be feeling the effects of that kiss quite possibly for the rest of eternity. Who would have thought the sweetest guy on earth could kiss like that? Keeping her tone even, she cleared her throat. "What about Ozzy?"

"I heard what happened. I hope you know he was only trying to protect you."

"Then let me tell you what I told him." She turned her head. "I don't need anyone's protection. He can be a hero with someone else. I don't need one."

"That's kind of my point." Jed stood up when one of the system installers called out for him. "Ozzy doesn't think of himself that way. In his mind, he's just doing what he believes everyone should do—the right thing. There's no point in trying to change him or asking him to be something he isn't."

"Do I look like a damsel in distress who needs a knight in my life?"

"No ma'am." He held up his hands and headed off to the security camera installers. "Just offering a little food for thought."

Food. If she was going to be stuck not working for the next couple of days, she would have to stock up the fridge. "Might as well make the most of the rest of the day."

A half hour later, she'd changed into her walking shoes—somehow managing to lace them up—and, reusable bags and food list stuffed into her purse, headed down the road to Duskywing Farm.

It took her a good twenty minutes to get her head clear. She'd done all she could do, made all the necessary calls, organized the appointment for the investigator, rearranged next week's schedule to accommodate the shift changes. There was literally nothing else for her other than pushing the thoughts of what could have happened out of her mind.

The extra stress wasn't doing anything to help her or the baby.

She came to a halt along a fence line that allowed her a stunning unobstructed view of a bounty of rich farmed goodness only a few steps away.

She didn't know what she'd been expecting as far as Calliope Costas's organic farm, but as she drew closer to the wooden gate and welcoming arbor, she knew this wasn't it. She could smell lavender, thyme and lemons in the air. The faint buzzing of bees and clucking of chickens drifted from just beyond.

A gentle mew preceded a sleek gray cat leaping up and onto the fencepost. She immediately scrubbed her head against the wood, offered another mew as the bell dangling from the purple collar around her neck tinkled.

Ozzy had said the farm had an open-door policy, and she did see a small open shed filled with baskets just inside. She bit her lip, glanced at the cat. "I don't suppose anyone's here to ask?"

"Mew." The cat dropped to the ground, quickly tootling off toward the stone cottage covered in thick ivy twining around a bright red door. She should come back, Jo thought, but found herself drawn to the peaceful setting. Wind chimes sounded.

"Well, the worst they can tell me is to leave." She clicked open the latch and pushed on the gate. Almost immediately, the cottage door burst open and a red-headed girl bounded outside, her bare feet barely touching the ground as she raced toward Jo.

"Hi!" Bells and baubles were threaded through her long red curls. Freckles dusted her nose and accented the brightest pair of green eyes Jo had ever seen. She was tall, thin and looked about ready to cross into that preteenage stage. "Welcome to Duskywing Farm. I'm Stella."

"Hello, Stella. I'm Jo."

"Oh, you're the new lady at the butterfly sanctuary." Stella twisted and twirled the hem of her rainbow-bright skirt around her fingers. "My brother-in-law Xander drew up the plans." Stella grinned. "That's architecture talk for he thought up the building. Come on in."

"I wasn't sure if you were open."

"We're always open. Calliope's making iced tea. Decaf. Cause she's having a baby and she can't have the regular kind anymore. You're having a baby, too!"

"I am." Jo nodded and rested a hand against her stomach. "Not until later this year, though."

"Calliope's due in December. We're going to have a Christmas baby! I can't wait. Except Alethea'll be moving out." She scrunched her face and beckoned her forward. "But she said I could come and stay with her some weekends when she has her own place. Come on, come on. I can help you shop if you want. I got my homework done already, but helping fill baskets is my favorite part of the job."

Stella darted over to the shed and plucked up a thin wooden basket with a large curved handle. "Do you know what you want?"

Jo dug around for her list. "I have an idea. I wrote down a few things I definitely want."

"Great! For how long? One week? Two? We also have a delivery service you can sign up for. Daily, weekly or however often you want. Oh, good. You like eggs. I got chickens a few months ago. We still have a bunch of fresh eggs left from this morning. I'll go grab you at least half a dozen."

"Um, thanks?" Jo called after her as Stella raced around the side of the house.

"I hesitate to recall how much energy she had before I eliminated excess sugar from the house." The gentle, almost melodical voice that drifted from the cottage door seemed to make the wind chimes ring. "It's nice to meet you, Jo. I'm Calliope." An ethereal vision of red hair and colorful swirls of fabric strode out of the house. The woman's bare feet were adorned with silver toe rings and a thin bejeweled chain around her right ankle. "Welcome to our farm. Your list is in good hands with Stella, I can assure you. Come sit down." She gestured to an outdoor table holding a tea tray and cups. "Have some tea and cookies. We're just waiting for Xander to get home."

"Thank you." Jo was grateful for the offer of a chair and went with the flow. She sat at the checked-cloth-covered table.

"It's a dandelion and agave tea. It seems to be good for circulation and getting rid of toxins." Calliope sat across from her.

"Stella says you're having a baby," Jo said. "Congratulations."

"And to you." Calliope's smile lightened Jo's heart. "I heard about the accident up at the site. I'm glad everyone's all right."

"So am I." Jo shouldn't have been surprised that word had already gotten out. "It's a good thing I don't believe in curses." Great. Now Gil had her thinking that way.

"Curses? No." Calliope offered a plate filled with a variety of golden baked treats. "The white chocolate and cashew are my new favorites," she urged as if Jo needed enticement. "They're also low in sugar and sodium. Cheyenne's usual pregnancy regime recommendation."

"I got my walking orders earlier today." Was that just a few hours ago? "I'm a passable cook so hopefully I won't starve." She bit into the cookie and reveled. "These are delicious."

"Calliope, look!" Stella ran over to the table and held out her hand. "We got pink eggs!"

"Really?" Jo had never heard of such a thing. "Eggs come in colors other than white or brown?"

"Chickens lay rainbows," Stella laughed. "I'll leave these here, so they don't break." She lifted ten eggs in varying colors onto the table before dashing off again.

"You were saying about curses?" Calliope asked Jo.

"Oh, nothing." Jo shrugged and resisted the urge to snag another cookie. *Hmm, what the heck.* She'd taken a walk. "I'm not a big believer in coincidences, I suppose. I was brought to town because of one accident, then another happens soon after I arrive? I can't imagine what someone would have against a butterfly sanctuary."

"There was some disagreement about the project at the beginning." Calliope sipped her tea. "Fortunately, enough of my fellow town members agreed that my farm shouldn't be sacrificed for the sanctuary."

Jo nibbled on a stray crumb, then reached for her cup. "You're kidding. That's…" She looked around the paradise Calliope had created for herself and her town. "Just the suggestion is downright criminal."

Calliope toasted her. "Gil's made his share of enemies over the years. It runs in the family, I suppose you could say. He's continued that unfortunate family tradition. How did you find him?"

"Gil?" Jo sat back in her chair and snapped her cookie in two. "Not what I expected. Younger certainly and not quite so..." She struggled for the right word. "Ruthless."

"He's had some recent awakenings in that department," Calliope confirmed. "He was almost killed in a fire at his office last year."

"I heard about that. What caused it?"

"The building was old and hadn't been well maintained." Calliope tilted her head. "I don't know that an official cause was ever reported."

"Hey, Jo?" Stella called from where she stood ankle deep in kale. "What kind of kale do you like?"

"A question I don't think I've ever been asked," Jo said to Calliope.

"Come." Calliope got to her feet, picked

up her cup and motioned for Jo to follow. "Let's help you find out."

"KNOCK, KNOCK." Ozzy stepped inside the hospital room. From his bed, Kenny Vogelman turned his head and offered Ozzy a dazed, definitely drugged smile. Visiting the people he helped on the job had become part of his routine.

"Hey, it's the Oz-man." Oh, yeah. Kenny had definitely had some serious painkillers.

"Seeing as I was in the neighborhood, I thought I'd check in on you." Ozzy's own exam in the ER had gone about how he'd expected. Bumps, scrapes, bruises and a more serious contusion on the back of his shoulder. Nothing that wouldn't heal. "How are you feeling?"

"Like I'm floating on a cloud. Broke three ribs and punched, pucted, punc-tur-ed," he enunciated deliberately, "my lung. Doc says I'm lucky I didn't bleed out. And I didn't even thank you." He punched out a hand as if making for a fistbump. "You saved my life, Oz."

"Just doing my job."

"I know, right?" Kenny's voice had that high-pitched quality of disassociation. "Man, who's ever going to believe fat old Ozzy Lakeman came rappelling down a rope to rescue me off a cliff. That's stellar story fodder for sure."

In the blink of an eye, Ozzy was back in high school, his back pressed up against his locker as Kenny and his friends found new ways to harass him. "Glad you're okay." He turned to leave. The sooner he made himself scarce, the better. "Oh, hi, Lisa."

"Yes?" The slight blonde with large teeth and even larger…eyes, who'd come into the room, blinked up at him. "Oh, Ozzy! I'm sorry. I didn't recognize you."

Kenny snickered.

Maybe it was time to rethink his recovery visits. First, he'd hauled his childhood bully off the cliffs, and now he was face-to-face with one of his massive teenage crushes. He was glad he'd moved on from those times, even if others hadn't. "Just seeing how he was doing."

"So it was you who saved Kenny?" Lisa blinked disbelieving lashes. "I thought that was just the medication talking. You know I haven't been home much these last few years. I had no idea about…" She stepped back and motioned at him. "Well, about this. You look great." The shift in her expression, from disbelief to sudden interest, was one he'd imagined thousands of times over the years. To be seen as something other than the fat kid who had never fought back, the one with a big target—sometimes literally—on his back. "I should take you out for a celebratory drink. You know, thank you for saving Kenny's life."

"Hey, yeah." Kenny raised his fist again. "The three of us for sure."

"Uh-huh." Lisa flipped her blond hair over her shoulder and did that head-tilt thing as she looked up at Ozzy. "What do you say, Oz? I'm free now."

"Sorry, Lisa. I have someplace I need to be." The odd satisfaction he felt at watching her face fall probably didn't do him much credit, but he didn't ignore it. "Kenny, hope you're back to work soon. Have a good evening, you two."

He got out his cell and texted Jasper that he was on his way down. There had been days he'd have sold his soul to have Lisa Faraday bat those lashes in his direction and ask him out. Now that it had happened, there was only one thought in his head. To close out his shift and head up to the construction site.

To see Jo.

"Hey, Ozzy?" Jasper poked his head into the office where Ozzy was finishing up his report. "Someone here to see you."

"Oh?" Ozzy frowned. "Who is it?"

"Some guy. Said you called in a favor about a dog?"

"Right. On my way." Ozzy hit Print, waited for the papers to pop out, then scribbled his name and left them stapled on Frankie's desk. He was already two hours beyond his extra twelve, and he was about as close to crashing as was humanly possible. He'd showered, changed and gotten something to eat so he could hit the mattress the second he got home.

But some things were more important than sleep. "Sawyer Tuckman." Ozzy held out his hand to greet his longtime cyber friend. "I told you I'd come to you. You didn't have to drive this far."

Sawyer pushed his thick glasses higher up on his nose and adjusted his stance. "Saw your hero bit on the news and thought I'd give you a break." He lifted his chin and looked around. "Can't believe you work here now. Showing us math fans what's what, am I right?"

"Doing what I can do." Ozzy slapped him on the shoulder and turned him to the door. "Just like you. Who do you have for me?"

"It took some wheeling and dealing, and you definitely owe me." Sawyer strode to the van parked in front of the firehouse and clicked open the door.

Perched on the back seat, sitting at full attention, was a gorgeous glistening dark dog with bright, attentive eyes. A mix, Ozzy saw. Definite German shepherd in there, maybe some rottweiler. "He's only three," Sawyer said, "but his partner was killed in the line of duty and he was injured. He hasn't bonded with anyone else on the force, so they retired him. He's been fostered ever since."

Sawyer made a clicking sound and the dog dropped to the ground and plopped his backside down. He blinked up at Ozzy, who nearly fell to his knees to give the dog a hug. But that wasn't the right tactic to take. Not when he wasn't the one the dog needed to bond with. "His partner was a woman," Sawyer added. "One reason I think this'll work."

"Sawyer, you are the man. I can't thank you enough."

"Hey, you're the one who parted with a collectible number one comic." Sawyer held up his hands in surrender. "I got the better end of the deal for sure. Hang on. He comes with stuff." He rounded the back of the van as Ozzy reached down and picked up the dangling leash.

"You're about to luck out big-time, fella," Ozzy told the dog. The two of them walked to join Sawyer, who was unloading three boxes and a bag of dog food from the back. Thinking of Jo's limited living space, Ozzy repressed a wince. "He have a name?"

The dog whined as Sawyer dived farther into the van and came out with an oversize stuffed dragon.

"Lancelot. Here you go, boy." Sawyer held out the toy, and with a whimper, Lancelot grabbed hold. "That's his coping mechanism," Sawyer explained. "He'll need some paw holding for a while, but he's protective and well trained. Trust me, your lady will be safe with him around."

His lady. Ozzy normally would have flushed at a comment like that. Instead, he found himself offering his hand once again in thanks. "You need anything, you call me, okay?"

"Deal," Sawyer agreed. "See you online."

Lancelot whined as Sawyer drove off. "Don't worry," Ozzy told him. "You're going to be just fine."

Lancelot sighed and looked up at Ozzy as if he needed convincing.

"What's going on, Oz?" Jasper asked as he and Frankie emerged from the station, then came to a halt at the sight of man and beast standing side by side. "You got a dog? Man. Oh, man, he's a—he?" Ozzy nodded his confirmation. "He's a beauty. I can't wait to get a place of my own so I can have a dog."

"Do you have time for a dog, Oz?" Frankie glanced uneasily toward the top of the fire truck where Sparky was perched, sitting regal-like, watching everything as if from his throne.

"Not really, no. He's not for me." He grinned, bent down and gave the dog a good scruffy scrub. "I got him for Jo."

"Right," Frankie said slowly. "Because

with a baby coming and a house the size of a postage stamp, she has room for that." She shook her head.

"She'll love him," Ozzy declared, pushing away the worry. "Won't she, boy?"

Lancelot dropped to the ground and rested his chin on his dragon.

Jo STARTED AWAKE.

She blinked into the darkness, trying to remember falling asleep. She groaned, started to roll onto her back, only to be stopped by the stack of pillows she'd stuffed behind her that had done little to no good to relieve her discomfort.

The urge to get to the bathroom went from mild to urgent with the kick of one foot, but that wasn't what had woken her up. She was certain of it.

Dragging herself out of bed, she walked as quickly as she could to the bathroom, eventually recalling she'd meant to simply take a nap after getting back from the farm. She'd put her cold items in the fridge, left everything else out and wanted to rest her eyes.

She glanced at her watch. That was ten

hours ago! No wonder she was wide-awake at 4:00 a.m. She *never* slept that long.

"It's like I'm training for a vampire's arrival, rather than a baby's," she muttered. The stress over yesterday's events must have taken a bigger toll than she'd realized considering she was still wearing yesterday's clothes. She took care of business, strode barefoot into the kitchen and grabbed a bottle of water. She yanked a sweater from under the pile of work papers she'd left on the counter. Her house looked as if a mini-mart had exploded, but even her hunger wasn't motivation enough to make her tackle the disaster.

She drank her water, looking out into the silent night that had crept up on her. A shadowy outline had her frowning and trying to peer over the counter to get a better look. She clicked on the outside light, went to the door and cupped her hand on the window. "What the…"

She yanked open the door and stood there, staring at the all-too-familiar SUV. "Ozzy Lakeman," she muttered. With the new security system installed, she could only imagine what the monitoring station must be thinking, considering one of the cameras had been attached to the north corner of her house. What was he doing? They'd had this conversation. She was not defenseless or unwise as to the ways of the wicked, evil world. Clearly the man needed a refresher course in Jo Bertoletti 101.

Jo grabbed her slip-on shoes and exited, then walked around the front of the car. The motion lights that had also been installed blinked to life and shone a spotlight on Ozzy's vehicle.

She lifted a hand to knock on the passenger window, then stopped. A smile spread across her lips at the sight of him, arms folded across his chest, fast asleep behind the wheel.

A second face popped into her line of sight. Jo yelped, jumped back and covered her mouth as the canine moved closer and pressed its damp nose against the glass.

Ozzy didn't stir. Not even as the dog planted both its significant paws on Ozzy's thigh. Jo tilted her head to the side. The dog did the same. She tilted to the other side. The dog mirrored her actions. Laughing, Jo couldn't help herself. She reached out and tested the door, found it unlocked and opened it.

The dog dropped out and, after giving Jo a

significant sniff, pushed its head firmly into her hand.

"Well, hello, Ozzy's dog." She bent over, as far as she was able, and gave the dog a good long pat. "You're gorgeous, aren't you? Your owner didn't tell me about you. What's your name?" She angled the dog tag up into the light. "Lancelot." She rolled her eyes. "Obviously a knight would have a dog named Lancelot."

"He's not my dog."

Jo yelped again, and this time the dog sprang into action, planting himself firmly between Ozzy and Jo. "Ozzy! What are you doing here? It's okay, boy." She stroked the dog's head.

"Well, I came originally to continue our discussion." He scrubbed his hands down his face and slowly unfolded out of the car. "But you were asleep—"

"How do you know that?" He hadn't been peeping in her windows, had he?

"Because I knocked numerous times, and even though people saw you go in, you didn't answer. I figured I'd wait for you to wake up." He stretched his arms over his head and in so doing tugged his T-shirt up and exposed his six-pack stomach.

Jo pressed her lips together and forced herself to look away. She did not need to be distracted by Ozzy the fireman's firm abs. "I only meant to take a short nap. You didn't have to wait."

"Listen, we have a creeper around here cutting brake lines in the dead of night. Could be dangerous, and I didn't like the idea of you being all alone."

"How sweet." She purposely used the word she knew would set him on edge.

"Sorry, sweetheart." He brushed a finger under her chin. "That won't work anymore. Can I use your bathroom?"

"Sure, *sweetheart*. You know where it is." She stepped back and let him head inside while she motioned for the dog to follow. "Might as well come in, too, Lancelot." The dog remained where he was, looking into the cab of the open SUV. "What's wrong?" She looked in and spotted a bright purple-and-blue dragon on the floor. "This yours?" She grabbed for it, held it out and watched in befuddled amusement as the canine grabbed hold and carried it into the house. "Should have named him Linus with his blankie."

She closed Ozzy's car door and headed inside just as Ozzy emerged. His hair and face were damp as if he'd ducked his head under the faucet.

"So whose dog is he?" Jo asked, sitting down, as Ozzy made himself at home by attacking her coffee maker.

"What?"

"You said Lancelot isn't yours. You must be dog sitting, then? Who does he belong to?"

Lancelot whimpered from his declared space in front of the sofa. "Yeah, I know, boy," Ozzy said. "He's yours."

"Mine?" Jo nearly fell off her stool. "What do you mean mine?"

"A friend of mine trains police dogs. Lancelot's a bit of a dropout. No shame in that," he added at the dog's rare growl. "He lost his partner and—"

"Gained a dragon?" Jo teased.

"Something like that. He needs a good, strong female household and you need…"

She arched a brow at him. "Go ahead. Say it." She quirked her mouth. "I dare you."

"I can't believe I'm saying this about Butterfly Harbor, but yeah, you need protection."

"And seeing as you wouldn't fit on my sofa, you found someone else to do the job." She sighed, rested her cheek in her hand. "Ozzy, I can't believe I'm saying this, but it's a very swee—er, nice gesture. An appreciated one. But I'm not set up for a dog. Certainly not one his size. I mean, he's bigger than me." She looked down at her stomach. "Almost."

"You can adjust accordingly. He comes with plenty of toys and food that we can store outside. He'll be good company and he'll make me feel better."

She couldn't help it—she laughed. "Well, of course, this is all about you," Jo countered. "What about the baby?"

"What about it?"

"If the dog's protective, he might not be so welcoming to an infant. There's no telling what his reaction will be."

"So we test him. Lots of babies around this town to introduce him to. Safely," he added. "He's a former police dog, Jo, not an extra from *Cujo*."

Jo snorted. She must really be out of it to even be considering keeping the animal.

"I'll be around to help out with him whenever you need. Besides, I bet Cheyenne suggested walks, right?"

"For me or the dog?" Jo teased but went on before he could answer. "Let's agree to play it by ear? See how it goes? With you as backup. Always good to have a plan B."

"Fine. Worst case, we do joint custody. After the way he was snuggling me in my car, we might be halfway to being engaged, anyway."

This time, Jo didn't even try to stop it. She laughed heartily and made Ozzy smile in a way that made doing so every day from here on her life's goal. "I'll get changed." Her stomach growled noisily enough for him to grin. "Forget you heard that, please."

"Not possible. You get going and I'll get started on breakfast." Lancelot was on his feet in an instant, padding over to sit beside Ozzy. "Make that we will. Hurry up. I think he's starving."

CHAPTER ELEVEN

MAKING THE DRASTIC changes he had over the past couple of years meant Ozzy had made himself comfortable in the kitchen. And not just his own, it turned out. It took him a few minutes to put away the groceries she'd left on the counter, but he hadn't changed anything. Instead, he'd followed her surprisingly logical organization system and was digging into her refrigerator like a man on a culinary mission.

He'd seen enough of her food selection to understand she'd cook if she had to, but she preferred to grab and go. Made sense considering her long work hours, but grab and go didn't always mean healthy. He found the wrinkled food list in one of her reusable bags when he'd folded it. He scanned through it, noticed the foods she was not supposed to eat during her pregnancy and did a quick cabinet check. Other than tuna, he didn't find anything Cheyenne had mentioned as objectionable.

Lancelot gave a soft whine as Ozzy pulled out the fresh eggs, tomatoes and various other vegetables he could throw together into a frittata. By the time she emerged from the bedroom, he was popping the fancy tomato, asparagus and onion frittata into the oven. "Tea's brewing," he told her. "I found the box from Calliope's stash."

"I might actually find one I like as much as coffee." She smirked, then shook her head. "Nah. That won't happen." She tugged at the hem of her oversize sweatshirt that almost, *almost*, hid her baby bump and part of the snug-fitting leggings clinging to her.

"Seahawks fan, huh?"

"Naturally." She looked at him as if there was no other choice. Sitting on her usual stool, she stretched out her hand to scratch the top of Lancelot's head. "I'm a legacy. Sundays were football days with my grandfather."

Ozzy grabbed two oversize slices of hearty grain bread, another of Calliope's homemade offerings, and dropped them into the toaster. He poured Jo a cup of tea and handed it to her. "You've mentioned your grandfather quite a bit. You two were close?"

She nodded and sipped her tea. "Hmm, good choice. Very. After my father died, he stepped in and stepped up. Good thing, too, since my mother wasn't particularly interested in being a parent."

"Sorry about your dad." He peeled a banana and handed her half. She looked at the fruit as if she wasn't entirely sure what to do with it. "It's potassium. Eat."

"Yeah, yeah." She nibbled and shrugged.

"How old were you when you lost your father?"

"Eight." She hesitated. "My eighth birthday, actually. We were supposed to go out to this fancy dinner. My first big-girl dinner. Cloth napkins and everything. He was late getting home from work because he'd stopped to get my birthday present." Her voice shifted, became almost distant. "A monogrammed tool set he had special ordered. Nothing fancy and nothing pink. I loathe pink." She met Ozzy's gaze with a hint of the ghosts that haunted her. "He was crossing the street to go to the store and was killed by a hit-and-run driver."

Ozzy had no words. His relationship with his own father wasn't ideal, but at least he was there. "Do you still have the toolset?"

"No." She took another bite of banana. "The store had it sent to my mother, but she didn't want it. She didn't want any reminders, so she gave it away. My grandfather was livid."

He had every right to be, Ozzy thought. So did she.

"My mother and grandfather did not get along. My father was his only child, and how she unfortunately dealt with his death was to pretty much try to erase his existence. She was going to move out of the state, but my grandfather put his foot down. He had a successful business, he had an established life and he wasn't going to lose me on top of losing my father. So he paid her to stay, even bought her a new house closer to his. When I was thirteen, I went to live with him full-time, then moved out when I went to college."

"I take it he's gone now, too."

"New Year's Day when I was nineteen. We were watching football." A slight smile curved her lips. "The last thing he did was swear at the refs. I went to get him another beer and when I came back, he was gone."

"Jo." Ozzy rested his hand over hers and squeezed.

"He was a really good guy, you know? Always there. Never let me down. Not once. He did create unrealistic expectations, too," she added with a bittersweet laugh. "Leah's diagnosis," she explained. "And that concludes the maudlin portion of our morning." She pulled her hand free and swiped at the dampness on her cheeks. "What about your parents? They're still in town, obviously. I dream of that pie, by the way."

"Same house for the past thirty-seven years. Dad's retired from the city."

"And your mom?"

"Housewife. Devoted to my father twenty-four seven. I was a late surprise," he said. "They didn't think they could have kids and then there I was. I think I confused them in a lot of ways. Still do."

"They should be proud to have you for a son."

"It's difficult to be proud of someone you don't understand. But I turned out okay. Eventually." If he made the joke first, then it lessened the odds someone else would make it. "It took me losing a ton of weight for my father to finally engage with me. Too bad I'm still not the son he wants."

"I'm sure that's not true."

He shrugged, not wishing to answer. He didn't like doing a psyche deep dive any more than she did. "You know what I should have fixed? Potatoes." He snapped his fingers and retrieved a large russet from the basket by the sink. "It's a splurge for me, but what the heck." He wiggled the potato in the air. "We're both worth it."

"That we are." She lifted her feet to examine her ankles. "Still swollen. Not quite so bad, though."

"How did your appointment with Cheyenne go?"

"Good, I think. Fine. Well, you saw my food list. Yum."

He chuckled at her lack of enthusiasm.

"She's running lab tests, but told me to stay off my feet as much as I can. And I'm to take her prenatal yoga classes. Since there's no site work this weekend, I guess I don't have any excuse not to go. I'm also, as you guessed, under strict orders to get an hour of walking in every day. How that goes along with keeping my feet up, I can't fathom."

"I bet she recommended the beach." Ozzy zapped the potato in the microwave for a few minutes, set another pan on the stove with a drizzle of oil. "It's nature's depressurizer. Blood pressure remedy extraordinaire. I've gotten my best workouts running on the shore."

"Ha, I won't be running anytime soon." She stood up and retrieved her bag from the floor. "I have a picture, if you're interested. It's totally okay if you're not."

"A picture of what?"

"Of the baby. Cheyenne said I should share it with someone and, well, other than Leah, I don't really know—"

"I am absolutely interested." He wiped his hands on a dish towel and plucked the small manila envelope out of her fingers. He felt his breath catch as he pulled out the two grainy black-and-white sonograms.

"See, there's an arm and…" She peered closer. "Nope. Still not getting it."

"I am." His heart swelled. "Arm, arm, leg and foot. Looks like someone's camera shy. Did you find out if it's a girl or boy?"

"I don't want to know."

"Oh." He looked a bit disappointed, but in the next instant he shifted and held the photo up to her stomach. Lancelot, having been ignored long enough, came over and pushed his muzzle between them to get his own look. "From where I'm standing, it's a perfect match," Ozzy announced. "All three of you."

"Ozzy." She shook her head. "You really don't have to…"

"To what?" He asked when she went quiet, "Care? Is it really so hard to believe that I do?"

She shrugged and glanced down. "This is complicated. And you being here, doing all this, watching out for me, it's too much. You have a life, Ozzy. What are you doing in mine?"

It was a good question. One he'd asked himself frequently since he'd met her. He'd spent most of his life longing for someone he felt truly comfortable with, someone he could create a life with. For so long that had felt out of reach, partly because he hadn't even tried reaching for it. But he'd since overcompensated and turned over every stone and found no one who fit. But Jo did. He couldn't figure it out. He didn't really want to, either. He just wanted to go for it, for once in his life, and take the chance.

"I'm here because it's where I want to be," he said finally. "Not because I think you need me, but because…" He set the photo on the counter, careful not to crinkle the edges. "Because I think maybe you might want me." Ozzy reached out, caught her hands in his and tugged her toward him. Lancelot heaved a sigh and backed up.

"Kissing you yesterday, for me, it was like everything I'd been waiting for fell into place." He lifted a hand to her face, stroked her cheek. "You're amazing, Jo. You're stunning and fun and challenging. I like watching you and listening to you and talking with you. Did I mention I enjoy challenging you?"

"You might have. You really know how to say all the right things." Even as she said it, he could see the doubt swimming in her eyes. "We're so impractical a match, Oz. I mean, I'm older than you for one thing. And not by a little."

"What does that even matter?"

"It just does."

"Not to me. And I don't care what other people might think."

"That's not true—you do care," she countered and hit a nerve. "The changes you've made in your life, the man you've become, it's partially because you want people to see beneath the shell. I'm simply another shell to hide behind." She pushed away from him. "I'm further along in life than you are. I know who I am. I'm set, Ozzy. I know what I want and where I'm going. And where I'm going is away from here. I live on wheels, not to mention I come with a serious attachment."

"Kidlet's a bonus," Ozzy said with a grin. "You're acting as if I didn't know you were pregnant from the start. No offense, but it was hard not to notice."

She twisted her mouth. "Ha ha."

But she was struggling with where this conversation was going, and his pushing her into something that distracted her wasn't going to get him anywhere but kicked completely out of her life.

"Give us a few weeks. Isn't it worth maybe seeing if there's a chance this works?"

"Despite my obvious dubious history with men?" Jo said in a somewhat strangled voice.

"I've barely scratched the surface on me and Greg. How can you want to—"

"You'll tell me when you're ready," he said easily as he grabbed onto the hope she offered. The hope he needed.

The oven timer dinged. Neither of them moved. They stood there, in her kitchen, a foot away from one another, and waited.

"Fine, all right. Whatever." She tossed up her hands as if she'd surrendered. "We'll see where this goes."

"Hear that, Lancelot?" Ozzy crouched down and held out his hand. Lancelot dropped his paw into Ozzy's and Ozzy swore the dog winked at him. "We're gonna give this a shot."

He heard Jo mutter under her breath about "not knowing what he was getting into" as she went over to the oven, but she was wrong.

Ozzy knew exactly what he was getting into. And he was already halfway there.

CHAPTER TWELVE

How was it, Jo wondered as she stared up at the community center ceiling, that some women carried pregnancy as effortlessly and gracefully as a prima ballerina balancing on tiptoe and she felt like an elephant on ice skates?

She also wondered how she was going to get up off the floor and resume her regular schedule. Maybe listening to her fellow mommies-to-be collecting their yoga mats and belongings would inspire her to try to move.

She heard the clack of canine claws on the floor a moment before a cold nose nuzzled her cheek. Lancelot dropped onto his belly, rested his face on her shoulder and let out an encouraging whine. He'd waited patiently by the door, leash looped around a nearby chair for the class to finish.

Jo lifted her hand to pet him, reveling in

the unconditional love she could feel coming from the animal. She couldn't easily recall what her life had been like without this whacky, lovable dog. Whatever might happen with Ozzy from here on out, she'd never be able to thank him enough for bringing Lancelot into her world.

Her body ached, but in a good way and, as she flattened her hands on either side of her stomach, she could feel the baby shifting as if to tell her she'd done well. Jo took a long, deep breath, closed her eyes and tried to cling to the relaxed mindset Cheyenne's yoga class had put her into.

Something hard poked into her arm, as if she was a stuffed turkey being tested for doneness. When she opened her eyes, she looked up into a group of old, wrinkled, curious faces. She chuckled at the sight of some of the Cocoon Club peering down at her.

"You still alive down there?" Delilah, a former town council member with a penchant for glamour and glitz, blinked perfectly outlined eyes at her.

"I'm alive," Jo confirmed and pushed herself up on her elbows. Lancelot whimpered and shifted aside. "Just pondering the effort it's going to take to get up."

"I remember when I was pregnant with my first." Myra, known for her teased orange hair and take-no-prisoners attitude nodded in understanding. "Didn't think I'd ever move right again." She grabbed hold of Harvey's arm and did a butt-shaking boogie. "But it all came back."

Jo laughed, appreciating the encouragement.

"You going to be down there for much longer?" Delilah, tall, slim, and looking as if she'd stepped off a 1950's film set, glanced around the room. "We've got a class to set up for."

"Give me a sec. Oh, hey, Alethea. Great." Jo waved the food truck chef over. "Give me a hand? I might topple one of them over."

Alethea grinned and abandoned her task of setting out folding chairs to assist Jo.

"I doubt I'll be able to do even those simple stretches in a couple of months." Though Jo had to admit that despite her reluctance to attend the yoga class to begin with, she felt good, inside and out, and, well, calmer.

"You never know," Alethea joked. "Abby

swore by these classes when she was pregnant with David. Cheyenne might just have you doing backflips by then."

"Never going to happen." Jo collected her mat and bag, slipped Lancelot's leash over her hand. "What kind of class are you guys taking?" She asked the elderly group as they made their way around a group of teenage students setting up long tables and arranging chairs.

"Vlogging 101," Myra announced. "We're thinking about starting a YouTube channel."

Jo stared wide eyed at Alethea, who only shrugged her shoulders and grinned some more.

"We've got loads of life experience to share," Harvey added. "Now that we're guest lecturing at the high school again, we thought we'd branch out. Lots of history among us on all sorts of topics. I was a Marine, you know."

"And we've run out of people to talk to in town," Myra finished. "We're going to take the Internet by storm!"

"Maybe we'll even be featured on one of those special segment stories on the news," Delilah added, pushing a short strand of silver hair behind her ear. "Wouldn't that be wonderful?"

"We have to be a success first," Myra stated. "Which means we have to know what we're doing. Harvey, let's get that laptop of yours set up." She moved off on the cane she'd used to poke Jo.

"They're so much fun," Alethea whispered as the group organized themselves. "When they aren't wreaking havoc on the town, that is."

Affection welled up inside Jo. Her grandfather had never acted old. He'd rarely admitted to even being old, but he'd worried, as the years passed, that the perception of him, of what he was capable of, would decline. Had he lived, he'd have fit right in with this spirited group of seniors.

And no doubt he'd have had a ball.

"Are you taking the class, too?" Jo asked Alethea as they walked toward the door, Lancelot in the lead.

"No. I was only dropping off leftover food from the truck. Holly's dad, Jake Campbell, he runs the place, has volunteers who will deliver meals to seniors who can't get out and about, both here and in Durante, the next town over."

"That's a nice system."

"Gives me extra cooking practice, too. And it's win, win since Jason hates throwing food out."

The community center, from Jo's understanding, was an expanded version of the original building that the town had quickly outgrown. Both buildings were situated close to the beach, which Jo personally appreciated as it allowed her a leisurely walk post-yoga class. Of course, it didn't cross her mind that her walks tended to coincide with Ozzy's swimming sessions as he trained for his water rescue certification test.

"If you don't have anything else going on, come by Flutterby Dreams for dinner," Alethea said with a hint of nerves in her voice.

"Okay." Jo glanced at her, curious. "Any particular reason why?"

"I'm filling in for Jason. First time on my own. I mean, I'll have our kitchen staff, but this is the first time the menu's been all mine." She twisted her hands together as if she couldn't keep them still. "I could use a few friendly, understanding customers. Besides, I owe you for all the time you've spent teaching me about business plans and budgets."

"You don't owe me anything. I've enjoyed it." It had been nice to make another solid friend in town. In fact, Jo was beginning to add quite a few friends to her contact list. "Do I need a reservation?"

"Nah, you've got an in." Alethea smiled as they strolled the curving planked path that meandered around to the beach. "I'll put you on the list. But would I be making that reservation for one or for two?"

Before Jo could answer, she found her attention drawn to the shore. Lancelot whined and, despite sitting beside her, was clearly eager to be rid of his leash.

There, in the distance, amidst the lapping waves and late morning sun, she caught sight of a dark head bobbing in and out of the water. Wet or dry, she'd recognize that hair anywhere.

"Never mind," Alethea said. "For two, it is." She walked backwards from Jo. "See you later!"

"Yeah, bye."

Jo was about to head across the sand to

where Ozzy would emerge from the ocean, but she spotted an older woman nearby, also watching the firefighter.

She was a little shorter than average, but a little more round in size, and held what looked like an insulated food bag in her hand. It didn't take Jo much more than seeing the woman's affection-filled face to connect the dots. *Ozzy's mother.*

Impulse nearly had her approaching the woman until nerves and uncertainty stopped her cold. She'd only met Greg's parents a few times and she hadn't exactly gotten the warm and fuzzies.

She didn't know why, but the idea of meeting Ozzy's parents felt like too large a step to take, especially since they were still determining exactly...whatever it was she and Ozzy had going on between them.

Besides, what was it Ozzy had said about his mother? That she considered Jo a curiosity? Yeah, she wasn't sure she could handle being micro-examined today.

Lancelot looked back at her, a "what's going on?" expression on his face, but all Jo could bring herself to do was watch as Mrs. Lakeman's smile grew and lit up her eyes as Ozzy emerged from the ocean and approached his mom.

He wore long board shorts the color of the ocean, blues and greens wrapping low around his waist and almost down to his knees. He was, Jo finally confirmed after her previous quick glimpse of skin, beautifully and perfectly toned and that spark in his eyes had been accentuated by what was surely frigid morning ocean water.

Ozzy grabbed a towel off the sand, scrubbed his hair, then draped it around his neck, engrossed in the conversation he and his mother began.

She didn't want to intrude. That was what she told herself as she nudged Lancelot away before Ozzy noticed them. She could meet his parents another time.

Maybe when she didn't feel quite so insecure about what the future held. Or… maybe she'll have packed up her home and have gone before she had to confront the opportunity again. "Come on, boy." It was time to do what she did best and they left.

She was grateful there was work waiting for her as she and Lancelot retraced their steps along the path. Maybe she'd have a quick power nap first. There hadn't been any further "accidents" or mishaps or weird in-the-middle-of-the-night sounds at the site, although Jo had found other reasons to not sleep. Hence her added gratitude for the yoga classes. She even felt confident enough in the project's progress that she could take a day off, too. She'd ask Jed to notify her if anything came up. Out of sight didn't always mean out of mind, and Jo was rarely far from work mode.

Her walk took her through town and on to the marina, where seagulls cawed in the air and the wind rustled raised sails.

With the sun streaming from a cloudless sky and the tide a gentle ripple against the shore, she dropped her bag and walking shoes onto the sand, longing for the days she, too, could simply drop down and relax. Instead, she stood there, strategizing how to do it, feet braced apart, hands on her hips. She arched her back, lifted her face to the sun.

Something cold and damp fell onto her bare feet. She looked down and there was Lancelot standing in front of her, tongue lolling, tail wagging as he nudged the stick closer to her.

"You heard Cheyenne say bending over was considered exercise, didn't you?" Jo accused the dog. "Fine. Just give me a second." She did better than she anticipated and straightened back up with relative ease. "Well, what do you know?" She chucked the stick out into the ocean and Lancelot leaped into action. It was, she thought as he bounded back to her, as close to a perfect moment as she could remember.

They resumed their walk. Jo kept half an eye on the time. She had a date to meet Ozzy at the diner at noon, but before that, she wanted to do a little exploring. Her wanderings took her the length of the beach and up the path to the harbor marina. A picturesque area that looked as if it had come out of a storybook.

"Okay, boy, come here." Jo sat on a bench at the marina's entrance and slid her sand-caked feet into her shoes. When she had Lancelot's leash clipped in place, she removed her sweatshirt and wadded it up in her bag.

Overhead, a colorful bird swooped in and around the smattering of boats. The collection of houseboats caught her off guard. She wouldn't have expected so many, all rather inviting, from an elegant two-story gray-painted vessel to a smaller wood-paneled version that looked like the ones she'd seen in Seattle.

A flap of wings had her sitting back on the bench and Lancelot straining at his leash. "Easy there, boy," Jo murmured and stroked the dog's head. "It's just here to say hi." She tilted her head toward the bright green-and-red parrot, who appeared as curious about them as Lancelot seemed to be about it. Was Lancelot thinking of trying to replace his dragon? "Hello there."

"Hello there," the bird squawked. "Drop and give me twenty."

"Oh." Jo frowned. "Maybe you aren't so friendly after all. Sorry, bird. No can do." It seemed even the bird thought she needed exercise.

"Let's get physical!" The bird trilled. "Guaca-mooooooleeee!"

A female voice said, "Duchess, go home."

"Oh, that's all right." Jo turned to the voice as she laughed. "She's so cute."

"She is, the first ten times she says it." The woman who approached had dark, expressive eyes and thick brown hair that tumbled around her shoulders. She wore bright yellow capris and a matching white-and-yellow sleeveless sweater that accentuated a figure Jo found herself envying. "I'm Sienna Fairchild. You must be Jo."

"I must be." She'd gotten used to the introduction process of this small town. "Early congratulations. I hear you're the bride-to-be." Ozzy had mentioned the upcoming wedding between Sienna and Monty Bettencourt on more than one occasion, no doubt hinting he expected her to go with him.

"That's me. Second time's the charm," she added with a teasing grin. "Inside joke. This time I'm getting it right. Mind if I join you?"

"Sure." More than happy for the company, she scooted over. "This is Lancelot, by the way. He's harmless." Perhaps too harmless for the guard-dog role he'd been assigned.

"Hello, Lancelot. Handsome boy, aren't you?" Sienna set her small, expensive-looking purse down and offered her hand to the dog, then a pet. "Monty's due back any minute so I thought I'd meet him at the marina for lunch. He's got a small group out for a sightseeing tour to Abbot Point. You meeting Ozzy?"

"I am. Later at the diner." Again, she wasn't surprised her agenda had shown up on the town's social calendar. "Do you mind if I ask you a question?"

"I love questions. Shoot."

"Just how vested are folks in Ozzy's social life?"

Sienna flipped her hair over her shoulder and shifted her gaze to the water. "On a scale of one to ten, I'd put it at about a thirty-five. Granted, I haven't known him for very long, I'm a relative newcomer myself, but he and Monty are pretty good friends. Monty's made mention of the fact Ozzy's never really been a social butterfly."

"Still coming out of his shell, so to speak?" Jo pressed.

"It's a change. I provided some entertainment for the town for a little while. I was a bride on the run in San Diego until I spotted Monty's boat and a means of escape, so to speak, and the rest is history. I guess I have you to thank for the shift of topic of conversation. Congratulations on the baby."

"Oh, thanks." Jo touched her stomach. "Sometimes I almost forget. Then I try to move."

"Monty and I are talking about how many we would like to have." There was something wistful in Sienna's voice. "We're stuck somewhere between a baseball team and a quartet."

"Four?" Jo's eyes went wide. "Wow. That's... I have enough trouble wrapping my brain around having the one."

"I'll be happy with one." Sienna's voice was so soft, Jo shifted to face her. "Sometimes I'm scared of having too many kids, other times I'm terrified of not having any at all. Sorry," Sienna said quickly. "My mother passed after having me, so the whole thing makes me a bit nervous. You aren't my therapist. Boundaries. I have this habit of saying things I shouldn't to perfect strangers."

"Sometimes it's easier to talk to strangers than it is to those we love." Provided you had those people in your life. After her grandfather's death, Jo had pretty much been alone. She'd had friends, Leah being the closest, but beyond that, Jo had gotten quite used to being on her own. Until Greg. And that had turned out so well—not. "You know what this baby's taught me?"

"What?"

"That sometimes what you need most finds a way to show up in your life." She had no doubt that what was happening with her and Ozzy would burn itself out. It was inevitable, and that certainty was as much a part of Jo's life as the air she breathed. What she needed most was the child she carried. Building a family of her own was all she'd ever wanted, but never believed possible. "Maybe don't worry until you have to? And maybe it isn't as difficult as you think it might be to talk to Monty about it."

"We all seem to have baby fever in this town," Sienna said. "We've got kids and babies and pregnancies all over the place."

"And each one feels like your heart breaking when you don't think that'll be you." Jo nodded at Sienna's shocked expression. "Told you. I've been there. Have faith, Sienna. And when you run out of that, don't close down. Turn to the person you love. He'll help you through."

Tears glistened in Sienna's brown eyes. "Wow. A few minutes on this bench with you has paid off more than years of therapy. Next time maybe we can talk about my father's social life? He's started dating again, after more than twenty years! Can you believe that? And with Ezzie Salazar no less."

"In this town?" Jo asked, laughing. "I'll believe anything."

"WHEN YOU SAID we'd be taking a walk at dawn, I assumed we'd be going down to the beach for you to swim." Jo dropped out of Ozzy's SUV, and after a warning look at Lancelot telling him to stay put, she followed Ozzy around to the back of the vehicle.

"We'll head there next. Just have to drop this off first." He popped the trunk.

Glossy orange and black paint glimmered against the rising sun. "You finished it!"

"Last night." He pulled the bike out and lowered it to the ground. He ran his hand over the handlebars accented with sparkling streams of glittery black plastic. "I was waiting for the baskets to arrive. Custom order from Etsy."

One of the precisely woven faux wicker baskets was displayed perfectly on the front, the other situated at the back. Both were ac-

cented with tiny hand-painted monarch butterflies, and on the front basket, "Butterfly
Girl" was spelled out in beautifully painted
letters.

Tears burned Jo's throat. "It's beautiful, Ozzy. Charlie's a lucky little girl." She
touched his arm. He'd spent hours restoring
this bike simply because he saw a need that
he could fill and while Charlie's original bike
had been pink, he was pretty sure she'd be
okay with the changes. "But why are you de-
livering it so early? The sun's barely up."

"You need to brush up on your magic, Jo.
Don't you know fairies only deliver at night?"
He winked and headed across the street to a
yellow cottage with a white picket fence. Jo
remained by the car, admiring the beautiful butterfly stained glass window above the
front door. The monarch on display in the
glass spread its wings against the cresting sun
and bathed the garden below and around the
house like a winged guardian angel.

Ozzy lifted the bike over the fence and
situated it out of the way. When he returned
to the car, he motioned for her to jump back
in. No sooner had they closed the doors and
lowered the windows than the front door of

the house swung open and a very pregnant woman emerged. Bright blond hair knotted on top of her head, she had the same gapping-robe issue Jo had been dealing with as of late.

"That's Paige Bradley, right?" Jo asked. "She's an ER nurse at the hospital?"

"Yep," Ozzy confirmed. "She's married to one of the town deputies, Fletcher."

Paige gripped the doorframe, started to bend down, then looked at the ground. Even from a distance, Jo could imagine the woman's sigh.

"Fletch?" Paige's voice carried along the silence of the morning. "The newspaper's all yours today." She started to turn back into the house, then stopped. She stared, blinked, took a step out, then stopped, her hands covering her mouth. "Fletch!"

"Yeah, yeah, I can only move so fast myself." A man hopped into view, his khaki shirt still unbuttoned and hanging open over his matching pants. He grabbed hold of Paige's arm. "What is it? The baby? It's coming now?"

"No, look." Paige pointed to the bike. "I can't believe you did this."

"Me?" Fletcher shook his head. "No, honey,

this wasn't me. I've been looking for one similar, but just haven't found..." Fletcher's gaze shifted to the street as if casing it.

"Uh-oh. Duck." Ozzy dropped behind the wheel, but peered over the edge of his window.

"Yeah, that's not happening," Jo muttered, unable to take her eyes off the family. "It's okay. He's too preoccupied to notice."

"Charlie!" Paige disappeared inside the cottage and Fletcher came farther out to take a closer look at the bike. He stood there, shaking his head, as a springer spaniel bounded outside, yipping and yapping as if being let out of jail.

A few minutes later, a young girl with a sleepy expression wandered out the front door. Scrubbing her hands over her eyes, she frowned. "What's going on?"

"Someone left you a present—" Fletcher stepped back "—butterfly girl."

Jo felt Charlie's gasp of joy all the way down to her toes. Squeals of happiness swam through the air as Charlie leaped off the porch and grabbed the bike, swung it around and back.

"Oh, wow, Dad, it's perfect! I love it! You

found it! You promised me you'd find one and you did! Thank you thank you thank you!" She set down the bike and jumped onto the porch. She practically dived at him to give him a giant hug.

"This wasn't me, baby girl." Fletcher kissed the top of her head. "I wish it had been, but someone else did this. And you know why they did it?"

"No." She looked thoroughly confused that her father had not left the bike.

"Because you have such a big heart. People love you, Charlie. Because you're kind and you're funny and you're you. Don't ever take that for granted, okay?"

"Okay. Can I go for a ride now? And can I ride it to Holly's for the barbecue?"

Fletcher glanced at his watch, then back at Paige. "You can. Just go get dressed first, okay? No bike riding in your pajamas." He ushered his daughter and wife back inside, shooting another glance up and down the street before he closed the door.

Ozzy resurfaced. "Is it safe now?"

Jo leaned across the console and caught his face in her hands. She drew him toward her and kissed him. Not just a quick "you're amazing" kiss, but one filled with all the emotions and gratitude she felt for having met this man. When she released him, she stroked her thumb across his lips. "She's never going to forget this morning for as long as she lives."

"She's happy. That's all that matters."

"You are a wonderful man, Oswald Lakeman." She kissed him again. "Don't you ever let anyone convince you otherwise. Now—" she sat back and readjusted her shirt before she lost all composure "—how about breakfast at the diner after our walk? My treat."

"YOU TWO HAVING your usual?" Brooke set a tea service in front of Jo and filled Ozzy's waiting coffee mug. "Pretty soon I'll be setting my clock to you guys."

"We had a great morning," Jo said before Ozzy could. "Poor Lancelot's feeling left out, though, I think."

Ozzy looked out the plate glass window to his car, where a forlorn-looking Lancelot had his head sticking out the window. He'd gotten that pathetic "poor me" expression down pat.

"He had his morning bath in the ocean," Ozzy reminded her. "He's fine. Besides, he's going to be well fed this afternoon at Holly's.

They usually grill up a couple of special treats for the dogs."

"We'll see you guys there, then," Brooke said and moved off to greet the early morning customers coming through the doors.

Ozzy watched Jo, who seemed a bit fidgety all of a sudden. "What's wrong?"

"Nothing. Nerves, I guess." She wrinkled her nose. "Feels a bit strange, going to a party when I'm here to work."

"Hey, you've gone above and beyond in the work department the last few weeks." He reached out his hand palm up and waited for her to take it. "Last time I had lunch with Gil he was almost giddy with praise. Having a full, solid frame in place and the electrical going in next week has him thinking you all might meet that deadline after all."

"It's still odd, though, don't you think? About the excavator?"

He did think so, which was one reason he spent as much time as he did at the site when he wasn't working. "You still believe Jed was right and that the brake line was cut?"

She nodded, poured her brewed decaf lemon tea. "I've come to trust Jed implicitly. The inspector's report was inconclusive. The truth must be somewhere in between. I mean, I'd be lying if I said I hadn't been spooked a few times right when I first got here. There were a couple of nights I could have sworn I heard weird noises. And that guy the morning after I got here."

"Guy?" Ozzy frowned. "What guy? You didn't mention him before."

She shrugged. "Didn't seem important. He was walking around the site, near the tree line and cliffs. He moved off right away. Didn't give me any trouble." She eyed him as if expecting him to argue. "Don't go overreacting, Ozzy. I haven't seen him since so I'm sure he's long gone."

"And the noises?"

"I wasn't sure if I'd been dreaming. My sleep pattern's a bit off these days and my canine alarm system hasn't gone off." She sighed. "Maybe it was kids playing pranks."

Or maybe, Ozzy thought, *whoever it was had gotten scared off by a combination of the security cameras and the presence of a former police dog.* The entire incident with Kenny should be well in Ozzy's rearview mirror, but now that Kenny was out of the hospital—and temporarily on disability—

he'd been regaling anyone who would listen with the story. A story Ozzy had been tempted to point out that Kenny had been unconscious for during the last part.

"So am I supposed to bring anything today? Is it a potluck kind of thing?"

Ozzy thought it was cute how nervous Jo seemed to be about being around his family and their friends this afternoon. "Can if you want to, but it's not required. Believe me, there will be plenty of food."

"Sounds like Charlie's going to be showing off her brand-new bike, too." She reached her hand out, something she didn't often do in such a public setting, and touched his arm affectionately. "Charlie must have really struck a chord with you at some point."

"That's one way of putting it." He sipped his coffee as he found the words. "She saved my life."

Jo's eyes went wide. "What? When? What happened?"

"Not in a dramatic cliff-dangling way."

It wasn't something he'd ever talked about before. Not with anyone. But now, sitting across from Jo, seeing the combination of concern and curiosity on her pretty face, he realized it was probably time he told someone the real trigger behind the changes he'd made in his life.

"Shortly after Paige and Charlie moved here, Charlie heard the town legend about the magic wish box hidden in the cliff caves. As the determined kid that she is, she took it upon herself to find that box so she could make her wish come true."

"Must have been some wish."

"She wanted a dad." Ozzy found himself smiling at the memory. "And she had her sights set firmly on Fletcher. She just thought her mom needed an extra nudge. So she and Simon, that's Holly's oldest boy, teamed up and went into the caves to find the box. Long story short, the tide came in and Charlie got trapped."

"Oh, no." She gripped Ozzy's arm. "Paige must have been frantic."

"To say the least. We had dozens of people turning up, helping with the rescue. Filling sandbags, keeping Paige together. I wanted to help. It was my job, after all, as a deputy. But one look at that cave opening and I knew I couldn't." He turned his hand over, grabbed hold of Jo's. "I couldn't do my job because I couldn't fit into the cave."

"Ozzy." There it was. The sympathy he loathed. The sympathy he didn't deserve. "I'm sure you did what you could."

"Sure. I stood out there with Paige, directing people with sandbags while my team was in those caves risking their lives."

"But it all turned out okay. Charlie's fine. Fletcher and Luke are fine. If there was something you could have done—"

"There wasn't. Not at the time. So once Charlie was safe, once everything was okay, I made the decision that nothing like that was ever going to happen again. I didn't want to ever feel helpless anymore. That night I went online and I made myself a plan. You name it, I changed it. It took me a few years, and more than a few mistakes, but I got there. And when the opportunity to join the BHFD came up, I jumped at it. All because of Charlie and her magical wish box."

"You want to know what I think?"

"I don't know," he joked. "Do I?"

She slid her fingers through his and held on. "I think that while Charlie's situation was a wake-up call, you're the one who answered it. You didn't have to pay attention, Ozzy. You could have kept going and you'd have been okay. Your heart is the same, Ozzy. I can see that even though I didn't know you back then. Your desire to help her then, the way you fixed that bike for her now, the way you literally jumped over the edge to help Kenny, that's who you've always been no matter what the packaging on the outside shows."

"You can say that now, after seeing those pictures of me?"

"Yes." She reached her free hand up to his face. "I can. The wrapping is great, Ozzy. But it really is who you are inside that I—" She broke off, yanked her hands free and sat back. Whatever she was going to say vanished as Brooke arrived with their plates.

Ozzy bit back the frustration. He wanted to hear the rest, wanted to know what she'd been about to say. But it was obvious that not only had she surprised herself with the next words that were to come out of her mouth, she was scared. Somehow, some way, he needed to show her that it was okay to feel whatever she felt.

Because chances were, he was feeling exactly the same way.

CHAPTER THIRTEEN

JO SCRAPED THE melon rind into the garbage and dumped the last of the fruit into the oversize bowl on the counter. When a knock sounded on the door, she called to Ozzy to come in, but it was Leah who entered.

"Expecting someone else, obviously," Leah teased and set her bag down on the table. "You going to Holly's later?"

"That's the plan. My first barbecue in Butterfly Harbor." Never mind that she was as nervous as a kid on their first day of school. Socializing, at least in the Butterfly Harbor way, was a new experience for her. Usually she was all about work 24/7, but she'd definitely cut that back a few hours in the past few weeks. Not that she'd had much choice. Cheyenne had pretty much put her on restricted hours and insisted she get at least a good eight hours in bed, whether asleep or not.

Too bad she spent a lot of that time shooing Lancelot off the sheets. Speaking of her dog—and he was *her* dog now—the oversize pooch came bounding over to Leah for one of her obligatory pets.

"You're so domesticated," Leah joked and grabbed a bottle of water out of the fridge. Today's ensemble consisted of casual slacks and a tank the color of a tangerine along with that familiar thin chain of gold shimmering against her skin. "What's happened to the Jo I welcomed to town last month?"

"She's still here," Jo said. "Nowhere for me to go until the construction's completed."

"Speaking of—" Leah wandered over to the window "—it's looking amazing. I can see that circular shape beginning to take form. Everything running smoothly now?"

"It is." And that's what had her worried. Too many times she'd gotten complacent and settled and then wham! Something roared up and knocked everything off course again. Maybe that's what was bothering her. She rubbed the side of her belly. She kept waiting for the other shoe to drop. "Inspector's due out next week to sign off on our progress. With the frame up for all three stories, people will be able to get a feel for what the entire place will be like."

"No other creepy incidents, then?" Leah returned to the kitchen, snagged a grape out of the salad. "Your guard dog's keeping the bad guys away?"

"Ha ha. Which one?"

"Word around town is Ozzy's off the market." Leah swayed back and forth, arching a brow at Jo. "You two getting serious?"

Jo's frown deepened. She didn't know what she and Ozzy were other than... Oh, heck. She sighed and set her cutting board in the sink. "I'm in deep trouble, Leah."

"Oh?" Leah grinned. "This sounds promising." She sat on one of the stools. "What kind of deep trouble?"

"The kind I told myself I'd never be in." How did she explain it? That she felt all squishy inside when she merely thought about Ozzy. Or that she watched the clock incessantly until she saw him next. Or that instead of mapping out plans for her future and returning calls from Montana, she was spending as much time out of the office as she could. It was only now, feeling what she did for Ozzy, that she realized she hadn't loved

Greg. He'd been safe and easy and practical, and until he'd fled after her baby bombshell, he'd rarely even irritated her. "I can pretend all I want to, but I have this horrible feeling this won't end well between me and him."

"Why does it have to end at all?" Leah's frank question caught Jo off guard. "Relationships—"

"I'm not in a relationship," Jo snapped. At Leah's focused look, she cringed. "Darn it. Sorry."

"Relationships aren't time bombs, Jo. They don't explode at some unexpected moment because some imaginary force has decided you've had enough happiness. What's wrong with just enjoying what you have with him? What's wrong with letting yourself be happy?"

"I am happy when I'm with him." But she wasn't sure she should be. The happier she was, the more she had to lose, and with a baby on the way, there was a lot at stake beyond Jo's heart. "But you know me, Leah. I'm going to mess this up. I always mess it up."

"Okay, let's get something straight." Leah brushed off her hands and pointed her firm lawyerly finger at Jo. "You didn't mess anything up with Greg. That's all on him."

"I know. I know that." Was she trying to convince Leah or herself?

"Good. I hope Ozzy's been able to convince…" Leah's eyes narrowed. "You have told Ozzy what happened with Greg, haven't you?"

"Most of it." At Leah's moan of irritation, she added, "He hasn't asked. He's said he'll listen if I want to tell him, but I…I know it sounds weird, but I want the past to stay in the past. What happened with Greg doesn't have anything to do with Ozzy."

"If that were true, you'd be honest with him. If you want my advice—"

"I really don't."

"Tough. Here it is anyway. You're worried about messing things up with Ozzy, but it's a monster of your own making. You have to trust him enough to share how much Greg hurt you. Otherwise, it'll be a wall that's always there between you two."

"None of this matters," Jo insisted. "I'm going to be leaving, I'm going to be moving on and he'll forget about me and go back to his online dating and hardware store girls and diner servers—"

"Nope, I don't think he will." Leah shrugged. "Word is he canceled all his online dating accounts and pretty much confirmed he's off the market, so you, my friend, have some decisions to make."

"HEY, OZZY. I'D ALMOST forgotten what you look like." Monty Bettencourt, owner of Wind Walkers Boat Tours, sidled up to Ozzy at the barbecue and tapped him on the shoulder.

The Saxons' backyard was filled with family and friends. The intricate wooden playground set replete with swings, a rope bridge and monkey bars, brimmed with young ones ranging in age from barely walking to nearly ready to drive. "Been a while since we've had a fishing trip."

"Hence my scheduling another one the other day. Besides, my freezer was full." Ozzy shifted to keep Hunter MacBride away from the grill. Over Hunter's tall head, Ozzy met Kendall MacBride's gaze and grinned at her silently mouthed "thank you."

"That's code for he's got himself a girlfriend," Hunter said in a clear attempt to distract him. "Come on, Oz, let me man the tongs for a while. I promise—"

"Nope." Ozzy yanked the metal utensil

away. "I have my marching orders and they're from your wife."

"With a backup from mine." Sheriff Luke Saxon passed around bottles of beer. "I'm under strict orders to let only Ozzy or Jason man the grill, and seeing as Jason has his hands full…" He trailed off and the group of men turned to where Jason Corwin and his wife, Abby, were showing off their baby boy, David. "Ozzy is the man. Although I bet Jo could give you a run for your money."

"On so many things," Ozzy agreed. His gaze automatically slid to where Jo was seated under one of the backyard trees between Calliope Costas and Kendall Mac-Bride, all of whom were sipping on lemonade tinged with rosemary. Lancelot was racing around behind them with Cacius, the sheriff's golden retriever, as if they'd been best canine mates forever.

Ozzy had attended dozens of these get-togethers over the years and had never once brought a date. He was happy to be part of the crowd and watch the kids while the adults decompressed from their week. But walking in this afternoon with Jo and Lancelot nipping at their heels had felt… Well, he couldn't remember anything feeling quite so right before.

His friends had often teased him that when he fell, it would be hard and fast and probably for good. Ozzy was in absolutely no state to argue.

"You can almost see the cartoon birdies flitting around his head," Luke quipped. "Are those hearts exploding in his eyes?"

"Thus concludes the female part of our male bonding ritual," Hunter joked. "Hey, where's Deputy Matt and Lori?"

"Matt's holding down the office and Leo had a late karate class," Luke said. "They should be here later. Hey, Kyle. Come and take over for Ozzy."

"Now hang on," Ozzy protested as Kyle gave his girlfriend, Mandy, a quick kiss on the cheek and joined them. The crutches were gone, replaced by a rather cumbersome walking brace, but he was getting around a lot better than he had been a few weeks ago. "I don't need replacing."

"No. We just need someone easier to intimidate." Hunter reached for the tongs again only to get slapped back by Luke.

"Anything happens to this grill and my

name is beyond mud. Go play with my kids if you need something to do."

"How about I grab my camera and take some pictures." Hunter backed away, then nearly tripped when he spotted a not-so-familiar face walk in through the gate. "You invited Gil? Sorry." Hunter waved his hands as if he could erase the question. "I mean, you invited Gil."

"I did." Ozzy passed the tongs to a curious looking Kyle.

"Your secret backgammon dates aren't enough one-on-one time?" Monty grumbled. "Next thing I know, you'll be bringing him along on one of your...no." Monty balked. "Oh, man, you invited him to go fishing with us?"

"What can I say?" Ozzy shrugged. "He's growing on me. And he's trying, guys."

"It's like you have a squeeze toy for a heart." Luke shook his head. "But he's here, so I should help make the best of it. Someone signal us if Leah's around. I hear they've been butting heads over town business. Guy does look like he's waiting for someone to accuse him of something."

"I'll go with you," Ozzy offered, "and take him a beer. Kyle?"

"Yeah?"

"You don't let Hunter anywhere near that food, you hear me?"

"Roger that."

"Man." Hunter shook his head and retrieved his camera. "You ruin one grill…"

"Three," Kendall called out as if she had heard the entire conversation. "You've ruined three grills."

Ozzy headed to the cooler to grab a bottle for Gil. When he stood up, he cast a satisfied gaze. Kids played, laughed and squealed over Charlie's new bike, which she was showing off like a prize-winning attraction at a fair. Friends joked, teased and talked. The food spread out across three picnic tables would be enough to feed two armies, and there, just along the edge of happiness, sat Jo.

He wondered if she realized she often rested her hand against her stomach. A stomach that in the few weeks he'd known her had grown significantly. Every day he saw her he reveled in the changes, both to her body and to her spirit, which had eased and settled, as most everyone's spirits did when they found some peace in this town.

Butterfly Harbor, Ozzy thought, just had its own special brand of magic.

And it was that magic, along with his friends—his family—he was counting on to convince Jo she'd found where she belonged.

"IF YOU WEREN'T already pregnant, you would be now with the way Ozzy keeps looking at you." Kendall MacBride kicked up one foot onto the edge of her lawn chair and toasted Jo with her lemonade.

"Kendall." Calliope's gentle warning tone had Jo's blush fading beneath her laughter.

She liked Kendall, an army vet who had a no-nonsense manner that Jo appreciated. Kendall was thin, taller than average, with thick dark hair worn in a ponytail. The black tanktop and gray-green fatigues, from what Jo had heard, were a bit of a uniform for Kendall, while the significant burn scars on her arm and the side of her neck were an unfortunate reminder of a dark day in her military service.

"He does have a way about him." A way she liked more and more as the days went on.

"Oh, Kendall, that reminds me—I was wondering if you'd be up for giving me a tour of the lighthouse when you have a chance. I'd like to see what elements we might be able to incorporate into the sanctuary and education center."

"Anytime." Kendall rattled off her address. "Drop on in and we'll head on over. With Phoebe in school on weekdays, I'm pretty open to anytime."

"No projects in the offing, then?" Calliope sipped her lemonade and crossed her legs.

"Uh, there could be." Kendall tapped her fingers against her knee. "I'm honestly finding the personal communication aspect of the construction and remodeling business trying." She cringed a bit. "I love the work, restoring or redesigning or whatever, but Kyle had gotten really good at being the middleman with the clients. Until he's back, I'm keeping things to a minimum. I'm not the best people person," she added for Jo's benefit. "I do better when I'm left alone."

"That's interesting because I'm the opposite. I love the challenge of personalities," Jo said. "One of the jobs my grandfather gave me on a site was to be the go-between for a union rep and the workers and management. Sharpened my debate and communication skills for sure. Everyone's always right and everyone's always wrong." She shrugged. "Once I learned that, the rest was just navigation and translation."

"Sounds as if you two are different sides of the same coin," Calliope observed. "What a shame you didn't meet up sooner. You could have worked together. Excuse me. Xander and Alethea have arrived."

"She's a bit sneaky, isn't she?" Jo watched the rather ethereal Calliope move off in a tinkle of bells and chimes. "You don't think she's hitting you over the head with anything and then wham!"

"She does have her talents. Speaking of—" Kendall eyed Jo "—do you know if it's a girl or a boy yet?"

"No." Jo stopped rubbing her stomach. "Not yet." But she was getting more curious by the moment.

"FYI, Calliope's a baby gender psychic. She can tell you what it is, no test required. If you want to go that route."

"Mom! Mom, guess what?" A little girl with big blue eyes raced up to Kendall and clutched her arm. "Mandy said there's new kittens at the bookstore. Three of them!"

"No more cats, Phoebe." Kendall smoothed a hand down Phoebe's hair.

"But Mooo-ooom." Phoebe bent herself like a pretzel to get Kendall's attention. "I bet they're so cute and they need a home. And we have so much room!"

"Mandy will find them a home, Phoebe. She always does. Besides, if we get any more cats, we won't be able to get a dog, remember? We can only take care of so many animals."

"Oh." Phoebe's round face scrunched, then she caught sight of Lancelot and Cacius. "Ooh, look. A new puppy."

Jo choked on her lemonade. She wouldn't call Lancelot a *puppy* by any stretch of the imagination. "That's Lancelot," Jo told Phoebe and clicked her tongue. Lancelot trotted over and sat beside Jo. "Lancelot, Phoebe. Phoebe, Lancelot." She moved her hand to the leash, just to be safe. Phoebe held out her hand and giggled at the significant sniff and lick she received.

Then Lancelot dropped to the ground and

rolled onto his back, turning his big doe eyes to his newest fan.

"If only all men were so easily swayed," Kendall murmured as Phoebe bent down to rub Lancelot's belly. In the next second, the girl was racing off, Lancelot on her heels. The perfect image of a perfect Saturday.

Butterfly Harbor, Jo had to admit, was going to be a very difficult place to leave.

"I THINK YOU were the unofficial hit of the party," Ozzy told Jo as he drove her back home.

"I was a curiosity," Jo said. "But I'm glad I went. It was fun. They're taking bets on who Charlie's fairy godmother is, by the way."

"I know." Ozzy grinned. "I put ten bucks on Monty."

She playfully slapped his arm. Lancelot let out a big yawn and rested his head on the console between them. "It's only a matter of time before they find out it was you."

"Hopefully, you're wrong. There's not enough mystery in life. I'd rather Charlie believe in the magic."

Jo rolled her eyes. "How are you for real?"

"Huh?"

"They don't make guys like you, anymore, Ozzy. They just don't."

"Not entirely sure how I should take that. What standards am I being judged by?"

She pinched her lips tight as he turned the corner and headed up the hill. "You never ask. About the baby's father. Beyond what I've told you."

"No." A knot in Ozzy's belly tightened. "I don't. I don't want to push you into saying something you don't want to."

"It's not that I don't want to…" She surrendered at his look. "Okay, you're right, I don't really want to, but not because I don't trust you."

"I'm not going anywhere." He reached over and took her hand, squeezed and hoped she felt the promise where it mattered most: in her heart.

"You're really not, are you?" She smiled, looked out her window, but not before he saw the flash of sadness in her eyes. "He was comfortable. Greg."

Ozzy kept his expression passive. That was the first time she'd told him the baby's father's name.

"We were never going to be the kind of

couple like your friends are. Funny, how I see that now, in hindsight. I think maybe I assumed he'd only said he didn't want kids because we both knew I thought I couldn't have them. Stupid of me, I guess. Now that I look back on it."

"You thought he loved you," Ozzy said. "You trusted him and he let you down. I'd say I was sorry, but I'm not. No, that's not true." He lifted their linked hands and pressed his lips against her knuckles. His anger at the man who had abandoned her simmered low and deep, but he kept that for himself; she didn't need to know about that right now. She needed his understanding. "I feel sorry that he's missing out on all this. Whether he wants to be a part of it or not, it's still his child. But if that's the kind of man he is, it's probably best he's gone. There's nothing else you aren't telling me, right? About the baby? Everything's okay?" He didn't want to pry beyond what she was willing to share.

"Slightly elevated blood pressure and the doc's watching my potassium and blood sugar." A casual shrug lessened the tension in his body. "If I get lots of sleep and try to lessen the stress, and go to all my appointments, everything should be fine."

"Good." He dropped their hands onto Lancelot's head and earned one of the dog's canine sighs of happiness. "For what it's worth? This Greg guy sounds like a real dolt."

The smile she gave him could have brightened the entire night sky. "That's my Ozzy," she said and squeezed his hand.

LANCELOT'S LOW GROWL dragged Jo out of a deep sleep. "Aw, man."

She groaned and yanked the pillow from behind her and pressed it over her head. In the week since the barbecue, she'd had barely enough time to breathe let alone sleep. Between the frenetic pace at the construction site and Ozzy covering for a fellow firefighter at the station house, she hadn't seen him in three days and boy, was she cranky about it. That alone irritated her.

Now what sleep she'd finally fallen into had been cut off at the quick. She glanced at her clock: 11:00 p.m.

"This does not bode well for my doctor's appointment tomorrow," she muttered at the dog as she shoved out of bed, grabbed her cell phone.

Add to the fact that it had taken her more than a half hour to finally get comfortable and she was about ready to evict her canine roommate.

Lancelot barked, once, twice, sharp, insistent. "Yeah, yeah, I get it. Believe me, I get it." She slugged her way to the door. Lancelot was out like a shot.

The cool night air had her shivering and reaching for a sweater. She shoved her feet into slip-ons and in the beams of the motion-lights, followed Lancelot outside. "Okay, dog, where'd you go?" Lancelot barked again, but this time the sound was followed by a rustling and crash. Thinking the dog must have injured himself, she hurried toward the storage shed. "Lancelot!" She clicked on her flashlight app, shone it around as a shadow burst out and headed right for her.

Jo froze.

Lancelot erupted from behind the shed as a flicker of light exploded from the back of the building. The shadow knocked against her as he raced away. Jo spun and stumbled, unable to catch her balance. She hit the ground at the same time Lancelot leaped over her. Jaws snapping, the dog snarled and caught the back of the shadow's jacket. She heard a rip and a shout, definitely male, and then a muffled *whumph*.

Lancelot let out a whine. Footsteps raced away as the shadow disappeared beyond her house and into the thicket of trees.

Dazed, shaken and trembling, Jo ran her hands around the gravel and dirt, searching for her cell phone. "Where is it? Where is it? Lancelot? You okay?" She could barely see beyond the stars exploding in her eyes, and the over-bright lights, but there he was. Lying a few feet away. "Lancelot!" She pivoted onto her knees, scrambled forward to the animal, who lay there panting and whining. "Are you hurt?" He had to be. The dog never stood still, let alone lay prone. "Don't worry. I'm going to get help. Don't worry, boy." Tears burned her eyes.

The glass of her cell caught the light. "It's okay, boy." Trying to breathe deep and keep her focus, she stretched out and grabbed her phone. She blinked to focus, opened her contact list and dialed Ozzy. Just as the phone connected, she felt the first cramp.

"WHAT SAY YOU, oh, dungeon master?" Jasper O'Neill let out a cackling laugh that had Ozzy thinking back to his less mature days. Had he sounded this ridiculous when he'd played D&D as a kid? Then again, what were the odds he'd be working as a firefighter and, during his downtime, joining in on a ruthless game of fantasy and mayhem?

"I really should be recording this for Tik-Tok," Frankie muttered. "No one on the planet would believe it."

"Au contraire," Ozzy said and rolled his ten-sided die. "There are plenty of people who would." He glanced at the clock. Only seven hours to go until he was off shift. With a full two days out ahead of him, the world was his and Jo's oyster. Well, maybe the ocean was. She'd finally agreed to go fishing with him as long as they stayed relatively close to shore.

"Nine," he announced to Jasper, then he kicked Roman under the table to jerk him awake.

"I'm here, I'm here." Roman nearly toppled back in his chair. "Where's the fire?"

"My hero," Frankie snorted.

Ozzy's cell phone buzzed. "Maybe you

should have recorded that instead," he teased Frankie.

"I'm sure I'll have another chance." She went back to flipping through TV channels.

One glance at his phone screen and Ozzy was grinning like a fool. "Hey, Jo. Miss me?"

"Ozzy. I need help." Jo's gasp had Ozzy on his feet.

"Jo? What's wrong?" He snapped his fingers, pointed to the emergency vehicle and the station's oversize SUV nicknamed Dwayne after Frankie's favorite action hero movie star. "Is it the baby?"

Game forgotten, he ran for his locker.

"I don't know." Her voice cracked. "Someone tried to break into the shed...the shed. Oh, no, Ozzy! I smell smoke. Someone set fire to the storage shed."

"I'm on my way. Don't hang up, you hear me? You stay on the phone with me." Frankie, Roman and Jasper were already suited up and jumping into the vehicles. "Jasper, call an ambulance and Luke," Ozzy ordered. "Have them meet us at the construction site. Jo?"

"I'm here. Ozzy." The way she whispered his name sent a wave of panic surging through him. "Ozzy, something's wrong with the baby. I can feel it."

"I'll be there soon, Jo, I promise."

Frankie, behind the wheel of the main engine, pulled out of the garage as Roman started up the SUV. Ozzy jumped into the passenger seat beside Roman, straining to hear Jo. "We've got sirens rolling, okay? Can you hear them?" The lights spun into the darkness as Roman sped behind Frankie.

"Faster, faster," he pleaded. Roman glanced over at him.

"Going as fast as we can, Oz."

"I know." Never had a ride felt so long. "Jo? Tell me what happened."

"I thought Lancelot had to do his business. Lancelot." There was another sob. "He's down, Ozzy. I don't know how, he jumped between me and whoever was up here."

"He'll be okay," Ozzy lied. As crazy as he was about that mutt, his first concern was Jo. "You said you have pain. Tell me where. Did this guy hit you?"

"No. He knocked me down. Just ran right at me. I can see flames in the window, Oz. The shed—the supplies…"

"Get as far away from it as you can."

Ozzy's mind raced. He cupped the phone against his hand. "Is there anything explosive on a construction site?"

Roman shook his head. "Shouldn't be. Not with this one, anyway. Jo would know. She'd have signed the permit for it."

"Right." Stupid. "Jo? Are there explosives... Jo? Jo!" His phone beeped as the call disconnected. "She's gone."

"Time to make this thing fly." Roman hit the gas and took a sharp turn. They cut around the fire engine, taking a shortcut down Leaf Glen Lane. Roman blasted through stop signs, siren and lights blaring. Ozzy glanced into the rearview mirror, saw the engine coming up fast behind them once Roman had veered back onto the main road. "Man, I'm going to pay for that later."

Ozzy barely heard him. He dialed Luke's cell, not surprised when his former boss answered immediately.

"I'm on my way, Oz."

"Jo said someone was up here, Luke. They started a fire."

"I'll get Matt and Fletch on it. Is Jo okay?"

Ozzy swallowed hard. "I don't know."

"Hang on," Roman ordered and took the

last hill like a Hollywood stuntman. As the car skidded into the gravel lot, Ozzy could see the flames licking up the back of the shed. "You find Jo!" Roman yelled. "We've got the rest."

"But—"

"Go!" Roman ordered and dived out of the car. Frankie's truck abruptly stopped beside them. Ozzy was out of the car, using the glow from the headlights to lead him to where Jo lay on the ground, curled up on her side, her hand stretched out toward Lancelot.

"Jo. Hey, Jo, I'm here." He dropped to his knees beside her, thought for a moment she was unconscious until she blinked open her eyes and turned her head. "Hey. Told you I'd be here."

She shook her head. "The cramps won't stop, Ozzy." Tears streaked down her cheeks.

"I've got an ambulance coming." But he already knew it would take too long. He wasn't going to be too late this time. He wasn't going to stand by, wait and do nothing. "Do you trust me, Jo?"

That she didn't hesitate before she nodded filled him with both hope and confidence.

"Okay." He slipped his arms under her

knees and shoulders. "Grab hold of my neck. I'm going to take you in myself."

"Okay."

He had no idea where he got the strength, but he scooped her up, tried to ignore the sound of her gasp as he shifted his hold. He walk-ran toward the SUV and set her in the passenger seat. "Roman!"

"Go!" Roman yelled back as he, Frankie and Jasper grabbed the truck hose. Jasper raced toward the house and connected a second hose to the water line into Jo's home.

"Lancelot's hurt," Ozzy yelled.

"We've got him," Frankie called, her voice muffled by the face shield on her helmet. "Go, Ozzy. Go."

He slammed into the car, shoved it into Drive and peeled out of the gravel lot.

"Ozzy, I'm scared."

He could feel her trembling from where she sat. "I know, Jo." He reached for her hand, felt both relief and terror as she grabbed hold of him. "So am I, but it'll be okay."

Please, he prayed silently. *Let it be okay.*

HOSPITAL COFFEE SUCKED.

There just wasn't any way around it. Nor

was there any way around the unease and fear circling inside Ozzy like a ravenous shark. Jo had looked so pale in the blazing lights of the hospital's parking lot and she'd still been shaking when he'd wheeled her into the emergency room.

He'd made this trip dozens of times, but it never got any easier.

He walked beside the stretcher, clutching Jo's hand. She'd gone quiet in the car, so quiet after she'd confided her fear. She was the strongest person he'd ever met. He didn't want to see her in pain again.

"We've got her, Ozzy." A young female nurse in blue scrubs he vaguely recognized stepped between him and the swinging doors into the triage room. "Let us take care of her."

"I promised..." He stopped, hands on his hips, as he tried to catch his breath. "I promised I'd be here."

"You can wait right here. I'll let you know what I can, all right?" She touched his arm. "You don't remember me, do you?"

"Ah, no. Sorry." He shook his head.

"Allison Cavanaugh. We had a date last Christmas. You took me to the tree-lighting ceremony at city hall."

"Right, Allison." He couldn't for the life of him place her. The only person, the only woman, he could think about was Jo. "Sorry."

"Are you the father?"

"No." The answer came out automatically and with far more regret than he'd anticipated. "I mean, yes. Kind of." He cringed. "It's…" He was actually going to say it. "It's complicated."

"Life often is. Someone will be out when they can."

"Okay." He patted his chest for his phone, remembered he'd left it in the car, and paced back and forth as he debated going out to get it.

Minutes, or maybe hours, ticked by. He didn't go far because he wanted Jo to be able to see him if she needed to. Even with his training, he couldn't make sense of the doctors' and nurses' movements on the other side of the door. The clock ticked slowly and loudly to his ears.

"Ozzy." Leah Ellis rounded the corner, her normally pristine appearance a bit haggard, her sweater on inside out and her shoes completely mismatched. "Paige called. She told me what happened. How is she?"

Leah looked as pale as Jo had.

"No idea. Leah—" He let out a long, controlled breath "—if she loses the baby—"

"You stop it right now," Leah ordered. "This baby is a miracle and I don't believe for a second it won't arrive safe and sound at the right time."

"Now's not the right time." Ozzy shook his head. "It's too early." He was far too familiar with preemie statistics, and very few of them were on Jo's side.

"I know." She linked her arms around Ozzy's and held on. "I know. We just have to think positive, right? How about we go into the waiting room, get some coffee?"

"They said they'd tell me when they know something."

"Then they'll find you. Excuse me." Leah stopped at the registration desk and spoke to an older, rather dignified-looking nurse. "Would you let the doctors know Jo Bertoletti's family is in the waiting room?"

"Certainly. I have her paperwork here." She handed a clipboard to Leah.

"Great. Thanks." Leah took it and Ozzy into the waiting room. "You want to give this a shot?" They sat in two linked chairs under the television that was set to family-friendly cartoons.

"The forms?" Ozzy frowned. "I don't know any of this information."

"Me, either. Oh, hang on a second." She disappeared around the corner. "Cheyenne just got here," she said when she returned. "She's going in to see Jo now. That's good. That'll reassure Jo." She sat down, set the clipboard on her lap and grabbed hold of Ozzy's hand. "I don't know if you're one for prayers—"

"Ahead of you already." He leaned his head back and closed his eyes. "Way, way ahead of you."

CHAPTER FOURTEEN

"Gil."

Leah's startled voice shot Ozzy out of his trance. He checked his watch. Cheyenne had made one quick appearance to let them know Jo was stable and that as far as the ultrasound had shown, the baby was fine for now.

For now. Those words continued to echo in Ozzy's head as he looked to Gil. Then at the dog at the end of the leash. "Lancelot." Relief surged through him as the dog padded over to him and stuck his wet nose in Ozzy's face.

"Got him special permission," Gil said. "Since he's a former police dog and all." "Boy, you scared years off me," Ozzy muttered. Lancelot had a tight bandage around his torso, making him look like he was wearing a mummy costume. "He's okay, then."

"Had the wind knocked out of him," Gil said. "I took him to Doc Campbell. He has a cracked rib. He'll be in some pain for a while, but all in all, he's pretty lucky."

"Thanks." Ozzy held out his hand. "I appreciate it. Jo will, too. She was so worried about him." He grabbed hold of the dog and hauled him in, gently, so as not to hurt him. The dog had done precisely what he'd hoped he'd do in a situation like tonight's, what he'd hoped wouldn't be needed. Lancelot had lived up to his name and protected Jo. If the dog hadn't been there...

"He's a hero." Gil tossed an uneasy look at Leah. "Oh, there's this, too." He handed over Jo's cell phone. "They managed to stop the fire before it spread to the treeline. The losses were minimal."

"So far," Leah whispered.

Ozzy focused on the mayor. "Anything else you can tell us?"

"Luke found a metal lighter near where you found Jo. It had teeth marks in it, so Luke thinks whoever set the fire had it in his pocket when Lancelot chomped his...butt." Gil poured himself a cup of sludge from the coffeepot, examined the cup's contents, then changed his mind and dumped it. "Luke's going to run it for prints and I'm hiring a private security company to set up shop until the project's done, or whoever is responsible is caught."

"I'm surprised there are funds in the budget to cover all that," Leah said, then held up a hand. "Not criticizing. Just saying."

"There aren't," Gil told her. He started to say something else, then seemed to reconsider. "I'll make it work."

"I don't understand why anyone would want to stop the sanctuary," Leah said. "I've gone over it in my head a hundred times, and no one wins if it doesn't get finished. But a whole lot of people lose."

"That's one thing we can agree on," Gil said. "Look, I'm going to head into the office, see if I can get the lab results on the lighter expedited through the system. It's better than me sitting around here doing nothing. Or worse, annoying you."

"Appreciate you bringing him by." Ozzy stood as Lancelot sprawled slowly onto the linoleum. "I'm going to have to cancel our fishing trip for tomorrow, obviously."

"We'll do it another time. You take care of your family, Ozzy." Gil's eyes flashed before he ducked his head. "It's the only thing that matters."

"Okay," Leah said when the mayor had left. "Who was that and how did the Pod People replace Gil Hamilton?"

Maybe Ozzy's advice all those weeks ago had struck a chord. He held up Jo's phone. "She mentioned her mother in Florida. Should I call her?"

"I can do that. When I have more information."

She was right, Ozzy thought. Until they knew something for certain, there was no use raising the alarm. Then again, Ozzy couldn't stop putting himself in another man's shoes. Another man who didn't deserve Ozzy's consideration, but was involved in this whether Ozzy liked it or not. He tapped in Jo's passcode, earned an impressed arch of brow from Leah.

"How did you know that?"

"It's the date the Seahawks won their first Super Bowl." He found himself smiling. "She mentioned it one time as a life-defining event for her grandfather. She's not as sneaky as she thinks she is."

"Uh-huh." Leah stuck her tongue in her cheek.

"Okay, I might have been looking over her shoulder once or twice. But she did it to me first."

"Hey, Ozzy. Leah."

Ozzy's smile faded as he looked up and saw Dr. Miakoda standing in front of them. Ozzy had been the bearer of bad news often enough to recognize the expression that came with the role, and thankfully Dr. Miakoda did not have it. The steel bands that had locked around his chest eased. "She's okay? The baby, too?"

"She's better than I expected her to be," Cheyenne said. "The fetal heartbeat is steady and strong. Jo's blood pressure isn't that great, but then it hasn't been. She has experienced some bleeding, so until that stops, I'm reserving complete optimism."

"Does she know?" Ozzy asked.

"I told her before we had her sedated. I want her resting for as long as possible until the bleeding stops. We're moving her into a room on the third floor. If you want, I can get you special visiting privileges so you can be there when she wakes up. Both of you. It's always good to have friendly faces around."

"Yes, please," Leah said.

"Him, too?" Ozzy motioned to Lancelot, who lifted his head slightly.

"Him, too." She reached down and touched the dog's head. "You got her here fast, Ozzy. It made all the difference. Believe me."

Ozzy could only nod as Cheyenne left them.

"I'm going to call Paige," Leah said. "Have her spread the word. Ozzy? You all right?"

He stared down at Jo's cell phone, torn between doing what was right and doing what was easy. "I'm fine. I'm going to stick around, walk up with her."

"All right. I'll go to Jo's and get her things. The less she has to worry or think about, the better. For all of us."

When he was alone, he walked to the swinging doors, touched his fingers to the glass as he watched Jo sleep. She was curled up on her side, her skin still pale, but not nearly as drawn as it had been when he'd brought her in. They had an oxygen mask on her face, her hair was beyond messy. He'd never seen a more beautiful sight in his life.

Love, when it hit, landed with a devastating force and reshaped everything in its wake. Nothing, absolutely nothing would be the same.

He loved her. Probably had loved her from the moment she'd dropped out of that truck on day one.

He loved that baby, too. He couldn't love that little life more if he'd been the father. He trailed his thumb over her cell phone, clicked open her contacts. He found what he'd expected, what he'd told himself he'd take as a sign. Under ICE, in case of emergency, was the name he needed.

After an encouraging nod from Cheyenne letting him know Jo was all right, Ozzy moved off and made the call.

Jo FELT AS if she were being dragged to the surface of a particularly murky lake. Her head hummed and her tongue felt thick. She tried to move her head but had to settle for prying open her eyes, and when she did, the sun had her closing them again.

"Don't you dare tell Mom or Dad about this." The female voice had a familiar ring of frustration to it. "I mean it. Eat it up quick or we'll both be in—"

"What are you feeding my dog, Leah?" Jo lifted a hand to her face, but the skin on her arm tugged and kept her from moving very far. It took a moment for her to understand she had an IV. "Oh, wow." She frowned, memories flashing in her mind like an old filmstrip. "I'm all tied up."

"Only for a few days." Leah moved from her chair and perched on the edge of Jo's bed. She slipped her hand in Jo's and held on tight. "Hello, sunshine."

Jo laughed weakly, then sucked in a breath when she realized she shouldn't be moving. She froze, waiting, thinking, wondering when the next cramp was going to hit.

"How do you feel?" Leah tucked Jo's hair behind her ear.

"Thirsty. Hungry." How could she be hungry? The fog in her brain dissipated and she gasped. "The baby?" She moved her other hand to her stomach and, feeling the familiar, strong flutter, let out a shuddering breath. "It's okay?"

Leah nodded. "You've been out for the past twenty-four hours. The bleeding's stopped.

Your blood pressure's down. Looks like you both dodged it, Jo."

Lancelot poked his head up onto the mattress and rested his chin inches from Jo's face. "Hey there, boy." She reached out to scratch his head. "You really lived up to your name, didn't you? I thought for sure whoever that was was going to barrel right through me."

"He almost did," Leah said. "What on earth were you doing out there, anyway? You should have called—"

"I thought Lancelot needed to pee." She leaned in and sniffed. "Did you feed my dog peanut butter?"

"Who, me?" Leah blinked wide innocent eyes at Jo. "I wouldn't do that. But for future reference, he's a snob about it and definitely likes the high end stuff."

"No more people food for you," she chided the dog, who whimpered and returned to his makeshift bed in the corner of the room. "Ozzy'll pitch a fit. Where is Ozzy, anyway?"

"I sent him home to take a shower and change. And hopefully get a little sleep. He's been here since he brought you in. His parents, too."

"His… parents?"

"They were worried about you. And him," Leah said.

"Why would they be worried about me? They haven't even met me."

Leah frowned. "Because they know Ozzy cares about you. All right, it wasn't exactly your particular experience, Jo, but parents do tend to care when their children are hurting. However old they get."

"I guess it'll just take some getting used to, is all."

"What? Being cared about? Kind of comes with the territory in this town." Leah patted her arm. "It took a lot of persuading to get Ozzy to agree to go home."

"I have no doubt." Jo's sleepy smile was automatic. "Glad he listened to you, though."

"I also figured it would get him out of the line of fire." Leah shifted on the mattress. "You were touch and go for quite a while, Jo. We weren't sure what might happen, and Ozzy…"

"Ozzy what? Leah, what are you talking about?" Dread pooled in her chest. "Oh, no. He didn't call my mother, did he?"

"No, I did that. Don't worry!" Leah added

quickly when Jo groaned. "She's not coming out here." She hesitated. "Ozzy called Greg."

Jo heard the words. She understood the words, or at least their basic meaning, but she couldn't quite comprehend the implication. Just in case she'd misheard, she only had one question. "Greg who?"

"You know which Greg. For the record, I didn't agree with Ozzy, but he only told me after the fact and, well, Greg got here about an hour ago."

"He's really here?" Jo shifted slightly, then remembered she didn't want to move. "I don't want to see him. Or talk to him."

"I know you don't," Leah said quietly. "But clearly Ozzy thinks—"

"I'm not particularly interested in what Ozzy thinks." What was it with the man that he thought he knew the best thing for her or this situation? "He had no right calling Greg."

"He was listed as your emergency contact," Leah explained.

"Because I hadn't gotten around to updating my phone. Who's your contact, might I ask?"

Leah's spine stiffened. "Well, that's something I'll be fixing this evening, obviously.

But that's beside the point. Greg's here now and you need to talk to him. He looks stressed, Jo. Like he's worried about you. Maybe you misjudged him?"

"Maybe he's realized he made a mistake by walking out on me and our baby?" Jo considered it. Was it possible? And if so, how did she feel about it? Was Ozzy telling her she should give the man another chance? Or giving her the opportunity to finally close the door forever?

"Can I tell him to come in?" Leah asked.

"Okay." She tugged her hand free and covered her face. "You'd better take the dog with you," she added when Leah stood up. "Better safe than sorry."

Leah retrieved Lancelot's leash and clicked it on, then nudged the animal with her as she headed out. She stopped at the door, said something and then, like moving in slow motion, Greg Chambers strode in.

He hadn't changed in the months since she'd last seen him. He was still tall, still blond, wearing that Ken-doll haircut that made him look like a Robert Redford screen double. The fact that he was wearing one of his expensive tailor-made suits and it was wrinkled possibly beyond pressing had her thinking perhaps he'd had a change of heart after all.

"Hey, Jo." He offered her his trademark smile, the one that had charmed her but never thrilled her. Not the way Ozzy's smile did every time she saw him. "How are you doing?"

"Better than I was a little while ago." She refused to move, didn't want to budge and risk bringing the pain back. It was as if she'd turned into petrified stone in this bed, curled on one side, her knees drawn in. She didn't plan to go anywhere for a long while. "You didn't have to come."

"I know." He drew the chair Leah had vacated earlier closer to Jo and kicked the makeshift dog bed out of the way as if it were nothing more than huddled blankets, which, of course, it was. "That Ozzy guy was pretty insistent that I be here considering…" He started to reach out, to take her hand, then changed his mind. "Jo, I'm so sorry."

"You are?" Jo blinked. It wasn't what she'd expected to hear. Was it possible… Had Ozzy been right? Had she misjudged Greg, and all he'd needed was time to get used to the idea of becoming a father?

"More than I can say," Greg told her. His silver-blue eyes narrowed in concern. "I can't imagine how hard this must be for you, but as soon as he told me you were in the hospital and that they weren't sure about the baby, I took it as a sign." Now he did take her hand and held it between his. His skin felt clammy, nowhere near the comforting, gentle, pulse-pounding assurance Ozzy's provided.

"A sign of what?" She swallowed, difficult to do with such a dry mouth.

"A sign for us to get back to where we were. Jo, you know we make sense. My family, my coworkers and bosses love you. Heck, they ask about you more than they ask about me. They were really disappointed when I told them we'd broken things off."

"*We* didn't break things off, Greg. That was all you."

"I guess it was." He shrugged. "But none of that matters now. We can move past this. Together. We can make a new start and—"

"So you've changed your mind." Jo cut him off. At his blank stare she felt her temper catch. "About the baby. You've changed your mind about being a father?"

"No. No way." Greg looked baffled. "I'm sure you're no doubt devastated, but obviously this wasn't meant to be. Just like we thought from the beginning. We have a clean slate now, Jo. We can—"

A shivering coldness draped her from head to toe. "You don't know." The whispered realization landed like a weight on her heart. "How is it you don't know? Didn't Ozzy—"

"He told me there had been an accident and that you were in the hospital. He said I should be here to help with any decisions that might have to be made. I've been trying to get here ever since. Changed flights, hopped all over the place. I only recharged my cell phone—"

"And when you got here? Who did you speak with?"

"No one. Just Leah. Ozzy wasn't around and…" He stopped himself, as if putting the pieces of the puzzle together. "You're still pregnant."

"Yes." She choked the word out. How could she ever, ever have had feelings for this man? A man who looked devastated all over again—not to hear she'd lost the baby, but to hear she hadn't. "I think," she said, clearing her throat, determined to get the words out. "I think this time we can agree that we're done. Consider yourself absolved from any responsibility for this baby. I'll make sure my attorney draws up the necessary paperwork that ends your parental rights. You don't have to worry about ever being known as this child's father."

"Jo, I'm sorry, I—" The befuddlement returned. "I'm just not cut out to be one. I…" He hesitated. "I don't want to be one."

"Glad we've cleared that up once and for all," Jo told him, and breaking her promise to herself to stay put, she rolled onto her other side and closed her eyes. "Goodbye, Greg."

She could hear the squeak of his shoes as he left the room, heard the muffled voices and the questions in the air. When someone knocked on the open door, she couldn't stop herself.

"I hocked the ring, Greg. Live with it."

"Jo?"

Ozzy.

She squeezed her eyes shut until she saw stars.

"I'm so sorry."

She could feel his presence, even from several feet away. But she couldn't look at him. Not right now. "You shouldn't have called him. I didn't want you to."

When Ozzy didn't answer, she opened her eyes and looked down to the foot of the bed. He had a ridiculous stuffed panda tucked under his arm and a small "get well" balloon sticking out of an anemic vase of flowers.

"He had a right to know, Jo."

"It wasn't your place." Anger continued to bubble around the disappointment and pain that resurfaced at the second rejection, not of her, but of her baby. She touched her stomach, wishing she could hold this infant in her arms and promise it everything was going to be all right. "He doesn't want this baby. He doesn't care if it lives or dies. It was devastating enough to hear it the first time, Ozzy. I didn't need to hear it again." The words, the detachment, the coolness in Greg's eyes— how had she ever thought she loved him?

Because she hadn't known, she told herself. She hadn't known what it was like to truly love someone before Ozzy. And she did love him. More than she thought possible.

And far more than she wanted to.

"What did he say to you? I'm sorry, I should have been here. I meant to be," Ozzy continued. "Jo, what did he—"

"He thought I'd lost the baby." She closed her eyes again because she couldn't stand to look at him. She'd never thought Greg could inflict another round of pain, but he had. "He came here thinking we could get back together because the baby was gone."

She heard him swallow, then the panic rose in his voice. "Jo, I had no idea. I was afraid… I was worried that if a decision had to be made, that as the baby's father he should know what was happening."

"You were wrong." She swiped the tears off her cheek. "I'm tired, Ozzy. Please just let me sleep."

"Jo, I don't want to leave you like this. I—"

"I'm not giving you a choice," Jo whispered. "You did the one thing I didn't want done. And you did the one thing I knew you would. You disappointed me, Ozzy. I didn't call Greg when I was in trouble up at the site. I called *you*. That should have told you everything you needed to know."

"Maybe it should have," he said. He set the bear and the vase on the table beside her bed.

"And I'm sorry I've disappointed you. I guess you finally got what you've been waiting for."

She glared at him. What was *that* supposed to mean?

"If you're going to go through life just waiting for people to let you down, you really will be alone. Calling Greg was the rational thing to do."

"For you, maybe."

"For all of us. I wanted us to be a family, Jo. Greg or not, I wanted to make this work because I love you. And I love that life you're carrying around inside of you. But I guess maybe that isn't enough for you, is it? You expect perfection, and believe me, I am far, far away from that." He reached out his hand, stroked a finger down her cheek.

Before he turned and walked out of her life.

CHAPTER FIFTEEN

"Ozzy, YOUR MOM AND I weren't expecting you tonight." His dad stood up from weeding around his rosebushes as Ozzy climbed out of his car. Ozzy felt as if he'd gone ten rounds with a heavyweight champ, and as he'd already run five miles on the beach and didn't feel like answering a million questions from his friends, this seemed the best place to escape to. "Is everything all right?" his father asked.

"Rough day." Rather than heading into the house like he normally did, he leaned back against the hood of the car.

"We heard about the excitement up at the construction site the other night," Lyle said, pushing up the brim of his baseball cap. "Your mother's been baking up a storm since we got home from the hospital. She's looking forward to you bringing Jo to dinner. How's she doing?"

"Better," Ozzy choked out. "Baby's just fine, too."

"Wild times we're living in these days, that's for sure. Your quick thinking probably saved them both."

Ozzy shrugged.

"Can't believe someone would have attacked her like that." Lyle paused, then looked at Ozzy. "Something on your mind?"

Heart-to-hearts had never been on the list of father-and-son things for them to do. They'd never quite understood each other, not from the beginning. Maybe that was why Ozzy had let himself get so attached to Jo and her baby. Because he wanted that kind of connection with someone. No. There was no maybe about it. He wanted a family of his own.

He loved Jo and her baby.

"I did something, Dad. Something I knew in my gut was the right thing to do." He shoved his hands into his pockets and shook his head. "Turns out, it wasn't." Doing the right thing had cost him everything.

"You could always be counted on for that, Oswald—doing the right thing, even when you took it upon yourself to rescue your friend Jonah's frog when you all were kids." Lyle obviously thought he was making a joke, but it didn't land. When he realized that, he set his tools down and approached his son. "Would you do it again? This, whatever it is you've done?"

"Yes." That he knew that made it worse. He short-storied it for his father, leaving out most of the personal details. "She blames me for hurting her again. If I hadn't called him, we'd have kept moving forward, right in the direction I was hoping for. Now?" He shrugged. "How do I get through to someone who's afraid of being happy?"

"Do you know what I've always admired about you, Ozzy?"

Ozzy's eyebrows shot up. His father had admired him? Since when?

"Whenever you set your mind to something, you got it done. Half the stuff you were interested in I didn't understand, could barely fathom, but that determination you had?" Lyle nodded in what looked like amazement. "You were the most tenacious kid, maybe person, in this town. Look at when you decided to take control of your health and lost all the weight. It wasn't you losing weight that made me proud of you, Ozzy. It was that you made a decision and kept going in the face of daunting odds." He gestured to the house where Ozzy's mother was baking and cooking up a storm. "Do you love her?"

"Jo?" Ozzy didn't hesitate. "From the second I saw her."

"Then you'll find a way to work it out. Just like you did with your computer motherboards and your D&D dungeon master challenges and losing half your body weight. If she's worth it—"

"She is."

"Then fight for her, Ozzy. And while you're at it, think about making things legal."

Ozzy snort-laughed. "She's barely talking to me at the moment, so I don't think we're at the marriage threshold just yet."

"She's got a baby on the way, doesn't she? Best pick up some speed. Especially since your mother's realized she could easily become that child's grandmother."

The front door opened and his mom stepped onto the front porch. "Ozzy!" Her face glowed when she saw him. "Oh, how lovely. I just got off the phone with Leah Ellis. She said Jo's going to be fine."

"She is, yeah." He didn't realize how hard it had been to breathe the past few hours until now.

"Will you stay for dinner?"

It was on the tip of his tongue to ask what was on the menu, but it didn't matter. "I'd like to, if that's good?"

"Wonderful! I'll go set another place."

"Hey, Dad?" Ozzy called to his father when Lyle went to retrieve his tools and clean up. "You want to go fishing next Saturday morning? I've got a standing reservation on one of Monty's boats. It'll be early, around six."

Lyle looked surprised for a moment, then smiled. "I'd like that. Come on. Let's go get washed up."

AFTER FOUR DAYS of being in the hospital, Jo was more than ready for a jailbreak. If she was going to be on bed rest, she'd rather be in her own home, with her things and surroundings and…her laptop so she could keep an eye on what was going on at the construction site.

Lancelot was being doted on, not only by

his Auntie Leah, but by the entire town who had declared the ex-police pooch a hero and showered him with praise and affection. She couldn't wait to get back to a schedule.

Not that she was going back to work yet, but she had no doubt there were hundreds of emails and details that needed attention. She'd had her share of visitors and updates from Jed and Kendall. And Alethea, too, who was putting the finishing touches on her solid marketing and business plan, which she would present to Jason Corwin when she got up the nerve. If Jo had to make a bet, she'd say Flutterby Dreams was about to get a new project up off the ground.

Despite the welcome visits from neighbors and friends—people like the Cocoon Club, who had made it their mission to teach her how to play bunco, bridge and canasta—every time she heard someone at her door, she found herself disappointed it wasn't Ozzy.

He had, much to her dismay, listened to her request and left her alone. Probably all part of his evil plan, she grumbled to herself on more than one occasion. Absence didn't make her heart grow fonder—it turned her into a sobbing sap who was too ashamed to admit she'd made a horrible mistake. She'd had plenty of time to think on it, and Leah had certainly helped her talk the subject into the ground. While she had no doubt that she wouldn't have called Greg, she couldn't fault Ozzy for being exactly the kind of man she'd fallen in love with in the first place. Making that call hadn't been the easy thing to do. It had been the right thing to do.

And she was most definitely not in an enviable position having reacted the way she did. But it's what she'd always done when she was scared or someone had hurt her. She withdrew and struck out. And did what she could to keep people away.

Well, Ozzy had stayed away. She sat on the edge of her hospital bed, dressed and ready to head home, Lancelot standing paws up at the window, looking outside.

She missed Ozzy so much that she ached. "What do you think, kidlet?" Her mind had been racing for the past two days. What was the best route to solve this? Would a simple mea culpa suffice? She needed to talk to him, one-on-one, in person. Except he wasn't taking her calls, and when she'd contacted the fire station, either Roman or Frankie or Jasper told her they'd give him the message.

Clearly a stronger message needed to be sent.

She'd spent so much of her time reveling in being alone, she'd never let herself truly feel what it was like to be part of something bigger, part of a community. Maybe even a family.

For someone who prided herself on being able to pick up at a moment's notice and move her entire life, the prospect of ending her nomadic ways felt oddly terrifying and...exciting.

She'd watched her mother lock herself and her heart away after they'd lost Jo's father. Even all these years later, there was still a part of her that remained unreachable.

That wasn't the kind of mother she wanted to be. It wasn't the kind of person she wanted to be. She wanted to be the woman Ozzy saw. That Ozzy cared about.

That Ozzy believed her to be.

After all he'd been through and overcome and dealt with, she owed it to the man she loved to try to be as brave as he'd been.

Jo picked up her cell phone, stared at the

contact name and number for a good while before she dialed.

Fifteen minutes later, she hung up, waiting for the regret or remorse or whatever came with changing the course of her life. But none of that appeared. If anything, that bubble of excitement she'd been longing to feel again burst to life.

Step one complete. Only a few more to go.

"Beep beep. Your carriage awaits!" Leah steered a wheelchair into the room and screeched to a halt. "I've always wanted to do this."

"Don't you have work or something?" Jo slid to her feet and took a seat in the wheelchair.

"I've got the week off. Been busy on a special project."

"It must be special. I've never seen you in jeans before." Jeans and a T-shirt. Had she really been out of commission that long that her friend had changed her style altogether?

"Yes, well, desperate times and all that. Oh, hey, Cheyenne."

"Good afternoon." Cheyenne Miakoda met them at the door. "Here's your list of to-dos, Jo." She handed Jo a stack of papers. "And your upcoming appointments. I'll see you next week at my office, all right?"

"Yep." She'd already updated her calendar on her phone. "Don't worry. Me and kidlet will be on time."

"Great."

"Oh, hang on." Jo called to her doctor before she turned away. "I was wondering if you could tell me one thing before I go?"

"If I can." Cheyenne crossed her arms over her chest.

"I'll grab Lancelot," Leah said and gathered up the last of Jo's things.

"What is it?" Cheyenne asked.

Jo's pulse pounded. "I've been thinking, it might be best, after all, if I knew. About the baby." She took a deep breath. "Do you know now if it's a boy or a girl?"

"I do. Would you like to know?" Cheyenne asked.

"I guess I could ask Calliope when I see her, but I'd rather have it official."

"All right, then." Cheyenne bent down and whispered in Jo's ear. When she stood up, she touched Jo's shoulder. "Congratulations."

Tears clogged Jo's throat. "Thanks. Okay, Leah, let's get this show on the road!"

"I SHOULD WARN YOU," Leah said as they drove around the corner and headed up the hill to the sanctuary site and Jo's house. "Things might look a bit different than the last time you were here."

"Jed said they'd made some changes to the site." Her hands were itching to get back on her laptop, but first and foremost was a shower. A nice, long, hot shower. Maybe followed by a nap. Then, *then* she'd get down to fixing things with Ozzy. "He'd normally be first on my list, but I'm letting my controlling self not get too far ahead," she added when Leah glanced at her. "Stop worrying so much. I know what's important. I've got people I can rely on." She had people she cared about. Equally nice, she had people who cared about her. "By the way, were you able to get those papers drawn up that I'd talked to you about?"

"The day you asked for them," Leah said. "I had them overnighted to Greg. I've already got the signed ones back. You can officially put him behind you."

"Good. Thanks." It would always make her sad that her baby's biological father would have nothing to do with her or the baby, but if things went as planned, Jo would be giving her child someone far superior in the parenthood department.

Leah drove up the final hill and had to pull the car over almost immediately.

"What on earth...?" Jo asked and peered out the windshield.

"Oh. We're having a community get-together."

"This isn't for me, is it?" Yoga pants and a football jersey did not make her well attired for company.

"Depends on how you look at it. Come on." Leah shoved out of her Mercedes and opened the rear door for Lancelot. The second he was on his home turf, he took off at about half his normal speed thanks to his still-sore rib.

"I've got your things."

"Thanks, Leah." Jo headed for her house and had to dodge dozens of people flitting through the construction zone heading to the eating area and the... Confused, she stopped and blinked. Her arms went slack and her bag hit the ground. *How is this possible?*

"Surprise," Leah whispered from behind her.

"But, how..." She remained flummoxed by

the sight of what she'd only imagined—and seen on her computer-generated designs. Before her, the playground she'd designed, the expansive custom-made structure of recycled materials, had come to life, from the cushioned platform base to the intricate winding and connecting platforms to the row of cool swings.

She saw the faces of all the friends she'd made. People she'd met from Holly's barbecue to customers she'd seen at the diner to the Cocoon Club passing around bottles of water on a warmish summer afternoon in the middle of the week—Butterfly Harbor had turned out in droves.

"Welcome home, Jo." Kyle approached slowly but steadily, her laptop tucked under his arm. "Surprise."

"What did you do?" she asked, shocked, and for an instant, she saw he was afraid he'd done something wrong. "Kyle, this is amazing, but how did you know about my plans?"

"We networked our computers into the same system, didn't we? And when you were in the hospital, I needed information I couldn't find anywhere else. Sorry." He shrugged.

"How are we paying for this? It isn't in the budget." She'd worked and reworked the numbers for hours trying to make it happen, but she'd given up, at least until after the rest of the sanctuary was complete. Now...in a matter of days, the playground was there and would be ready to open to the town's kids in no time.

"Ozzy and Gil and Jed recalculated a few things," Kyle replied. "There's also been an offered settlement from the supplier that shipped us the faulty materials. Gil's fed it back into the budget, which will allow for another ten hires if you decide we need them."

"And everyone just turned out to do this?" She was in awe.

"I put out the call over the weekend," Kyle said. "People rearranged their schedules so they could help. We should have it done by tomorrow."

"You should be getting off your feet," Leah reminded her.

"Right, uh-huh. In a minute." Jo waved her off, having caught sight of the one person she wanted—needed—to speak to. "I'll be right back."

"Hey, boss! Welcome back!" one of her

crew called from the sanctuary structure. He tossed her hard hat into the air. She caught it easily and plunked it on her head.

It took her longer than expected to reach the monkey bars that Ozzy was perched on top of. Power screwdriver in his hand, his dark T-shirt stained with sweat, Ozzy looked down at her, a slightly cautious expression on his face.

She stood there, hand on her hat, peering up at this man, this wonderful, beautiful, kind man, and wondered what she'd done right to deserve him. "I was hoping to talk to you," she said in a strained voice.

"All right." He jumped to the ground and handed off the screwdriver. "Thanks, Dad."

"Mr. Lakeman." Jo felt the heat rise to her cheeks. "I heard you and your wife came to the hospital. Thank you for that."

"You're family, Jo." Mr. Lakeman reached out a hand to grip hers for a moment. "And it's Lyle, please. My wife's anxious to get to know you. And feed you."

Jo laughed, acknowledging the woman Lyle Lakeman was gesturing to.

"So this whole thing is a family affair?" She pointed over her shoulder at the woman approaching his father. The affection in the older woman's eyes as she handed over a bottle of water had Jo smiling.

"I think by now you'd know, Jo." Ozzy touched a hand to her lower back. "This entire town is a family thing."

She did know. It had taken her a long time to accept it, but it had been on full display from the moment she'd driven through town, towing her home with her. "You did all this? Even after what I said at the hospital."

"I did." He slipped an arm around her waist and drew her close. "You were right. I never should have gone around you like that."

"We were both right," she corrected. "You gave me something I didn't know I needed. Closure. Thank you for that." She could lock Greg away now, into the past, where he belonged. Because her future, the future she wanted more than anything, was standing beside her. "I want to be happy, Ozzy." She turned into him, framed his face and looked into those breath-stealing green eyes of his. "I want everything I never thought I could have. I want you." She took a deep breath and, as if jumping off the high dive, took the plunge. "I love you."

The smile that split across his face lit up her heart. "Took you long enough." He kissed her, slow and deep, and earned a deafening roar of applause from the onlookers. When he ended the kiss, she could still see the question in his eyes. "Does that mean you're going to stay?" he asked.

"I called the company in Montana and told them I wouldn't be taking the job. They countered and offered me consult work on a job-by-job basis. It might mean some traveling, but they'd be short jaunts and it won't be for a while." She traced his mouth with her finger. "I want some time to get settled with my family."

"Are you going to be happy here? Once the sanctuary's done—"

"I'm going to start my own construction company, focusing on small businesses and homes. Custom-design and remodeling work."

"That's a lot to take on."

"It would be if I were doing it alone." Jo looked across the way to where Kendall MacBride was hefting a stack of redwood two-by-fours over to the plank bridge being assembled. "Kendall's going to be my partner. I hope to talk to Kyle and Jed about joining, as well."

"I thought keeping your laptop away from you would stop you from working."

Jo smirked. "I'll slow down, but I'll never stop. There is one more thing we have to discuss."

"Okay." He sounded confused as to what that might be.

"This bet going on as to who you're taking to Monty and Sienna's wedding."

"Oh, that." He grinned and tugged her closer. "That's already been settled. Ursula paid the winner yesterday."

"Oh? Who won?"

"Ursula. She put all her money on you the day after she saw us together at the diner getting takeout."

"Well…" She patted his chest affectionately and smiled. "As long as they realize you're off the market, I'm good with it." She was so happy, she couldn't stop smiling. "So, what do you say, Oz-man? You want to make this official?"

Panic jumped into his eyes. "I've been a bit busy to think about buying a ring."

"You don't need to give me a ring. You need to give me a name."

"A name?"

"Uh-huh." She nodded and pressed a quick kiss to his mouth. "For our daughter."

"Daughter?" He blinked. "It's a girl? You're going to have a girl?" He splayed a hand across her stomach. The baby kicked, swift and sure, as if recognizing him for who he was: her father.

"We're having a girl," she told him. "So? Do you need some time to—"

"Hope." Ozzy didn't hesitate, didn't second-guess himself. "Her name is Hope."

Yes, Jo thought as they joined the congratulatory crowd of coworkers, family and friends.

It most certainly was.

EPILOGUE

"Looks like things have turned out aces for all involved," Gil Hamilton commented to Sheriff Luke Saxon as the two of them ordered lunch at the food truck. It had taken him far longer than it should have to see what working with people could accomplish, but adversity often bred results. The past few years in Butterfly Harbor were proof of that.

"For most of us, anyway," Luke agreed. "Thanks, Alethea."

"No problem." Alethea focused her attention on Leah, her next customer who stood waiting to order.

Gil tried not to stare, but it was difficult where Leah was concerned. She was a stunning woman. Irritating, annoying, headstrong and tenacious to be sure. All the things he'd be looking for in a mayoral candidate if he wasn't one himself. Too bad he was running against her.

"I heard from the lab that they sent the results about the lighter," Gil said.

Luke smirked. "Should have known you were here for more than small talk and a bit of lunch. Yep. They came in this morning." He pulled out his phone, tapped to open the document. "Fingerprint analysis came up with Christopher Russo. Age twenty-seven. Arrest record includes everything from vandalism to burglary to suspected arson. No current arrest warrants out, but I'm about to change that."

Gil accepted the phone, looked down at the suspect's picture. He swallowed hard, blinking as he recognized the familiar face of the boy in the image of the man.

"Gil?" Luke frowned. "You know him?"

Gil had always thought this day would come; the time for keeping his father's secrets was over. Now it was up to Gil to trust someone with the truth.

Beginning with Sheriff Luke Saxon.

"Gil?" Luke said again.

"Yes, I know him." Gil took a deep breath and then said, "That's my half brother."

* * * * *

*Don't miss the next
Butterfly Harbor romance from
Anna J. Stewart and
Harlequin Heartwarming,
coming fall 2021!*

Get 4 FREE REWARDS!

We'll send you 2 FREE Books plus 2 FREE Mystery Gifts.

Love Inspired books feature uplifting stories where faith helps guide you through life's challenges and discover the promise of a new beginning.

FREE
Value Over
$20

HARLEQUIN SELECTS COLLECTION

19 FREE BOOKS IN ALL!

From Robyn Carr to RaeAnne Thayne to Linda Lael Miller and Sherryl Woods we promise (actually, GUARANTEE!) each author in the Harlequin Selects collection has seen their name on the *New York Times* or *USA TODAY* bestseller lists!

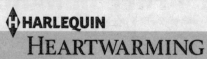
#387 THE RANCHER'S UNEXPECTED TWINS
Jade Valley, Wyoming • by Trish Milburn

Dean Wheeler is willing to marry Sunny Breckinridge and be a dad to her orphaned niece and nephew to own the ranch he loves. But is risking his heart in a pretend marriage part of the bargain?

#388 FALLING FOR THE LAWMAN
Heroes of Shelter Creek • by Claire McEwen

Gracie Long is impulsive and bends the rules. Deputy Adam Sears follows a strict moral code. As they work together to track poachers, Gracie starts to wonder if she can have a future with someone so different.

#389 THE TEXAS SEAL'S SURPRISE
Three Springs, Texas • by Cari Lynn Webb

Former Navy SEAL Wes Tanner loves his rescue horses—and they need his help. When pregnant Abby James arrives in town, seeking a fresh start, she lends a hand...but can she save Wes, too?

#390 THE REBEL COWBOY'S BABY
The Cowboys of Garrison, Texas
by Sasha Summers

When Brooke Young and Audy Briscoe become guardians of their best friends' baby, they have to set aside their rocky past to give baby Joy the family she's lost. But falling for each other wasn't part of the plan...

HWCNM0821

Visit
ReaderService.com
Today!

As a valued member of the Harlequin Reader Service, you'll find these benefits and more at ReaderService.com:

- Try 2 free books from any series
- Access risk-free special offers
- View your account history & manage payments
- Browse the latest Bonus Bucks catalog

Don't miss out!

If you want to stay up-to-date on the latest at the Harlequin Reader Service and enjoy more content, make sure you've signed up for our monthly News & Notes email newsletter. Sign up online at ReaderService.com or by calling Customer Service at 1-800-873-8635.